after the storm

Cottonwood Cove ~ Book 5

laura pavlov

 Created with Vellum

My raven had found her way home.
And I was going to keep her this time.
Forever.
Cage Reynolds

prologue

. . .

Cage

THEN…

"You're surprisingly skilled for a kid your age," Butch said, as I shoveled the hay in the stall that I was currently cleaning. I'd gotten hired at Duncan Ranch two weeks ago for a summer job.

"Thank you, sir," I said, as I reached into the wheelbarrow for a big scoop of fresh grass. It irritated the hell out of me that he kept referring to me as a kid, but Butch was the ranch foreman for the Duncans, so I knew better than to act like a dick to my boss.

I'd interviewed with both the owner of this place, Frank Duncan, and Butch Hall. The ad had said that I needed to be sixteen years old, but I'd shown up and insisted I was capable of doing the job. I wanted to start making money this summer so I could afford to buy a car once I got my license. So, I'd been working hard to prove that I was more than up for the task.

Because I was.

"Finish up in here, and then you can call it a day."

I nodded as he walked out of the stables, and I lifted my

hat and wiped at the sweat running down my forehead. I was meeting some friends at the cove later, and I couldn't wait to dive into the water and cool off.

"So, are you a real cowboy?" a voice said from behind me, and I whipped around to see the prettiest girl I'd ever laid eyes on.

Blonde waves rolled down her shoulders, and her skin looked like it had been kissed by the sun. She was petite and lean, wearing tan riding pants, boots, and a white top. She looked to be about my age, maybe a little younger.

My mouth went dry at the sight of her.

That had never happened before, and I'd met plenty of pretty girls.

But no one like this one.

"I'm a ranch hand here."

"Yeah? You work for my dad?" she asked as she strode into the stall and stood across from me.

"Is your dad Butch Hall or Frank Duncan?"

She chuckled and held out her hand. "My dad is Frank. I'm Presley Duncan."

I wiped my sweaty palm on the leg of my jeans and reached for her small hand. "Hey, I'm Cage Reynolds."

"So, are you a cowboy, Cage Reynolds?"

"I'm a ranch hand, but I guess it's not all that different from being a cowboy." I shrugged as my stomach wrenched in the weirdest way. I guessed it was because she was standing so close to me. I'd made out with Marcy Waters more times than I could count, and my stomach never did this shit. "How about you? Are you here for the summer?"

I knew the Duncans lived in San Francisco, and they'd just bought this place a few months ago, which I assumed would be a summer home, although they were adding a lot of animals to the barn, and her father had hired on quite a few people to look after the property. But I'd never seen his daughter here before.

"Yep. I usually spend the summer traveling because I'm a competitive jumper, but I wanted to have a summer off and be a normal teenager for once in my life. Actually get to spend some time at our new place and have a little fun." She smiled, and I swear I felt like I'd suddenly come down with a fever.

She was so damn pretty.

"A jumper? Like high jump and long jump?" I asked as I cleared my throat and tried to keep my shit together.

I'd never been nervous around a girl before. This was definitely new for me.

She chuckled, and I couldn't help but smile as I watched her. Her dark brown eyes locked with mine. "No. I ride horses. I'm guessing you know about equestrian sports, living out here."

"You're a horse jumper. That's cool."

"How old are you, anyway?"

"Fifteen. I just finished my freshman year of high school. How about you?"

"Same." She tucked her hair behind her ear. "Good. I don't know anyone here, so it looks like you're my first friend."

This summer was off to a great start. I'd gotten the job, and now the hottest girl I'd ever seen wanted to be friends with me.

"Well, I'm almost finished up here, but I'm meeting some friends down at the cove later, if you want to go."

Her eyes widened, and she shoved her hands into her back pockets. "Oh, that sounds like fun. But my mom was not pleased that I decided to spend the summer here, so she's doing what she can to fill my days with things just to prove a point."

That was kind of fucked-up. Why wouldn't her mom want her here for the summer with them?

"What kind of things?" I asked as I spread the hay evenly on the ground before setting the rake in the wheelbarrow.

"I have a riding lesson in a few minutes with my coach, and then I have a math tutor after that."

"Math tutoring in the summer?" I gaped at her as I gathered the rest of the tools and piled them in the wheelbarrow.

"Yep. It's ridiculous. She wants me to be prepared for law school in *seven years*." She rolled her eyes.

I knew the Duncans were wealthy; I'd heard people in town talking about them. But Presley seemed like a normal girl in the way she talked and acted.

"That's cool that you already know what you want to be."

"I thought you wanted to be a cowboy?" She waggled her brows.

"I'd like to do something with animals, and I think I'd love to have a big ranch like this someday. But I'm not sure I can make much money as a cowboy, even if I do look good in the hat." I smirked. I was normally a fairly cocky guy, but this girl had me acting all sorts of nervous.

Time to get my game face on. Who knew when I'd see her next.

"You do pull off the hat well," she said, her voice all tease. "But for the record, I've never thought about what I want to do when I grow up. That was pretty much decided for me long before I had the chance to decide for myself."

She followed me out of the stall as I dropped the wheelbarrow off where I'd gotten it, and I took my time hanging the rake and shovels on the wall. I didn't want to say goodbye to her just yet.

"I wouldn't let anyone tell me what I'm going to be when I get older. It should be your choice," I said, glancing around to make sure no one was listening. I sure as hell didn't want to lose my job, but I liked her, and she'd said I was her only friend here.

"Do you have siblings?" she asked, motioning for me to follow her out of the barn.

"Yes. I'm the oldest of five." I groaned.

"Oh, wow. I always wished for siblings. I'm an only child."

"I'll tell you what." I stopped when we stepped outside where the sun was shining brightly, and my bike sat a few feet away. "You can borrow mine anytime you want this summer. But you can't return them. Once you borrow them, you have to keep them."

"You've got yourself a deal." She laughed and shook her head. "I see Charlie is ready for me out there."

I glanced in the distance and saw the brown horse trotting around with a man I'd never seen before.

"All right. Have a good lesson."

"Hey. I don't have tutoring tomorrow. Are you working again?"

"Yep. Same hours."

"Would you want to go to the cove tomorrow after I finish my lesson with Charlie?"

My stomach wrenched once again, but I made an effort to keep my face from showing how excited I was. "Yeah. That sounds cool. Give me your number and I'll text you. If you have any questions, you can just text me back."

I pulled out my phone and handed it to her.

Had I ever been this nervous to ask a girl for her number?

Definitely not, although I knew everyone in Cottonwood Cove. When you grew up in a small town, you knew almost everyone.

So, there was no need to ever be nervous.

Until right fucking now.

"Presley, let's go!" the man yelled from the small, fenced training area.

"I'll be right there!" she shouted back and rolled her eyes again. "He's not happy that I'm not competing this summer, either."

She typed her number into my phone before handing it back to me. I quickly shot her a text so she'd have my number and tucked my phone into my back pocket.

She walked backward toward her coach. "I'll see you tomorrow, Cage Reynolds."

I held up a hand, and then I walked my bike slowly toward the driveway, taking my time watching her climb onto her horse. I heard the man lecturing her.

"I get it, but not everyone is as talented as you. You had a shot to win it all this summer. You're ranked now. That's nothing to take lightly," he said, but his words weren't laced with contempt.

He actually seemed like he was in awe of her.

"I know, but sometimes you just want to be a normal teenager. I'm burned out, Charlie. I want to have a summer like other kids my age."

"I know. And you deserve that. But we can still work on things so you'll be ready in the fall."

"Sounds like a plan." Her head turned, and her dark gaze locked with mine, and I just stood there gaping at her like a fucking idiot.

Because once she started riding, it was impossible to look away. She made jumping over the walls look like it was nothing.

She was moving fast toward the first hurdle. She leaned forward and moved over the first jump with complete ease. The sunlight was shining down on her, creating sparks of light as she jumped through the air, laser-focused on the next jump.

I'd just done a research paper at the end of the school year about ravens and the way they soared and glided with such ease. If Presley Duncan were an animal, she'd definitely be a raven.

I forced myself to look away and get on my bike just as she slowed a few feet from me, and I started pedaling.

"See you later, Cowboy," she sang out and chuckled when her coach scolded her for not being focused.

I nodded and held up a hand.

See you later, Raven.

one

. . .

Presley

"WHAT'S THE SAYING? When life gives you lemons, make yourself a gin martini?" I asked my best friend Lola, who'd been here for all of thirty minutes, listening to me whine about the current state of my life.

"Ummm… You're holding a bottle of vodka, and you're making a lemon drop, my love. Clearly, Harvard Law didn't teach bartending 101. It's all that fancy wine you wealthy people drink that has you clueless about the good stuff." Lola laughed as I handed her a glass, and we clinked them together. I wasn't much of a drinker, but with my life being a complete shit show lately, I was open to trying new things.

"Ahhh… good to know. And it's tasty." I licked my lips after taking a long pull. "Thanks for coming over."

"Are you kidding? I love coming to Chateau Country Duncan." She and I both sat down on the couch, facing one another. My parents had purchased this ranch decades ago, and it actually *was* one of my favorite places in the world.

I'd met Lola in Cottonwood Cove the first summer I'd started coming here. I'd grown up in San Francisco but had fallen in love with spending summers in the small town. Lola had become the sister I'd always wanted.

She'd moved out to New York after college, and I'd been thrilled to have her nearby. But she'd missed home, and she was looking to simplify her life, so she'd left New York a few months ago to return to Cottonwood Cove.

I understood the appeal of this town.

I'd always loved it here, until the memories of this place had made it so that I never wanted to come back.

"So, you're loving small-town life, huh? Any progress with finding a location for the spa?" I asked as I sipped my cocktail.

"Yeah, I just wish you'd consider doing it with me, and not just financially. Don't you remember that dream of ours?" she teased. Her dark hair was cut blunt at her shoulders. She was effortlessly stylish and naturally gorgeous.

"Um… I remember. We'd had it all figured out back then, didn't we?"

"Yep. We were going to be business partners, and you were going to tell your parents to fuck off because you didn't really want to go to law school or be a lawyer. You were going to marry Cage Reynolds, and I'd marry some bad boy who rode into town on a white horse. We'd raise our kids together and have a little nursery at the spa for all our beautiful, well-behaved, genius children." She set her glass down and fell back against the couch. "The good ole days."

"Please. That was a fantasy. Clearly, bad boys don't ride on white horses." I tipped my head back and finished the rest of my drink. "My mother already resented me for not being a pageant queen; she wasn't going to let me be the first family member not to attend Harvard, too." No, Presley Duncan was groomed to be an intellectual. All through school, I'd had tutors on the side to give me a 'step up', as my mother would say. Dad wanted me on the rodeo circuit. I was his champion jumper, and my mother eventually embraced my competitions, but only after I started winning.

Lola pushed to her feet and made her way back to the

counter, where she poured us two more drinks. "Barbie Duncan does not play around. She's such a freaking powerhouse, too, and she has a gift for making others feel like they've failed comparatively."

"It's her superpower." I chuckled.

"And your poor dad has had two major medical emergencies in his life, and the timing has been horrible. Although, there probably is never a good time for a medical emergency, right?"

"Yeah, very true. Maybe it's my life that's the problem." I shrugged. "First, he gets into a skiing accident and spends eight months in rehab. His so-called motivation to recover was to help his baby girl move into her new place to start law school in Cambridge, his alma mater. As if my parents would ever help me move anyway. They hired movers. But, boy, did my mom lay it on thick while he was recovering." Fortunately, his broken bones healed nicely without any complications, and they did show up when I moved in to take me to dinner.

"And then..." My best friend settles on the couch and hands me my filled-to-the-rim glass. "What are the chances that your dad has a stroke now with all that's happening?"

"Sadly, I don't think you get to choose your time for something like that." I still vividly remember getting the call from my mom and the complete panic that I felt. This was the most severe illness my father had ever encountered. "Wait, are you referring to *now* as the time when my husband decided to knock up his assistant, who then went and took the story public? Is that the now you're referring to?"

Yes, I'd married Wes Wellington, the famous music producer who was ten years my senior, and to say that life had not gone as planned would be a massive understatement.

"Are you really that shocked?" Lola asked as she studied me.

She knew everything about me. She knew my marriage

was a total fraud. Wes and I hadn't been in love in years, and I couldn't say for certain that I ever was in love with the man that I'd spent the last five years with. I didn't fully blame him for the demise of our marriage, but he sure took us out with a bang.

Literally and figuratively.

But I had a hand in this mess. Wes had been the one to fill a void when my heart was shattered into a million pieces, but he'd never been the love of my life, not in any way, shape, or form.

He'd known it on our wedding day, and one of the biggest gripes he'd had was that there wasn't room in our marriage for him, because he'd known that my heart already belonged to another man.

We'd spent a lot of time apart, as he traveled often, and I'd wondered if he'd strayed, yet he'd denied it vehemently. I'd always assumed it was just a coping mechanism for me to expect the worst.

But now, I really questioned if his dalliance with Corona was the first time he'd strayed.

Yes, his mistress was named after my favorite beer. Go figure.

I'd threatened to divorce him a year ago, but he'd insisted I was being paranoid, and honestly, it was embarrassing to admit. But Wes and I hadn't even been willing to take the time to end our marriage the way we should have a long time ago.

I worked crazy hours, and he traveled all over the world with clients.

We'd been living separate lives for the last few years.

Sure, we'd make public appearances together and present a united front when he was home, because that was important to him. Wes had become more like a friend than a spouse, but it wasn't like I wanted to go out and date someone else.

I'd given up on finding love a long time ago.

I'd found it once, and it had burned me bad enough to never want to go there again.

So, I'd settled.

And this is where you land when you settle.

"Am I shocked that he cheated? Not really. But a part of me believed that I was being paranoid for thinking it all those times. I mean, I wasn't happy either, but I sure as hell wasn't out there sleeping around." I shrugged.

"He's a selfish asshole," Lola hissed and shook her head with disgust. "And to get her pregnant and let you find out with the rest of the world? He didn't even have the decency to tell you privately."

"That's the part that surprises me most. He's the one who claimed he was still in love with me, and now he keeps sending texts begging me not to leave him. He never wanted to separate, no matter how many times I suggested it. Why wouldn't he have just let me go so we both could have moved on without having to humiliate me publicly? And what are the chances that all of this happened right when my dad had a stroke? When it rains, it pours, I guess."

She set her glass down and wrapped an arm around my shoulder. "Maybe this is a sign that it's time to make a change. You would have just stayed in an unhappy situation, and now he's forced your hand."

I nodded and drained the last of the liquid from my glass. My nose was numb, and my hands were tingling. "It's all so complicated. My firm represents his company. I'm about to be named partner, which is what I've been working so hard for all these years. I just want to be completely free of him, you know? I love my job, and I want to bury myself in work when I get back home. But I am glad that I was able to leave when the story broke, to get out of New York and come here for a couple of weeks to be with my father."

"Ahhh... Cottonwood Cove heals all." She turned to face me. "So, go ahead and ask what you're dying to ask."

"I have no idea what you're talking about."

"The man we never talk about. *Cage Reynolds.* No, I haven't run into him since I've been back, but I saw his brother, Hugh, and his wife, Lila, the other day, and they are too freaking good-looking for their own good. Damn, that family is so beautiful. It's just not fair."

"This is helping me, how?" I fell back on the couch and groaned.

"I did some snooping when I had dinner with Madison and Felicia, and I tried to find out if Cage was in a relationship." She hovered beside me, her cheeks all rosy from the booze. "But they said he's so private that they don't have any idea if or who he dates."

"Why would I care if he's in a relationship? I'm in a disaster of a marriage. I'm not looking for a new man." I bellowed out in laughter. "That's the last thing I need. *Especially that man.* He broke me once. I would never let that happen again. I've avoided this town for years because I can't go there."

"Yeah, yeah, yeah. Time heals all wounds. And let's be honest, he wasn't the only one who messed up, bestie. You know I love you more than chocolate mousse and good sex, but you played a role in that breakup, too."

I gasped. "Cage had a child with another woman. He's the one who made things final."

"You weren't together, and you know it. And you married the man he was ridiculously jealous of so fast all our heads spun. I'd say you *both* made things final."

We hadn't been together for months when I found out Cage was having a child with another woman. Time had never been on our side. But I always thought, always believed, he'd be my end game. But he went and had a baby with someone else, and I knew in my heart we were done. So, I'd made things final for myself, as well.

Why wallow in my misery?

Even if that was exactly what ended up happening, I'd done what I needed to do to survive that time in my life.

I sprung forward and rubbed my temples. "I don't want to talk about Cage Reynolds. First loves are never supposed to be the person you end up with. We both went our separate ways, and we're the better for it."

She pushed to her feet and laughed so loud it felt like the walls in this little cottage on my parents' property were vibrating. My dad had built the guesthouse so I'd come home more, but sadly, this was the first time I'd been here in years. I'd always visited them in San Francisco, so I didn't have to worry about running into anyone that mattered there. This house was a miniature version of their fancy, gigantic ranch house at the other end of the driveway.

They'd started spending a lot more time at the ranch over the last few years, though, so it was bound to happen that I'd end up visiting.

"This is you being better for it? You fled your home, filed for divorce, and came to take care of your sick father. You've got mascara under your eyes, you're wearing a dirty T-shirt, and your socks don't match."

"What are you? The fashion police? I flew on a red-eye to get here and spent all day at the hospital, and then I was chastised by my mother, who stopped by for five minutes in between Zoom meetings and world domination. Did I tell you? She claims she has an important meeting in Barbados later this week. I don't buy it. Everyone works remotely now, so I think she's full of shit. *And she's leaving him to fend for himself.*"

My mother ran one of the largest textile companies in the world. Her father had started it, and she'd become the CEO when I was young. She worked a lot and had a social life that most would consider a full-time job. She didn't think I had an eye for fashion and decided that when I was at a very young age, so she insisted I become an attorney like my father.

"He's coming home with a team of nurses tomorrow, and it will be better without her at the house, carrying on with her life while he's struggling. Consider it a blessing."

"Good point." I ran a hand over my face. "I'm a mess, Lo."

"You're going to be just fine. There is no one in the world tougher than you, my bestie girl. It was time for you to break free. And now you're free. You can work remotely. You can focus on your dad, and you can focus on yourself. It's about damn time."

A tear ran down my cheek, and I swiped it away. "I've been miserable since you moved. The daily FaceTime calls are not the same as happy hour downtown every week and lunches in the park."

Her eyes were wet with emotion. "You were the only good thing in New York for me. I hated my job. Hated my boss. Hated every guy I went out with. I needed to figure out what would make me happy. But being away from you has been the only negative to this move. So, as much as I'm sad that your dad is going through all of this, selfishly, I'm so happy to have you here."

"That's pretty messed up, Lo," I said with a straight face before we both fell back in a fit of laughter. "Let's have another drink."

"I have a better plan." She held out her hand and reached for mine. "Let's go to country night at Garrity's. There's live music and dancing there tonight. I've gone for the last two weeks, and it's been so fun. Madison and Felicia are dying to see you, and there's a big group of people going that you'll know."

"Cage's family owns that place. What if he's there?"

"I've never seen him there. Does Cage Reynolds strike you as a dude to go out line dancing in the middle of the week?" She chuckled, and a memory flashed through my mind of him and me dancing in that very bar when we were home from college one weekend. A heaviness always settled in my chest when I thought of Cage. My thumb stroked the tiny tattoo on my wrist absentmindedly. I'd grieved the loss of the relationship in a way. He was such an enormous part of my life, and then it was just all… over.

"He's actually a really good dancer when you can convince him to get out there and do it."

"Well, if memory serves, the cowboy only came to life for his wild raven." She chuckled. I'd met Lola right when I'd started dating Cage all those years ago, so she'd known everything, even the nicknames we'd called one another. "You were the only one that ever got that man to do anything. So, I'm guessing he doesn't do a lot of line dancing these days."

"I mean, clearly, he had a baby with someone else, so I must not be the *only one* who can get him to do things." I shrugged as that heaviness settled in my chest again.

She pulled me to my feet. "Come on. Let's get dressed up and do our hair and go out like old times. You could use it. Tomorrow, your dad comes home, and you'll be working with his team to get him back on track, and you'll be busy being the female superstar of the New York legal world. But for tonight, let's have some drinks and some laughs and forget about all this shit that will be there waiting for us tomorrow."

It was the last thing I felt like doing, but Lola was right.

Everything would be waiting for me tomorrow.

We made our way to the bathroom, and my phone vibrated for the millionth time today.

THE DEVIL

Baby. Please talk to me. I can explain. I'm not signing these papers until we talk.

So maybe I'd changed Wes's name in my contact list. I didn't claim to be the most mature person on the planet. There was nothing more to say to him. He'd showed up at our penthouse *after* the story broke, just in time to see me packing my bags to head home. I wasn't leaving because of him, of course. My dad needed me.

I wasn't running from my home because I wasn't the asshole who'd strayed. He would be the one moving out.

He'd admitted to the affair. Told me it meant nothing to him, and it was just sex.

He'd said it like he'd taken her to coffee or flirted with her a little too much.

She was having his child, for God's sake.

Why was he even trying?

We had nothing.

We hadn't for a long time.

I think, in a way, I was as angry with myself as I was with Wes because I'd allowed things to go too far. I was obviously embarrassed that the whole world knew about the affair, including the people I worked with. My family. My friends.

My mother.

But I realized it was the embarrassment that hurt the most. The lack of respect for the history that we'd shared, at the very least.

The friendship that still remained, or at least *had* remained, up until now.

But it didn't hurt that he'd actually been with someone else—at least not the way that it should hurt.

We hadn't been together in so long that I couldn't even remember the last time that we'd had sex. It had been over a year, so what did that say about me?

Why didn't I leave a long time ago?

I wasn't this girl.

I was ready to kick his ass to the curb.

But tonight, I just wanted to forget all of it.

Tomorrow was a new day.

two

. . .

Cage

"WHY CAN'T we just keep Maxine since she's been here so much anyway, and she loves us like we're her own family? Right, Daddy?"

This kid, man.

If Gracie weren't completely attached to this animal, I swear I'd give the Langleys a piece of my fucking mind. They'd been pawning this pig off on me for weeks now. First, it was a vacation. Now, Joe Langley was having some medical issues, and his wife, Martha, had come in crying yesterday, asking if I could keep Maxine for a few weeks.

Again.

I had this goddamn pig at my house more than they did because they had constant ailments.

Cry me a fucking river.

Why in the world an elderly couple decided to take on a seventy-pound pig as a house pet was beyond me.

But, of course, Martha following me around my veterinary office crying was not good for business, so I'd agreed to take Maxine for a few more weeks.

And my kid... my adorably big-hearted, cute-as-a-fucking-button-with-a-heart-of-gold little girl was in love with the little porker.

"Well, adopting a pig, one who lives in the home, is a big responsibility. We didn't sign up for that, the Langleys did. We are just helping them out right now."

Parenting meant that I had to take the high road more often than I would normally prefer.

"But we signed up for Bob Picklepants to live with us, didn't we?"

Bob mother fucking Picklepants.

How the hell I got talked into naming my dog that ridiculous name is still beyond me.

I swear this little girl was my kryptonite. Her chocolate-brown eyes and long curls bouncing around her, made her impossible to say no to.

And I'd never had a problem saying no to people.

I didn't wrestle with guilt or an overabundance of empathy. If I didn't want to do something, I didn't fucking do it.

Unless Gracie was involved.

"Correct. We did agree to make Bob part of the family." I set her plate down, and she smiled and rubbed her hands together when she looked at the spaghetti and garlic bread on her plate. I was happy to see that she'd finished the carrots and snap peas I'd given her while I was cooking.

I was that guy now… I got excited when my kid ate her vegetables.

I was living with an asthmatic mutt named Bob Picklepants, who snored so loud he woke me up most nights, a horny pig named Maxine, who humped my leg every chance she got, and the world's cutest kindergartener on the planet.

"I think Bob Picklepants really loves Maxine, Daddy."

Bob Picklepants did not give two shits about Maxine. My daughter was just a perpetually glass-half-full type of kid. Bob barely acknowledged Maxine's presence because he was a lazy bastard who only cared about belly rubs and dog treats. Gracie thought they were playing some kind of game when he ignored our unwanted houseguest.

They weren't playing a game, and my household was a real shit show lately. But Gracie thrived in the madness, so what the fuck did that say about my parenting style?

Bob wheezed from the couch, where he lay on his back because the dude was a pampered prince. Maxine was napping in her playpen, and I was grateful for the peaceful dinner with my daughter.

Gracie swirled her noodles around the fork and popped them into her mouth.

"Mmmm, you are the best cooker, Daddy. Piper said she loves to eat at our house."

Piper was Gracie's best friend, and her parents, Colton and Farah, were friends of mine. I happened to know for a fact that Farah prepared three-course meals for her family most nights because Colton mentioned it often. But apparently, five-year-old kids didn't care for things like baby hens and chicken dijon.

They wanted plain ole spaghetti and tacos and grilled cheese, which was easy enough for me to pull off.

"How was school today? Did you have your spelling test?"

"Yep. I got a hundred percent. But Preston spelled a bad word for lemon. Mrs. Clifton sent him to the office for some time to think about what he did."

"How did he spell lemon?" I asked because I was all caught up on the kindergarten drama lately.

My days consisted of crazy animal antics and hearing what that little shit, Preston, did at school, which had become one of my favorite things. The kid just looked like trouble. I'd drop Gracie off in the morning, though I preferred to walk her in if there was time. Preston always walked up and squared his shoulders at me, like we had some kind of beef. I knew trouble when I saw it. Hell, I had four siblings. I could spot a little hellion a mile away.

Gracie set her fork down and looked over both shoulders, as if this were the biggest secret she'd ever shared.

"He spelled lemons," she paused and cleared her throat, "B. U. T. T. That spells butt, Daddy. Like the butt you're sitting on. Or the butt we use in the bathroom."

I wiped my mouth with my napkin to hide my smile beneath it. She was so damn cute the way she took everything so seriously.

"Well, he certainly didn't sound that word out, did he?"

"He did not. Butt does not start with an L, right, Daddy? Lemon starts with an L. L. E. M. O. N."

Atta girl.

My little scholar.

"Correct. I think Preston likes to get attention."

"Well, you say Uncle Finny likes attention, but he doesn't spell butt for a lemon." She had a slight southern accent when she spoke, which my family found hilarious, seeing as we lived on the West Coast. But she'd always had this little twang, and I fucking loved it.

Loved everything about this kid.

I barked out a laugh. "I'm sure Uncle Finny and Uncle Hughey have both gotten into their fair share of trouble."

I let her finish telling me what everyone who sat at her table today ate for lunch, and my chest squeezed when she talked about the mothers of every kid in her class making their lunches.

I was doing this parenting thing solo, and I dreaded the day that Gracie realized she'd been shortchanged by getting me as her sole parent. My only hope was that my parents and my siblings being so involved in her life would make up for the fact that she'd been dealt a shit hand with just having one grumpy dad and no mother.

But damn, if I didn't try to make up for it by loving her fiercely.

"All right. Let's clean up, and then it's bath time, story time, and bedtime." I cleared our plates, and she pulled her little step stool to the counter and watched as I loaded the dishwasher, just like she did every night.

"Daddy, why do you have hair in your nose? I can see it up there." She was leaning over the sink, looking straight up my nostrils.

"Because I'm big and strong, and that requires hair in all sorts of places."

She giggled. "I don't want hair in my nose."

I leaned over and, with the pad of my thumb, raised the tip of her nose to inspect it. "I don't know. I think it's going to be extra hairy like your daddy's nose."

More laughter. It didn't take much to amuse her. She continued to tell me all the details about her day.

Tedious shit that I absolutely lived for.

It always surprised me because I would have never in a million years guessed that I'd be a single dad with a little girl, doing this on my own. Yet there had never been a single day since the moment this little girl was placed in my arms that I hadn't been fucking thankful for her.

I scooped her up and carried her to the bathroom.

Bath time was her favorite. There were bubbles and ducks and sponges and watering cans and a huge mess to clean up after, but it was her thing, so I went along with it.

If the simplest joy in her day was soaking in warm water with a shit ton of toys while telling me the reason that she had 1350 favorite crayon colors—halle-fucking-lujah.

I could make that dream a reality every day until she was too old for me to sit in the bathroom with her.

We went through the routine… I dried her off and pulled her nightgown over her head. She brushed her hair and then her teeth, and I was exhausted by the time I tucked her in and finished reading the final book on her list tonight.

Thankfully, she was worn out, and I kissed her forehead and made my way out to the family room to check on the high-maintenance animals.

I took the laziest dog on the planet out to the backyard and watched as he squatted to pee because Bob was too fucking lazy to lift his goddamn leg and pee like a normal male dog. Then I put Maxine out in the yard where she could spend the next few hours until we went to bed, and I turned on a college basketball game.

My phone vibrated, and I looked down to see a text from Hugh. It hadn't come in on the ongoing family group chat that my siblings were always blowing up. This was a solo text from him.

HUGH

> Hey, brother. I stopped by to check on things at Garrity's, and Presley Duncan is here. She's having a damn good time. She was very friendly to me, so I thought it might be a good time for you to come bump into her. Break the ice, you know?

I knew she'd show up after hearing that her dad had a stroke. I hadn't seen her in years. As far as I knew, she never came back here, as her family had multiple homes in different parts of the country, and I was fairly certain she made every effort to avoid me since we'd ended things.

And she lived in New York with her husband. The dude who'd recently gone viral for impregnating his much younger assistant. He was a famous fucking music producer who, apparently, couldn't keep his dick in his pants.

> Have you forgotten that I have a child I'm responsible for?

HUGH

Have you forgotten that I have a wife who happens to love you and is on her way to your house right now? Come on, brother. I know you want to see her. This way, you won't have an audience because everyone is too drunk to notice tonight, and it won't be awkward. Rip off the bandage. You have a history. You shouldn't avoid her.

I've never avoided her. She avoids me.

And she broke my fucking heart. So I should be the pissed-off one. I didn't say that to him because I didn't talk about it. About how fucked-up it all was in the end.

HUGH

She's at the bar that your family owns, so I'm guessing she'd be fine if you showed up. She wouldn't have come here if she wanted to avoid you.

I rubbed my hands together, unsure of what to do. Hell, a part of me wanted to see her, but the other part of me—the one who hated the way we'd ended things—wasn't sure it was such a great idea.

And I wasn't a guy who avoided shit or got nervous about how to handle situations.

But everything had always been different with Presley.

We hadn't spoken in years, and the last time we spoke hadn't been pleasant. There was a lot of hurt and a lot of finger-pointing.

The knock on the door pulled me from my thoughts, and my infamous guard dog, Bob "Lazy-Ass" Picklepants, was snoring on the couch.

I pulled the door open, and Lila stood there smiling. My brother's wife was a part of the family, and we all loved her.

"Don't argue with me. Go." She walked past me and pointed at the door behind her.

"When did you get so bossy?"

She raised a brow. "Hugh said you were going to fight me, and I'm not having it. You need to go see her. Stop being a baby."

"A baby? Oh, for fuck's sake. I'm not afraid of her. I just don't feel like putting myself or her in an awkward situation. She probably still hates me," I said, reaching for my coat.

"Sounds like the words of a big baby." She laughed. "And I could use some cuddles from Maxine and Ole Bob over there." She flicked her thumb at the lazy bastard, who had still yet to notice that someone had entered the house.

"I'm going. Gracie should be out for the night. I won't be long." I grabbed my truck keys.

"Take your time," she said, just before I pulled the door open and locked it behind me.

I drove the short distance to Garrity's and parked behind the bar. I yanked the back door open and held my hand over my head in greeting to Fred, the cook, and the two busboys who'd just been hired recently. Now that I was here, and I knew that she was here, I was suddenly in a hurry.

Would she want to see me?

I doubted it. We'd said some pretty horrible things to one another.

Hugh clapped me on the shoulder when I walked into the bar. "Hey, brother. She's had an awful lot to drink, so don't be a dick."

"Why does everyone always lead with that? I'm not a dick," I grumped, my eyes scanning the room.

At the very least, I hoped that I wouldn't have any reaction to her. That I wouldn't feel anything for the woman I'd loved fiercely in another lifetime. Feeling nothing for her would be fan-fucking-tastic. Hell, maybe her visiting would be a form of closure for me. Maybe I'd stop comparing everyone else to her, as if she sat on some sort of goddamn pedestal.

But it was the fucking parting of the seas when my gaze found hers on the dance floor.

There was nothing else in the room anymore. Not my brother's voice babbling in my ear about how I should act, not the fifty locals who had been on that dance floor surrounding her just seconds ago.

All I saw was her.

Raven.

She'd always been the prettiest girl in the room, but after years of not seeing her, I hadn't been prepared to have the wind knocked from my lungs.

Her dark jeans fit her like a second skin, and her white blouse accentuated her perky tits, with the button dipping low enough to make my mouth water at the sight of the pink lace peeking out. She had on tall brown boots, and her blonde hair fell in loose waves around her shoulders.

She looked up, as if she felt that same pull that I did. Her gaze locked with mine, and she raised a brow. Honey-brown eyes with pops of copper and gold brought me back to a time in my life I had tried hard to forget.

We both started walking toward one another, but her lips stayed in a straight line, giving away very little.

"Cowboy." The single word slurred as it left her lips, and she held her chin high. Presley had never been a big drinker, but I didn't know what she did anymore, did I?

"Hey," I said, shoving my hands into my pockets because the urge to touch her was strong. "You all right?"

"Am I all right? Do you mean because I've had more cocktails than I can count on two hands? Or do you mean because my father had a stroke, and my mother is the coldest human on the planet?" She narrowed her gaze. "Or let me guess, you're referring to the fact that my husband is having a baby with his assistant?"

Shots fired.

"I guess I'm asking about all of it."

"Well, I'm not your problem anymore, am I?" Her tone was harsh, and she stumbled a bit on her feet. "Obviously, I have a thing for guys who like to get other women pregnant."

That shit pissed me off. But she was drunk, and it was a stupid thing to say. We weren't together when I got Gracie's mother pregnant. Hell, Presley was in a full relationship with her current asshole husband at the time.

No one was unfaithful, and maybe it would have been easier if one of us had been. It was just bad timing. Bad luck. Life throwing us a shit-ton of curveballs. I narrowed my gaze as I studied her, but I bit my tongue before I said anything that made matters worse.

We'd always been explosive together. The way we loved. The way we fought. The way we existed.

Lola came running over and gripped her best friend's shoulders. "Hey, Cage. Uh, Pres, you look a little wobbly. Let me find us a ride home."

"No. You're having fun. You don't need to leave. I can walk. Stay and have a good time. I just haven't slept much, and I didn't eat today. And now"—she glanced over at me—"I'm aggravated. I'll walk home."

"I'm not letting you walk home alone," Lola said, her gaze shooting in my direction.

"I'll take you home," I said, wrapping an arm around Presley's shoulder to stabilize her as the sweet citrus scent that literally brought back every one of my teenage memories hit me all at once.

Presley groaned as she turned to her best friend. "I hate asking *him* for a favor."

"*Him* can hear you, so stop being a brat, and let's get you in the truck. It's not a favor; it's on my way home. I don't even have to stop the truck if you don't want me to. I'll just slow down and you can jump out."

Lola laughed, and Presley turned her head and glared at me as we walked out the door.

"You sure you don't mind taking her home?" Lola asked.

"I'm sure. I was leaving anyway," I said as I balanced Presley on one side of me and pulled the truck door open.

She attempted to lift her leg multiple times, all while remaining in the exact same spot, and Lola laughed hysterically.

I scooped her up beneath her thighs and lifted her easily into the truck, her hand knocking into mine as she reached for the buckle. Her fingers fought me for the strap, and my gaze locked with hers in challenge. She couldn't step into the truck two minutes ago. I highly doubted she could maneuver the buckle into place.

"Let go," I demanded, and she pinched my hand hard before letting me do it. Once I snapped it into place, I stepped back.

"You sure you've got her?" her best friend asked.

"I'm sure," I said.

"All right. I'll stay and hang out for a little longer. I'll call you tomorrow, Pres." Lola waggled her brows at me, and I rolled my eyes because the drunk woman in the truck was currently shooting daggers at me, so there was nothing funny about this.

I shut the passenger door and turned to wait for Lola to walk back inside. I might not be the cheeriest person on the planet, but I wasn't an asshole. I wouldn't leave a woman outside alone. "You sure you've got a ride home?"

"Yes, Dad," she said, her voice all tease. "Hey, Cage."

"Yeah."

"Go easy on her. She's had a lot on her plate lately."

I nodded. I knew it was true, even if Presley would never admit it.

Lola walked inside, and I moved around the truck and

climbed in before pulling out of the parking lot. I glanced over to see her watching me.

"Thanks for the ride," she huffed.

"Not a problem." I cleared my throat. Having her in this small space, with her scent all around me and her eyes on me, had me on edge.

"I saw the booster seat in the back. How old is your little girl now?"

"Gracie is five years old." I drove toward her parents' ranch.

"It's still hard for me to believe that you're a daddy. I mean, I always knew you'd be a great father." She stared out the window when I pulled up the driveway of the grand ranch house, and she pointed to the new addition. "I'm staying in the guesthouse."

Damn. The barn sat in the distance, and I had a vivid memory of the first time I met her. The first time I kissed her. Right there in that very place.

For the longest time, I was fairly certain Presley would be the last woman I'd ever kiss.

But life didn't always go the way you planned.

I had a little girl waiting for me at home that was proof of that.

I put the truck in park and turned to face her. Hell, even my body was on edge now.

It was unfamiliar after all these years.

Feeling things.

Wanting things I had no right to want.

"You doing okay?" I couldn't stop myself from asking. I already knew the answer. And as much as I hated that she'd married another man, I wanted to kill him for hurting her.

A feral need to protect this woman had always been there since the day I'd met her.

She shook her head, and a single tear streaked down her

face. I reached forward, but she held up a hand to stop me from touching her.

"I'm drunk. That's all this is. I don't want your pity, Cage." She sucked in a breath and squared her shoulders.

"It's not pity. I know you're hurting. Having your husband do what he did, and then the whole world knowing what happened… that can't feel good."

Her jaw clenched, and her gaze narrowed. "You know nothing about my marriage. You know nothing about me anymore. But know one thing for certain"—her voice was shaking now, and she scrambled for the door handle—"*you are the reason that my life is the disaster that it is.*"

She thrust her door open and stumbled to get out. I got unbuckled and hurried around to help her.

"Don't touch me!" she shouted, flailing her arms, which was causing her drunk ass to lose balance. I wrapped an arm around her shoulder, even though she fought me on it.

We'd always been like this, even when we were together.

We were both strong.

Both stubborn.

But always ended up wrapped around one another at the end of the day.

"Stop being a stubborn ass. I'm just trying to keep you from falling. You're drunk, and getting hurt right now is not going to help things."

She stopped fighting me, but I could see her chest rising and falling rapidly when I glanced over at her. Tears were coming down her pretty face, which caused a sharp pain to hit me in the chest. I could count on one hand the times that I'd seen her cry in all the years I'd known her.

Once we were standing in front of her door, she jerked away from me and held her chin high. "I'm fine. I haven't needed your help for a very long time."

She pushed the door open, and I fought the urge to scold

her for leaving it unlocked. It was a small town, but that didn't mean she shouldn't be careful.

"I'm more than aware that you don't need me. But I'm not the enemy here." My gaze locked with hers. I wasn't ready to walk away from her yet.

"Sure. You're not the enemy. Congratulations. You're just the guy that ruined me." She slammed the door in my face, and I stood there for a moment before shouting back at her.

"Lock the goddamn door!" I hissed.

She cursed from the other side, and I waited until I heard the lock turn before I walked back toward my truck.

I wondered if this would be the last time that I'd see her again for another couple years.

My chest tightened again.

Just like it did all those years ago.

three

. . .

Presley

MY HEAD POUNDED as the nurse went over all the medications with me that my father would be taking. He listened as well, but he appeared irritated that we were even here. Of course, there were going to be two nurses staying at the house around the clock. My dad didn't want me to be his caretaker, but he was happy that I was home. He preferred to growl at the people that he hired, not his only child.

He and I had always been close. My mother was a cold woman, while my father had always offered a lot more warmth. He'd been the one cheering me on at my horse competitions until she'd finally gotten on board when I started having success as a horse jumper. They'd been equally proud of my scholastic accolades, but I knew that my mother had never gotten over the fact that I hadn't enjoyed pageants the way that she had. She'd won the Miss Massachusetts pageant and went on to graduate at the top of her class from Harvard Business School, where she'd met my father while he was in law school. So even with all that I'd accomplished, I'd been a huge disappointment to her. Attending Harvard Law School and marrying a wealthy socialite had earned me a few points on the Barbie Duncan approval scale, but it hadn't lasted long. She'd always hated that I loved horses, that I loved to paint and be creative, but most of all, that I wasn't polished and put together like she was.

I rubbed my temples, trying to will away the dull pain that had been there for the last few hours. I'd woken up on the couch still wearing last night's clothes, and it was a quick reminder why me and alcohol didn't mix well. I hated feeling this way. I'd taken a long shower and tried to block out the conversation I'd had with Cage.

I hadn't seen him in years, and then the first time I saw him, I acted like a sloppy, bitter drunk. I remembered blaming him for my shitty life and possibly slamming the door in his face. It was mortifying. I'd yet again reached another low.

But I was here to help my father, so I'd forced myself to get up and go to the hospital early this morning to be there for his discharge.

My mother had been busy packing for her trip to Barbados, not a care in the world. She came around the corner wearing a baby blue suit and coat that looked like something the first lady would wear and probably cost more than most people's monthly salary. Her hair was slicked back in a neat chignon, and she wore her black Chanel sunglasses.

In the house.

Barbie Duncan was a bougie bitch, and she made no attempt to hide it. She was intelligent and could outwit just about anyone. She was the master at winning arguments, even with my father, who was a brilliant lawyer in his own right.

My mother never backed down and never admitted to being wrong.

I'd never seen her cry or show emotion either way— happy or sad. She was as even as you got. In control at all times.

It was her superpower.

Lexi and Carol, the two nurses who'd be working the day

shift, both turned to look at her. Their faces remained neutral, but I didn't miss the way they glanced at one another.

This is the rich wife.

The one who couldn't be bothered coming by the hospital.

The one who's leaving now that he's home.

Or maybe those were just my thoughts.

My mother wasn't a caretaker by nature, and she was proud of it. She wanted her husband and daughter to have accolades that she could brag about, and that was as deep as the relationship ran. My father, for whatever reason, loved her in spite of it all. Their relationship had never appeared balanced to me. She held all the power.

"Okay, darling. The car is coming to get me. You've got, hmmm…" She paused and glanced over at the two women who were still staring at her, and she lowered her glasses. She hadn't taken the time to learn their names.

Because it wasn't important to her.

"Lexi and Carol," I said, as I cleared my throat and shot them an apologetic look.

"Yes. You've got Lexi and Carol. And Presley is here, so she'll keep me abreast of your progress."

"I'll be fine," he said, but his words were slightly slurred from the stroke. He would be in intensive physical therapy and speech therapy over the next few weeks. He didn't want me to be there during his sessions, and he'd thrown a fit when I'd tried to argue.

I got it. He was a prideful man. So, I'd let him win this battle. I was going to be working remotely while I was home. But at least I could have breakfast and dinner with him and be an advocate regarding his medical care. Being here would allow me to check on him throughout the day.

To be present.

Unlike the diva who was watching me with pursed lips.

"I can't believe you left the house looking like that." Her

blue eyes scanned me from head to toe, and I glanced down to see how I'd offended her this time.

A pair of jeans, a blue hoodie, and my favorite tan cowboy booties that were pretty scuffed up.

What was her problem?

In her defense, my hair was pulled back in a messy knot, and I was makeup free. My mother didn't understand the concept.

"It's interesting that my physical appearance is your biggest concern on your way out of the country and not the well-being of your husband."

Most people would be offended by the statement, but my mother was impenetrable. She never reacted. It was her way of saying that you weren't worth the energy. And trust me, I'd tried many times over the years to get under her skin.

She was a stone wall.

"I wouldn't leave the property looking like that, especially with the whole world knowing that my husband impregnated another woman."

Did I mention that she could be cruel to her core?

Lexi gasped the slightest bit, and I forced an empathetic smile. This wasn't my first rodeo with Barbie Duncan, but I knew it could be traumatizing for someone witnessing her wrath for the first time.

"Thanks for the reminder. I'm sure it was the scuffed boots that led him to stray."

"I'm just saying, it's worth it to take some time to make yourself presentable." She dropped her glasses back down on her nose and kissed my father's cheek before doing the same to me.

He forced a smile and nodded, as if he were ready for her to leave. I knew that he hated for her to see him like this. She didn't accept imperfection, and right now, he was most likely feeling very insecure about the road ahead of him.

I never understood why he put up with it. They were both

ridiculously wealthy, so it wasn't for the money. It certainly wasn't for me. They hadn't tried to sugarcoat their relationship for me, ever.

She left, and I returned my attention to the nurses just as a tall man entered the room.

"Hey there. I'm Louie, and I'll be here every afternoon for speech therapy. I just thought I'd come by to introduce myself and go over a few things with you, and we'll get started tomorrow."

We spent the next hour speaking to Louie, and then Baxter stopped by to let us know that he was getting his equipment brought over this afternoon, and they'd be starting physical therapy tomorrow to try to get my father up and walking again as soon as possible.

Dad already looked exhausted from the day, and it was barely lunchtime.

This man had always been my idol. My rock. He was strong and determined, and I hated seeing him like this.

Fragile and vulnerable.

Maybe it was because I felt that way at the moment, too.

My life was completely turned upside down.

We ate lunch together, but he didn't say much outside of showing me some photos of a horse he was interested in. After we chatted for a bit, the dark circles under his eyes told me he needed rest. Lexi helped him get into bed, and she encouraged me to take off for a few hours. She reminded me that she'd be there until the night nurse arrived. I thought of moving my things over to the main house, but my father asked me not to do that, and I knew he needed a win right now more than I did.

I decided to go to Cottonwood Café to get some pie to go because it was my dad's favorite.

"Well, look at you, Presley Duncan. Just as pretty as ever," Mrs. Runither said as she wrapped her arms around me. The woman was one of the quirkiest people I'd ever met, but I'd always loved her. My mother was appalled by her, which only made me like her more.

"It's good to see you."

"You, too. I heard that weasel of a husband of yours strayed. Don't let that get you down, though, sugar. You're the whole package. Always have been. It's his loss."

It was hard knowing that everyone knew that my marriage had failed in such a humiliating way, but somehow, Mrs. Runither talking about it came off much kinder than the way my mother had thrown it in my face.

"Thanks for saying that." I cleared my throat. "I wanted to get a blueberry pie for my dad. You know it's his favorite."

"Yes. I heard he was back home today, and I was going to send one over for him when I took them out of the oven in an hour or so. Can I have it delivered to you?"

"Oh, that would be amazing. Thank you." I handed her my credit card, but she refused to take it.

"This one's on me, sugar." She squeezed my hand. "Have you seen that good-looking ex of yours, Cage Reynolds?"

I sucked in a breath at the mention of his name. "Yes. I ran into him last night."

"That is one sexy man, isn't he?" she gushed. "But so irritable. Every time I flirt with him, he acts like I'm committing a crime. The guy needs to relax. And you know what can take the edge off for a man like that?" She winked, and I couldn't help but laugh.

I remembered how horrified Cage used to be by her when we were in high school. She made him so uncomfortable, and I used to find it hilarious.

I wondered how he took the edge off now. I knew he wasn't married because that would be big news in Cottonwood Cove. But I wondered if he still hooked up with his baby mama. If he had a girlfriend. If he slept around. I didn't know anything about him anymore. I certainly didn't keep up with the gossip here, but Lola would occasionally fill me in if she heard someone was getting married or having a baby from the friends that she'd kept in touch with. Now that she lived here, I'm sure I'd be updated on the local gossip moving forward.

But I certainly never imagined that the first time I'd see him again after all these years would go the way that it did last night.

I wasn't above admitting when I was wrong, and I knew he hadn't deserved that.

"Hey, do you know where Cage lives now? I haven't been back in a long time, and I have no idea where anyone lives, outside of my parents and Lola." I chuckled, trying to keep it casual, like it was no big deal, but hoping she would tell me what I wanted to know.

The lawyer in me knew how to press, but I didn't want it to look like I cared.

Because I didn't.

I just wanted to apologize.

"Oh, yes. He built a beautiful home down by the cove where that old, abandoned pink house used to be. He tore it down and built a new one from the ground up."

My heart started beating double time at her words. Memories flooded me, making it difficult to breathe.

He'd built a house *there*?

"Ah, yes, I know the place. Thank you, and thanks for the pie. I'll let Brenda know you're having it delivered." Brenda was the house manager for my parents, and she made sure that the place ran like a fine-tuned machine. Even when neither of them was there for months at a time, the woman kept everything going. My father had started spending most of his time here in Cottonwood Cove over the last two years, as he'd retired from practicing law and was just overseeing the family investments now. He loved animals, and the ranch was his happy place.

"Sounds good, sugar. And you come back and eat real

soon. See if you can drag that sexy ex of yours with you. Just the sight of him gets my ticker moving faster." Loud, bellowing laughter escaped her over-lined tangerine lips, and it made me laugh right along with her.

I waved as I zipped up my jacket and stepped outside. It was breezy and gray today, and the weather matched my mood. I could smell the salty sea in the distance, and I walked a few blocks toward the water, toward the place that held memories I hadn't allowed myself to think about in several years.

I turned the final corner and saw the large redwood tree in the distance, and I sucked in a breath when the white ranch house with black shutters came into view. It had a wrap-around porch with four red Adirondack chairs that matched the color of the door. A red barn sat off in the distance, but it looked to be under construction. I swiped at the tear that broke free and trickled down my cheek, and then I cursed myself internally for being weak.

It was just a house.

Just a silly dream I'd had as a teenager.

I didn't know why it was hitting me so hard. I stood there staring as the lump in my throat made it difficult to breathe. I glanced beside me at the large tree with exposed roots poking through the dirt-covered earth. I moved closer to it and walked around the back side to find what I was looking for.

PD + CR with a heart around it.

I remembered the day that Cage had carved our initials into this tree with his pocketknife like it was yesterday. I traced the letters with my finger and squeezed my eyes closed. I could still feel his lips on mine when I allowed myself to go there.

Maybe it was the emotion of everything I was going through right now… I'd filed for divorce the day that I'd left New York. The whole world knew that Wes and Corona were having a baby, my father was not well, my mother was as cold as she'd always been, and my ex-boyfriend—the only man I'd ever truly loved—was living in the house that we'd always talked about building together someday.

It was a lot.

I dropped down to sit in the deep crevasse between two thick roots erupting from the ground. It had been my favorite spot so many years ago. I just wanted to stare at the place and take a minute to catch my breath.

I'd always been a survivor. Even when my world had fallen apart, I'd been able to pivot. To come up with a new plan. To hold my head high. To keep moving forward.

To be strong.

But right now, I felt completely lost. Completely alone. Completely unsure of what tomorrow would bring. Of what I even wanted it to bring.

I had no fight left in me.

Everything that I'd worked for professionally was a breath away. I was about to be named partner at one of the most prestigious entertainment law firms in the country. I'd been interviewed by a reporter for *New York Law* magazine, and they were printing the story about my success at the firm, about a step forward for all women in the legal world, which would be available for everyone to read in just a few days.

I should be celebrating. Over the moon.

Happy, at the very least.

Yet, even before news broke of my husband's infidelity, I hadn't felt any sort of joy about achieving what I'd wanted for so long.

Maybe I was burned out. In need of a break.

My boss, Phillip Harper, was the most senior partner at the firm. He'd encouraged me to work remotely and take all the time I needed with my father. I wasn't certain if it was out of genuine concern for my dad or because he felt terrible for me that my marriage was being splattered all over the press. Phillip had always been like a second father to me. We were very close. He'd taken me under his wing way back when I was just an intern, and he'd been the one to introduce me to his biggest client, my soon-to-be ex-husband, Wes. So, he was in an awkward position, as the two of them had always been close friends.

The other two partners, Grant Walker and Ben Beezley, were not excited about having a female partner who was also much younger than them, and they'd done everything in their power to stop it from happening. But Phillip had stayed true to his word, and I'd be an official partner at the end of the quarter.

Harper, Walker, Beezley, and Duncan.

It had a nice ring to it.

And I'd paid a hefty price. I'd traded in love and family and any sort of relationship to chase this dream.

I shook off the feeling and blinked multiple times to keep the tears at bay. I chuckled when I looked down to see my scuffed tan booties, knowing that my mother would be horrified that I hadn't gone back to the house to fix myself up before heading out.

I didn't care how I looked right now. I was doing my best just to keep it together.

I squinted up at the sliver of sunshine trying to peek through the dreary clouds.

It was the way that I felt. Like I was being sucked up by the darkness, and I was desperately trying to find the light. To find my way out of this.

"Presley?" A deep voice pulled me from my thoughts, and I looked up to see Cage walking toward me. "You okay?"

He shouldn't be concerned after what I'd said to him last night. And Cage wasn't a forgiving person by nature. He'd always been stoic and stubborn and strong. But for whatever reason, I'd always been the one person that he'd given a pass.

He'd called me his Achilles' heel back in the day.

From the first time we met, he'd been tuned into my feelings, yet he seemed completely unaware of everyone else's feelings most of the time.

It made me feel like the luckiest girl in the world, having this man's light shine so brightly on me.

And then it was all just gone.

"Hey. Yeah, I'm good," I said, pushing against the ground to stand, but he waved his hands for me to stay seated. He stood just inches in front of me and squatted down as his gaze locked with mine.

They'd always been the most beautiful eyes I'd ever seen. Sapphire blue with a dark green circle around the irises. His prominent jaw was covered in day-old scruff, and he still took my breath away, even all these years later.

"Yeah? I saw you sitting under the tree out here and thought I'd better come check on you."

"I hope it's okay that I'm here. Probably a little creepy that your ex-girlfriend is just sitting under a tree in your front yard." I chuckled and looked away because at the moment, looking at Cage physically hurt.

It made no sense.

Our ship had sailed.

We'd both moved on.

I'd survived the loss of him, and I'd promised myself I'd never allow myself to love like that again. So, this should be freeing. A form of closure. But that was not how it felt.

"You know you're always welcome. But I'm guessing you came here for a reason."

"I wanted to apologize for what I said to you last night."

"You want to apologize, huh? Which part in particular are you referring to?" Between his deep voice and the sexy smirk on his face, it was like I'd just been injected with a strong aphrodisiac.

Right between the legs.

I'd thought my body was beyond reacting to anything

anymore, but I'd just been proven wrong. Clearly, I wasn't completely dead inside, as I'd suspected.

I looked up to see him watching me and sucked in a breath before glancing out at the water in the distance. "You didn't ruin me, Cage. I'm just in a weird place right now. But it has nothing to do with you, and I shouldn't have lashed out at you."

But in a way, it had everything to do with him, didn't it? The reason I was in a miserable marriage. The reason I'd chosen a completely different plan for my life.

"Daddy!" a little girl's voice shouted, and she came running out the front door as she headed straight for Cage. All the air left my lungs as I watched her. She was wearing pink tights and a pink leotard and a pair of pink cowboy boots. Dark curls bounced all around her as she pumped her arms and ran toward him like he was the only person in the world that mattered. My heart clenched when she jumped into his arms, and he pushed to his feet and scooped her right up.

It was magical and sweet and so endearing. Like I was a witness to something that was rare in this world.

Cage and his little girl turned toward me, and I stood up, brushing the dirt off my behind.

"Who's that pretty lady, Daddy?" she asked as he held her on his hip.

"Gracie, this is my friend, Presley."

Her hands flew to her mouth, but I was mesmerized by her chocolate-brown eyes and her little cherub cheeks. She was the cutest kid I'd ever seen. She had a perfect mix of all the Reynolds' qualities all wrapped into the most adorable package. "Presley? That's your friend who shares your heart with me, right, Daddy? Her name is inked right by my name. We have the same birthday. We're your two girls?"

Cage's shoulders tensed, and I looked between them, trying to understand what she was talking about. She was obviously just repeating what Cage must have told her, and judging by his unease, I was fairly certain my guess was right.

"That's something else you're thinking of. Presley is my friend, though, and *you've* got Daddy's heart." He cleared his throat.

Inked on his heart?

What was she talking about? I wanted to ask, but this clearly wasn't the time or place, and he acted like she was just confused, so maybe she was.

"It's nice to meet you, Gracie." I rubbed her little shoulder in greeting because, for whatever reason, I wanted to pull her into my arms and hug her.

"It's nice to meet you, too," she said, and she had this cute little voice with a slight twang in her words. "Can Presley come inside and meet Maxine?"

My chest pounded so loud it flooded my senses. Did he live with a woman? Was Maxine her mother? I forced a smile and held my breath, desperate to suddenly run away. I couldn't handle seeing him with another woman.

Not today.

Maybe not ever.

Yes, we'd both moved on. But I'd never had to witness him with someone else. We'd lived across the country from one another. Just the thought was painful, but seeing it? Not high on my list.

The hits just kept on coming, so I'm sure Maxine was going to be a gorgeous woman who wasn't wearing jeans, a hoodie, and dirty boots, and she probably had her life all figured out.

Cage smirked just as a car pulled up the driveway.

"Piper's here!" Gracie squealed before wiggling out of her father's arms and lunged herself at me. "I have to go, Presley. I hope I get to see you again because we share the same heart. But I've got to go to dance class now. It's Piper's mama's turn to drive. Daddy takes us on Mondays, and Farah takes us on Wednesdays. And today is Wednesday."

"I hope I get to see you again, too." I blinked several times because just seeing Cage's daughter had me feeling things that had been buried so deeply I hadn't realized they existed anymore. "Have fun at dance class."

"Give me a minute," Cage said, as he took his daughter's little hand in his and led her toward the car. His long legs moved slow enough for her to keep up, and his broad shoulders were exactly as I remembered them. He helped his daughter into the car, buckled her in the back seat, and said goodbye before holding his hand up and waving as the car backed down the driveway.

The way his brows furrowed as he watched the car drive away had my heart threatening to burst.

The protective stance, the concern—it was everything I knew he'd be as a father.

But witnessing it was different.

Witnessing it hurt me in a way that I couldn't explain to even myself.

I was getting a glimpse of the life that should have been mine.

Time had never been on our side.

And that certainly hadn't changed.

four

. . .

Cage

FUCK. My daughter had a gift for spilling a shit-ton of information in a short period of time. It took everything I had not to laugh at how tense Presley looked at the mention of Maxine. Gracie also outed my tattoo, as well, but hopefully, I played it off well enough. My little girl had no filter. She said whatever came to her mind.

I'd taught her to speak for herself. To always use her voice.

So I couldn't fault her for not knowing what was off-limits.

Hell, I was still trying to wrap my head around the fact that Presley was here in town and that I'd found her sitting outside my house just now.

I'm sure it was a shock for her to see the home that I'd built.

Just because things didn't work out between her and me didn't mean I hadn't stayed true to my word about the other promises I'd made.

But seeing Gracie and Presley together—something I never imagined would happen—did strange things to me.

I'd never been a guy who liked surprises. I liked my routine. I avoided change.

But here we were, with Presley fucking Duncan standing outside my house, and she'd just met my daughter.

I walked back over to her, and she was sitting in the same spot I'd found her a few minutes earlier. I thought of inviting her inside but decided against it and dropped to sit across from her. She looked fucking stunning in her faded jeans and hoodie. Her hair was pulled back from her gorgeous face, which was makeup free.

I wouldn't lie and say I wasn't happy to see her. That my heart wasn't pumping harder than it had in a very long time. That my body hadn't come alive just being close to her.

But that didn't change anything.

Presley Duncan was off-fucking-limits for a multitude of reasons.

Even the fantasy of her.

I couldn't go there. Never again.

She didn't live here.

She was technically still married, as far as I knew, though it had been leaked in the press that she'd filed for divorce the day she left to come home. I only knew this because Finn and Brinkley loved to send me updates. But I knew nothing about her anymore. All I knew was that being around her again was having an effect on me. And I couldn't allow that.

Not anymore.

I prided myself on being in control, and she was the only woman who'd ever tested that.

But there was too much to lose now. Falling for my unattainable ex-girlfriend was not an option.

"Is Maxine Gracie's mother?"

That didn't take long. I raised a brow, enjoying how tense she looked as she waited for my answer. Hell, why did any of it even matter? We'd both moved on with our lives.

"I told you back then that I was going to be raising Gracie on my own."

"I didn't know that meant her mother wouldn't be around."

"Gracie's mother is not in her life."

Her gaze softened, and she let out a long breath. "I'm sorry about that. So, who is Maxine? The lady in your life?"

Goddamn, this woman hadn't changed a bit. I could still read her just as easily as I always could. She was trying so hard to stay composed. To act unaffected. I recognized it because I was doing the same thing.

"Maxine is a pig."

"Wow. I see you haven't lost your charm for complimenting others," she snipped, and I barked out a laugh.

"I'm not fucking insulting anyone. Maxine is an actual potbelly pig."

"You have a pet pig?"

"We do not have a pet pig. Maxine belongs to Martha and Joe Langley, who guilted me into watching her. For the millionth fucking time."

"Well, look at you... you've turned into a big softy, Cowboy." The corners of her lips turned up, and damn if I didn't still get off on making this woman smile.

"Whatever. I did it for Gracie. She loves that little porker."

Her head fell back in laughter, and I couldn't help but do the same.

"Gracie's amazing, by the way," she said, blinking several times before turning her gaze back to mine.

"She's a good kid. I'm guessing my family has more to do with that than I do." It was the truth. They'd all chipped in, and my parents were very involved in my daughter's life in every way possible.

"I don't doubt that they're great with her, but it's impossible to miss the way she looks at you."

"Oh, yeah? How does she look at me? Like the sappy bastard who agrees to babysit a pig to make her happy?"

"She looks at you like she's the luckiest girl in the world to have you for a daddy."

I paused at her words, and it took me a minute to pull myself together.

Parenting was not for the weak.

"She's got a big heart. But I'm the lucky one. I'd be lying if I didn't admit that I question every day if I'm failing her."

Why was I even sharing this? We hadn't talked in years, yet it had always just been easy with Presley. Like she understood me in a way that no one else ever had.

"I mean, all you have to do is look at her. She's bursting with joy. You've got yourself one happy little girl. Why would you even question it?"

I scrubbed a hand down my face.

"Remember how you always liked to be at my house when we were teenagers? You liked the stability you felt there. There were two parents and a lot of love under that roof. You said you didn't have that kind of joy at your house, and I guess it worries me that she doesn't have that perfect family setting."

Her gaze narrowed before softening so much that if I were standing up, it would have dropped me to my knees.

"Cage, I didn't like being at your house because you had two parents. I liked being at your house because it was full of love. My house had two parents, too, but it was filled with staff, and it was run more like a business. You have a pet pig staying here, and your daughter is a bundle of happiness. I'd say you're giving her exactly what you had as a kid. A fairy-tale childhood. And she knows how much you love her; it's impossible to miss."

"All right, that's enough about me. How about you tell me the truth about what's going on in your marriage?"

I didn't know why I'd asked, but I wanted to know.

Needed to know.

She blew out a long breath. "I'm not hurt the way you think I am, if that's what you're asking."

"Your husband knocks up his assistant and the whole world knows, and you aren't hurt? That doesn't sound like you. I know you're strong, but you always had the capacity to feel things deeply."

"Maybe you don't know me anymore." Her expression hardened, lips in a straight line, and I could tell she was trying to keep it together.

"You might be right. But not being hurt doesn't make a whole lot of sense."

At that, her shoulders sagged the slightest bit, and her eyes welled with emotion. "I didn't have a very happy marriage, Cage. Ironically, I ended up living in a home that was similar to the one I'd grown up in."

Presley had hated that her parents had a notably loveless marriage. It was more of an arrangement. Her father tried, and he was a good guy, but her mother was not a warm person. They appeared to be wealthy people living their own lives and throwing money at their daughter to overcompensate for their lack of family. She'd always been drawn to my family. My parents. My siblings.

Me.

My chest tightened at her words, because as much as I hated the idea of her with someone else, I hated the idea of her being sad or lonely more.

I reached for her hand, and my eye caught on a tiny tattoo on the inside of her wrist. It looked to be a small bird.

Raven.

I forced my gaze back up to meet hers. "I'm sorry to hear that. I know that all you ever wanted was a big family."

She shook her head and shrugged. "Well, in his defense, he tried. He tried harder than I did, if I'm being honest. I mean, outside of having an affair. I didn't want kids, and he did, but things were fractured long before that."

"You always wanted kids. What changed?"

"I rushed into marriage because I was hurting." She pulled her hand away from mine and straightened her shoulders. "It was the end of a long-time fairy tale when you and I imploded."

Her words startled me because she appeared to move on so quickly from where I was sitting at the time.

"You didn't wait long to get married." My tone was harsh because the sting was still there. All these years later.

"Well, you were a new dad. That ship had sailed. We just hadn't pulled the bandage all the way off before that. Are you really going to point the finger at me?"

"Fuck, Presley. It was a messed-up time. I don't think either of us knew what to do. Things don't always work out the way you expect, but I think we're way past pointing the finger."

"Agreed. I've got bigger fish to fry than you right now, anyway." She smirked. "I don't have the energy to hate you anymore, Cage. I let all that anger lead me into an unhappy situation."

"He didn't lay his hands on you, did he?" Anger coursed through my veins. Regardless of whether we spoke anymore, there wasn't anything I wouldn't do for this woman if she asked.

I'd fucking do it if she didn't ask.

"Hell no. I would never let a man lay a hand on me. You know that." She raised a brow. "But you always did want to beat up anyone who hurt me, didn't you?"

"Until I was the one to do it." I scrubbed a hand down my face. It felt like a million years ago. And there was too much water under the bridge now. But being with her here, right now, it felt like no time had passed.

"I think we both did the hurting." The tip of her finger moved, running along my knuckles almost absentmindedly. I didn't mind it. I'd never minded being close to Presley.

Never minded her witty banter or her stubborn determination.

Definitely never minded her body wrapped around mine.

My cock thickened in my jeans, and I jerked my hand away and moved to my feet in response. She looked startled by my brisk movement, and she cleared her throat and pushed to stand.

Hell, it had been a while since I'd reacted like that. Sitting close to a beautiful woman would do that to any horny dude who'd gone way too long without sex.

And involving my dick would be the quickest way to lose control.

I couldn't allow that. Not with this woman. I'd barely survived the first time I'd lost her. I couldn't risk that kind of hurt again.

Not when I had Gracie to think about.

"I should probably go check on Maxine." I shoved my hands into my pockets and took a step back, needing to put more distance between us.

What the fuck was wrong with me?

"Yeah. I need to get going. This has been enough of a trip down memory lane for one day." She chuckled.

"How long are you staying? What's your plan?" Wasn't that the million-dollar question? I knew she was a lawyer at her firm in New York, and from what I'd heard, she had a big, fancy penthouse there, as well. Finn had shown me an article about her and her husband, where they'd been photographed at their place in some entertainment magazine a few years ago.

They were living large, to say the least.

"As long as I need to. Probably a couple of weeks, maybe longer. There's nothing to rush back to, aside from work. I'm going to officially be named partner at my firm at the end of the quarter, which I'm really happy about. But my marriage is over. I'm just hoping he'll sign the divorce papers sooner rather than later. Wes doesn't like when he doesn't get his way." Her smile was forced, and she shrugged. Her honey-brown eyes looked gold with the bit of sunlight peeking through the clouds. So fucking pretty, with a body that would make any red-blooded man lose his mind.

And it pissed me the hell off that I was struggling this much from just being around her.

"Why wouldn't he sign the papers? He's having a baby with another woman." I crossed my arms over my chest, working hard to keep my erection under control.

"That's just the way he is. He likes things to happen on his terms. But don't you worry about me, Cage Reynolds. I'm going to be just fine." She took a few steps backward.

"You always are."

"Thanks for the chat. I guess I'll see you around." She held up a hand and turned to walk away.

And I didn't fucking move.

Couldn't fucking move.

I still hated saying goodbye to this woman.

She turned around and caught me staring, and chuckled. "You're going to watch me sail off into the sunset, huh?"

"It's what I always did best."

And that was exactly what I did.

I stood there, watching her leave, reminding myself that she'd be gone for good again in just a couple of weeks.

Because our time together had passed a long time ago.

five

. . .

Presley

WITH THE WEST COAST time difference, I was able to wake up fairly early and head out to the stables to check on the horses before getting in a few hours of work. My horse, Honey, had definitely aged since I'd seen her last, but I couldn't wait to take her out for a ride. She was a gorgeous golden-brown Dutch Warmblood, which was the best jumping horse money could buy. But she'd become more of a friend to me than anything. I'd won my last national competition riding her my senior year of high school, and I'd decided to stop competing after that.

There was a peacefulness that came over me when I was here, breathing in the country air with the morning sun just peeking through the clouds. The ocean sat in the distance, and there really wasn't much that compared to this beauty.

My father wouldn't be up and moving for a while, so the timing was perfect. I'd just finished a meeting with a client and my boss, Phillip, had wanted an update, so we'd agreed to have a Zoom meeting so we could meet face-to-face.

"Good work, Presley. I told you that you could have some time off while you're home, but from the looks of it, you're working quite a bit from there."

"Trust me, I'm not working nearly as much as I normally do. But I'd rather not cancel meetings with clients if I don't have to."

"That's the work ethic that has made it impossible not to make you partner." He chuckled. "How's your dad doing?"

"It's going to be a long road to recovery, but I think he's up for the fight. It's been a tough week, but I'm seeing improvement."

"Yeah, he's going to be just fine. Shall we discuss the elephant in the room?"

"I told you that we don't need to discuss Wes. I know he is your client and your friend, and this is… complicated." I fiddled with the handle of my coffee mug. "You knew him before you knew me."

"Yeah. But I like you much better," he said with a chuckle. "Obviously, we represent his production company. I'm assuming he's seeking his own personal legal representation since you've filed for divorce."

"I honestly don't know. He hasn't responded. We have a prenup, so this whole thing could be very simple if he'd just sign. But you know that isn't really Wes's style."

Wes wasn't a bad guy. Hell, it was the reason I'd agreed to marry him. I may not have loved him the way I should have —the way I'd loved Cage—but he had this vibrant personality that I'd always found attractive. When Wes entered a room, he captivated everyone in it. He was charming and funny and kind. But he was also arrogant and spoiled and entitled. He wanted to have his cake and eat it, too.

They say most people's strengths are also their weaknesses. Wes was a perfect example of that. He required a lot of attention, and he liked to win whatever conquest he found attractive at the moment.

I'd quickly learned that after I'd agreed to marry him. He still sought female attention everywhere we went, and after our first year of marriage, I poured myself into work and stopped traveling with him.

So, he traveled without me.

Which clearly brought us to our current situation.

At the end of the day, we grew apart. And we'd never had a strong enough foundation to make either of us fight for the other.

"Is Stew going to apply a bit of pressure?" he asked about my divorce attorney. Stew Bearman was one of the best, and he also happened to be a personal friend.

"Yes. And I have no doubt that he'll get it done."

"Good. You know I'm here for you. Veronica wants me to drop Wes as a client, but Grant and Ben are pushing back a bit, of course. They are all about the bottom line." Veronica was Phillip's wife, and she'd become a close friend of mine. The partners at the firm weren't loyal to me, nor should they be. This was a business, and at the end of the day, Wes was a good client.

He just wasn't a great husband.

But I certainly wasn't winning any Wife of the Year awards either, though I'd never strayed. I wouldn't disrespect him that way. I may not be in love with him, but I did care about him.

"Don't drop him as a client. This will all blow over, and we'll move on at some point. I just want to have it all behind me before returning home. I don't need to be sharing an apartment with him." I forced a chuckle, dreading everything that needed to happen before this was all over.

"That magazine article is going to press this week. No one will be talking about your creep of a husband when they see that you're blazing the way for women in the legal world." He smiled as he tapped his pen against the desk.

"Thank you. It's nice to have something going right in my life."

"You're tough, and you're going to be just fine. I'll let you go. Keep me posted. We'll talk soon."

I said my goodbyes and made my way to the main house. I wanted to be present for both speech therapy and physical therapy today, just to get an idea of how he was doing and what they'd be expecting of him moving forward. I'd stay out of the way so he wouldn't be embarrassed about me being there.

When I arrived at the house, Brenda was just setting out a fresh vase of peonies and hydrangeas in the entryway. My mother liked things run in a certain way, whether she was staying at this house or not.

"Good morning," I said, pausing to give her a hug. She'd worked for my family for a long time.

"Hey there, sunshine. I sure do like starting my days seeing your sweet face. I'm glad you're here. I think it's helping your dad a lot."

"Yeah. I'm glad I'm here, too. Is he up?"

"He is. I'll bring you some coffee up shortly."

I held up my water bottle. "No need. I'm good for now. And you know I'll help myself if I need anything."

I'd married a man who was as wealthy as the family I'd grown up in. But I'd always preferred to do things for myself when I could.

"All right. Come say goodbye before you head out."

"I will."

The next few hours were filled with progress and frustration. My father was a strong man, and he didn't like relying on anyone for help. I understood it. But he was also stubborn, and that could work against him.

"Nice work today," Baxter said, helping him back into the wheelchair. There was a layer of sweat across my dad's forehead, and he nodded.

Once we returned to his room, he tipped his head back and chugged some water. "All right, darling." His words were already getting much clearer, and it had only been a week since he'd started speech therapy. "I'm going to shower and make some calls."

"You're back to work?" I shook my head in disbelief.

"Work keeps my mind focused. I'm just going to check on a few things, nothing over the top. Don't you have to go meet Lola to see that property?" he asked, and his words dragged toward the end because the longer he spoke, the more tired he grew.

"Yes. I'm going to meet her in an hour. She's excited about it." My father was going to be an investor in her new business, as was I. My best friend was brilliant, and I had no doubt she would turn this spa into an attraction that everyone on this coast would want to visit.

"You sure you don't want to throw in the towel on law and move back here and partner up with her?"

My eyes doubled in size. "Says the man who once told me there would be nothing better that I could ever do with my life than to practice law?"

"Well, I said that when I was practicing law." He chuckled this raspy, hearty laugh that made my chest heavy. "I know you're going through a lot. That asshole husband of yours better not come around me anytime soon."

I rolled my eyes. "He messed up, but he isn't the only reason our marriage is done. I just waited too long to do it myself. We were over long before he had an affair."

He looked up at me with the same dark eyes as mine. "Life is short, sweetheart. Do what makes you happy."

"Who are you, and what have you done with my father?" I laughed and did my best to mimic his deep voice. "Life is short, so make a difference in the world while you can. Work hard. Make a name for yourself."

"You've already got my name." He smirked. "And you graduated from Harvard Law and work at one of the most prestigious firms in the country. There's nothing left to prove.

What I don't like seeing is the sadness in your eyes." His voice broke on his last word, and I reached for his hand.

"I'm fine. I just want you to be okay."

"I will be. You can count on it."

"All right. Get showered and get some rest. I'll be back in a few hours."

There had been a heaviness in my chest since I'd been home. Seeing my dad in his current state, my lack of relationship with my mother more apparent than ever, being in the same town as Cage, and meeting his daughter—it was a lot.

I said goodbye to Brenda as she fixed a tray of food for my father, and I decided to walk to meet Lola downtown. I was so used to being in the city with so many people, and it was nice to be out on a walk and hear the sound of the birds chirping and smell the salt water in the distance.

How long had it been since I'd walked somewhere and took my time getting there?

My phone vibrated, and I glanced down to see yet another text from Wes.

THE DEVIL

> I just spoke to your attorney. I will sign the papers if you hear me out. I'm flying into Cottonwood Cove tonight. Have dinner with me, let me speak to you in person, and I give you my word that I will sign the papers afterward if that's what you want. Tell me where to meet you, and I'll be there at 8:00 p.m.

I came to a stop and let out a long breath. I knew this was the only way he'd do it, so I could agree to these terms. I responded quickly, and I felt hopeful that this could be closure for both of us.

> Thank you. I'll be at Reynolds' Bar and Grill at 8:00 p.m.

THE DEVIL

Why am I not surprised you chose Reynolds'
as the meeting place? It's sort of ironic,
isn't it?

I didn't respond. Yes, he knew about my history with Cage. Hell, he blamed that relationship for all that had been wrong with ours. But Reynolds' Bar and Grill was the busiest place in town from what I'd heard, and I knew Wes well enough to know that he wouldn't make a scene in a restaurant with an audience. Wes was all about image and appearances.

I tucked my phone into my back pocket and looked up to see Lola waving at me as she stood in front of the old firehouse.

"So, this is it, huh?"

"Yep. Brax opened it up for me to show you, and he'll be back to lock up in an hour. He had an appointment." Brax was Hugh's best friend, and he'd grown up in Cottonwood Cove.

"Did you already go inside?"

"I did," she said. "You're going to lose your mind. It's absolutely perfect. I'm hoping it makes you want to be my partner and run this place with me."

"I am your partner," I said, shaking my head. "But my life is in New York, and you know that."

"You're my financial partner. I want us to work together like we always dreamed we'd do."

"Lo, I'm about to become a partner at Harper, Walker, and Beezley. It's everything I've worked for. Not to mention, there is an article going to press in a few days that will be singing my praises as having paved the way for women in the legal world. Have you forgotten about all that?"

"I know, and I'm so proud of you. I just… I don't know," she said, looking away as her teeth sank into her bottom lip.

"What? Say it."

"I think you've buried yourself in a miserable job, working endless hours all to avoid your unhappy marriage. Life is short, Pres. I want you to be happy. That's why I left the city and came here. I'm done with the rat race. I want to start living."

I raised a brow and reached for the door handle, pulling it open and stepping inside. "Don't put your issues on me. You hated Corporate America. I thrive in it."

"I'll bet you thrived having that talk with Cage, too, didn't you?" She waggled her brows.

"It was fine. I didn't want to leave things with me being a complete asshole to him while I was drunk. We got some... closure."

"Is that what we're calling it?" She chuckled and pulled off her coat, and I did the same. "And his daughter sounds adorable."

"Yeah. She's really something. He's a good dad, no doubt about it." I looked up as I dropped my coat onto the counter beside the door. "And... oh my gosh. This place is spectacular."

The old firehouse had massive vaulted ceilings and wide-open spaces. It would take a lot of work to make it what she had visualized for the space, but I listened as we walked through and she explained her plans for the layout. From yoga classes to several rooms for massages and facials and whatever else she could think of. There would be a juice bar and a small gift shop selling brand products she wanted me to help create. My inner artist couldn't wait to go sit at the cove and sketch some ideas for her.

"Isn't it fabulous?"

"It is. I can see it. Now, we need to come up with a name and brand idea and then figure out the budget. It's going to take a lot of work to get this place up and running, but I think it's going to be worth it."

"Does it make you want to jump ship on your boring life and join me?"

"It does not. But I will be cheering you on all the way." I bumped her with my shoulder as we moved up the stairs.

"Can we grab dinner and celebrate that we might actually have found the perfect place?"

I loved that Lola was always a glass-half-full person. We had a long way to go as far as figuring out the expenses and what this particular location would take to get it up and running. But her enthusiasm had always been one of my favorite things about her.

"I can't tonight. Wes is coming into town."

Her head whipped around, and her mouth fell open. "Shut the mother fucking front door!"

"Relax. He said he'd sign the papers if I agreed to meet with him. He's just flying in for dinner."

"How noble of him. Is he bringing his baby mama with him?"

"That would make for an interesting dinner, wouldn't it?" I shook my head and laughed. What had felt mortifying just a week ago, had somehow become comical to me now.

Maybe being back here in this small town that I'd always loved was having a healing effect on me.

My life was still a shit show, but somehow, I didn't feel so alone anymore.

six

. . .

Cage

MY PHONE VIBRATED as I sat at my desk, and I glanced down to see the never-ending text thread lighting up.

GEORGIA

Hey, I ran into Farah at Cup of Cove, and she told me she saw you talking to Presley Duncan when she picked up Gracie a few days ago.

BRINKLEY

WHAT? Why would you not tell us that? Why are we hearing it from a third party?

Because I didn't want to make it a big fucking thing.

HUGH

I know it didn't go well at Garrity's the other night. Did it go better the second time around?

It's fine. She met Gracie. We don't hate each other. There's not much more to say.

GEORGIA

You know you can tell us if you're hurting.

Oh, for fuck's sake. I'm fine. I don't need a therapy session, so don't go running to Mom and tell her about this. I'm fine. Presley's fine. There is nothing to dissect.

BRINKLEY

Hmmmm... You've loved one woman in your entire grumpy existence, and you expect us to believe that it's no big deal that she's here? I'm not buying it.

GEORGIA

Same.

You don't need to fucking buy it. Just because you two think something does not make it true. I. Am. Fucking. Fine.

BRINKLEY

Sure sounds like it.

I wasn't about to tell them that my daughter had become consumed with questions about Presley. She'd come home from dance and talked nonstop about my *special friend*. How the fuck was I going to get her to tone it down before Sunday dinner? The whole family would be all up in my business if this went any further.

FINN

I think he's given his heart to Maxine now. Last time I was over, that pig was awfully territorial.

HUGH

How much longer are you keeping that beast anyway? The Langleys were having dinner at the restaurant last night, and Joe looked absolutely fine.

Those fucking Langleys are trying to use my daughter to get me to keep this fucking pig. It's ridiculous. I'm going to stop by their house when I leave work today and return her. I'm lugging this damn pig with me to and from work every goddamn day because she loses her shit if I leave her home.

BRINKLEY

Go figure. She doesn't want to stay home with the ever-exciting Bob Picklepants? I can't imagine why. <laughing face emoji>

HUGH

Do not hate on Bob. That's my kind of dog. Last time I was over, he stuck his nose in my beer mug. He's a cool dude. He's just chill.

GEORGIA

Why don't you just agree to keep Maxine? Gracie loves her, and I think you like her more than you let on. I saw that cute peach bandana you got her.

It's just a bandana. I think I found it at Mom's house.

BRINKLEY

That's interesting. It has Maxine embroidered on it, Tough Guy.

Fine. Gracie saw it and begged me to get it for her. This is what I'm saying. My life is a shit show. I just spent an hour with Mr. fucking Wigglestein, trying to convince Mrs. Remington to get him fixed.

FINN

That fucker has knocked up more women in Cottonwood Cove than the Reynolds brothers have all together.

Don't be crude. He's impregnated multiple bitches, and she needs to get a handle on it and keep him contained, for fuck's sake. I've got to go. I have one more client before I can get out of here.

HUGH

See you tonight at dinner.

BRINKLEY

I think it's uncool that you have a men's-only dinner without us.

FINN

You're having dinner with Georgie, Reese, and Lila. What are you talking about?

GEORGIA

It's the point. You could have asked and allowed us to turn you down.

We have dinner every Sunday night with all of us. It's enough. You people are suffocating me.

BRINKLEY

Any chance you'll invite Presley to Sunday dinner? Now, that would be exciting. <winky face emoji>

FINN

Presley and Maxine in the same room. Let the fireworks begin.

HUGH

I think Maxine is more likely to put up with his grumpy ass than Presley.

You fuckers need to get a life and stay out of mine. <middle finger emoji>

I silenced my ringer and slammed my phone down before rubbing my temples.

"Dr. Reynolds," Kate said, hovering in my doorway.

"What's up?"

"Kressa Peterbaken is here with Chester, the latest stray puppy she's found and adopted. I put them in room two, and that's the last one for the day. But prepare yourself. I'm not a veterinarian, but something seems a bit off about this one."

"Great. Of course, it is. This day just keeps getting better." I pushed to my feet. "Did Mrs. Remington make an appointment to get Mr. Wigglestein fixed?"

"She made an appointment to come talk to you again because she has more questions."

I fisted my hand and held it to my mouth. How many fucking times could we talk about fixing this fucking dog?

"What is her goddamn issue with getting him fixed? I mean, half the town is outraged by the whole situation."

"I know. There are going to be little Wigglesteins coming in to see you for years to come," she said over her laughter, and I shook my head.

"Not funny. I will meet with her one more time, and then I'll refer her to my mother for emotional help. This isn't a Mr. Wigglestein issue at this point. It's a Mrs. Remington issue."

"Agreed."

I made my way into room two, and Kressa Peterbaken

was standing in front of her small dog crate, talking baby talk to Chester.

"Hey, you got a new pup, huh?" I asked as I closed the door and set the file on the counter before glancing into the crate to see a fucking raccoon looking back at me.

"Isn't he precious? I think he's part Maltese and part Terrier. What do you think?"

I cleared my throat. When I graduated top of my class in veterinary school, they could not have prepared me for the shit I was dealing with in Cottonwood Cove.

"I don't believe that he is part Maltese or Terrier," I said, raising a brow as I crossed my arms over my chest because I didn't have time for this shit right now.

"Really? Do you think he's part bulldog?"

I'd known Kressa for many years, as she used to work for my parents at Garrity's before retiring a few years ago. I didn't want to be cruel, but I also didn't have the patience to make this okay.

"This is not a dog, Kressa. You've got yourself a raccoon in there."

"What? Really? Well, he was hanging out in my yard for weeks, so I decided to get him into the crate and bring him here for shots before I let him in the house with the other dogs."

"Well, he isn't a dog, so that won't be happening."

"Will he need different shots?"

"No. He's a wild animal, so he needs to be set free. It's against state law to keep any wildlife as a pet."

"Well, isn't that ridiculous. He seems like a dog to me."

"But he isn't a dog. He's a raccoon."

And I'm a fucking doctor who doesn't have time to convince you that you lured a fucking wild animal into your dog crate.

"So, I guess I need to go fight this with the county?"

"I recommend setting him free to live the life he was meant to live." I pinched the bridge of my nose.

"All right, then. I hope he won't feel abandoned."

"I don't think that will be a problem." I nodded as I pulled the door open and shot a look at Kate, who was sitting behind the desk with her hand over her mouth to keep from laughing.

I shook my head and heard Kressa going on and on about what a shock it was that Chester was a raccoon. Then I finished up my paperwork and left for the day.

———

When I got to Reynolds' Bar and Grill, I was already exhausted. I'd just made my daughter dinner and dropped her off at my parents' house for a few hours so they could watch some new movie that had just come out and bake cookies. I was meeting Finn, Hugh, Lincoln, and Maddox at Reynolds' for a guys' night. We tried to get together at least once a month, without the girls, so we could shoot the shit without a million questions derailing the conversation. Sometimes we played poker, and other times we came to Reynolds' for the best ribs in town.

I'd completely wasted my time stopping by the Langleys' on my way home from work because when Martha opened the door, she started coughing profusely, and Joe had to go get her inhaler.

I'm sure the Langleys were milking it, but Maxine and I hightailed it out of there. I dropped her off at the house, leaving her outside in the backyard until I got home.

She was the houseguest that just wouldn't leave.

I tugged my coat closed as a gust of wind whipped around me as I made my way to the door. We were expecting a big storm in the next few days. Once I stepped inside, Hugh walked toward me quickly, and I could tell by the look on his face that something was wrong.

"Wes Wellington is at the bar. He claims he's here to meet Presley."

"Well, he's got some fucking nerve coming here, of all places." I stormed past my brother, and he gripped my shoulder, but I shook him off because I was on a fucking mission.

"Who the fuck do you think you are, coming here?" I shouted as I yanked him out of his seat.

His glass dropped from his hand, clanking against the bar as liquid splattered all around. I shoved him back, and he stumbled to get his footing.

My fist was raised, and there was nothing I wanted more than to knock this fucker out.

I hated him for marrying *my girl* all those years ago, and I hated him even more today for hurting her the way he had.

"Brother, you need to relax." Hugh clutched my shoulder hard, and I turned to see Finn, Lincoln, and Maddox all standing there now, watching me with concern.

"You must be Cage Reynolds," Wes said, holding his hands up before reaching for a napkin to wipe the red wine off his suit jacket.

"And you must be fucking insane to come here, to this restaurant, after what you've put her through."

"How about you sit down and let me get us each a drink before Presley shows up to meet me and we cause her more stress than necessary."

"She knows you're here?"

"She chose the restaurant."

Kline, the bartender, gathered the broken glass off the bar top, and I motioned for the guys to head back to the table. Hugh lingered before tapping me on the shoulder once. I took a seat beside the asshole that I desperately wanted to knock out.

Kline got Wes a new glass of wine and handed me a beer. Wes held his glass up like we were buddies, and I just stared at him before pulling the bottle to my lips.

We weren't friends.

I was still trying to figure out if punching him would be worth it.

He chuckled. "You're everything I expected. She clearly knows you well."

I narrowed my gaze. "I don't know what you're talking about, but you better be here to sign those fucking papers for her. You've done enough damage. Let her go."

He took a sip from his glass and forced a smile. "A part of me feels like I should be punching you in the face. You're probably the reason my marriage failed. But I don't believe in violence, so I'll restrain from getting physical."

The dude was a decade older than me, a few inches shorter, and I had a good fifty pounds on the asshole. He'd have more luck fighting Maxine than me. But there was humor in his eyes as he said it, so I sat back and set my beer down on the bar.

"I'm not sure what you're insinuating. Presley isn't a cheater, if that's where this is going. I haven't seen her in years, but I know who she is, and that's not her. So, I don't think you can use that defense to get away with what you did, if that's your angle."

"I know my wife pretty damn well, too, Cage."

"Soon-to-be ex-wife," I hissed.

"I brought the papers, and I'll sign them tonight if it's what she wants. I know Presley would never be unfaithful, but you can leave a marriage for other reasons. And she's been one foot out the door since the day we said our vows."

"Yet, she's stayed faithful. She doesn't have some asshole telling the whole world about an affair and humiliating you, does she?"

He shook his head. "I'm not a perfect man. But I can tell you that I have loved my wife fiercely since the day that I met her. But it wasn't reciprocated, and a man can only take so much." He held up his hands. "It's not an excuse. It's just the truth. There have been three people in my marriage this entire time, and there just wasn't room for me any longer. And that's the truth."

I listened and looked away because I understood it. I'd never moved on from her either. The connection we had was rare, but we'd made our choices, and life had taken us in different directions.

"You can't blame her for her past and then use that as a reason to be unfaithful. That shit doesn't fly. She's too smart for it. Hell, I don't think anyone is going to have sympathy for you on that one. I'm sure you have a past. An ex that you dated before her."

"I think we both know this was different. I'm not asking you to understand what I did, but I am not a stupid man, and neither are you, from what I've heard. What you two had was different, and I couldn't live up to that."

"That sounds like *your* problem, buddy. You should have manned up and proven you were worthy. If you love someone the way you claim to love her, and you're lucky enough to call her yours, you keep your dick in your pants."

He nodded and reached for his glass. "Do you know what Presley did two days before our wedding?"

"Got drunk and tried to flee the country?" I smirked because I just wanted to hate this asshole, even though I could tell he was devastated about losing her.

And it was his own damn fault.

"She got a tattoo on her wrist. This little raven. She said it was just something special she wanted. But years later, during one of our heated fights, she admitted Raven was a nickname that you'd given her. That it was a reminder of a time when she was actually happy." He sipped his wine. "How do I compete with that?"

My fucking chest squeezed at his words.

She'd run off and married him while I was alone and

trying to learn how to take care of a newborn and open my veterinary practice at the same time.

We'd completely cut off all contact from that moment on.

And knowing that on her wedding day, she had a piece of me inked on her body…

It fucking destroyed me to think about it.

"You should have showed up every fucking day and earned that trust. Instead, you just flashed your money and tried to buy her off. I'm sure her fucking mother loves you." I took a long pull from my beer.

"Barbie appears to like me a hell of a lot more than her daughter does." He chuckled, and I had to give it to the guy. He was laying his cards on the table and owning it.

"There's a shocker. But Presley isn't like her mother. That shit won't matter to her. She can make her own money. Make her own way."

"You're preaching to the choir, Cage. I have no doubt of her capabilities. And somewhere along the way, she gave up on one dream and replaced it with another. She's married to her job now, and that's her whole life. Her purpose. It's all she cares about. I just didn't want to give up, but it was over long before I strayed. She knows it, and I know it. But I'd still choose her over anyone."

"Good luck with that. She's not going to give you another chance to do this to her again."

"I know. But I've got to shoot my shot, right?" he said, as his gaze moved from me toward the door.

I turned to see Presley walking toward us, confusion in her honey-brown gaze.

Dark jeans, cowboy boots, and a white turtleneck sweater. Her camel dress coat was tied at the waist, and her hair was tied back in some sort of knot.

"Well, this is unexpected." Her eyes landed on Wes's suit coat, which had a large red wine stain.

Too fucking bad.

He could buy a new coat. He should consider himself lucky I didn't knock his teeth out.

"I thought it was time that I finally met the infamous Cage Reynolds."

Presley stared hard at him before turning to me as I pushed to my feet. "Have a good night. I'm right over there if you need me."

Because I wasn't going anywhere until this asshole was gone and I knew she was okay.

Old habits die hard, I guess.

seven

. . .

Presley

WES MOVED behind me as the hostess led us to our table, which of course, happened to be just a few feet away from my brooding ex-boyfriend. Cage was seething when I'd interrupted the conversation, and I didn't miss the wine stain on Wes's Armani tweed coat.

"Do you have a table in the back that might be a bit more private?" Wes asked, and the hostess was notably uncomfortable as she glanced over at Cage and then back to us. Hugh owned the place, so clearly, Cage had requested that we sit nearby.

Once a cowboy, always a cowboy.

"I, um, this is the only available table for two," she said, and her voice shook, making it obvious she was not being truthful, especially with there being several open tables on the other side of the restaurant.

"Oh, for fuck's sake. What does he think I'm going to do?" Wes shook his head and squeezed his eyes shut.

"It's fine." I nodded at her. "This is perfect. Thank you."

"Well, you certainly didn't exaggerate when you described him." Wes pulled out my chair, and we both took our seats.

I reached for the wineglass that Wes had ordered for me and brought over from the bar and took a sip. "We aren't here to talk about Cage. We're here to talk about the ending of our marriage and you signing those papers."

"Can I plead my case, and at the end of this, if you still want me to sign them, I give you my word that I'll do it?"

His word wasn't something I would put a lot of stock in right now, because I knew Wes well enough to know that he would say or do whatever he could to get what he wanted. But I'd agreed to meet him here, so I was willing to hear him out. There was nothing he could say that would change my mind, but I'd listen and then ask him to sign.

The server approached, and we paused to order dinner before handing him our menus. I looked up at Wes. "Go ahead."

"First and foremost, no matter what happens, I want you to know… No. I *need* you to know that I love you, Presley. I have loved you since the first time I laid eyes on you."

I knew that he loved me as much as he was capable of loving someone. When I first met him, he was possessive and wanted to be with me all the time. And maybe because I was heartbroken about Cage, it felt like love at the time. But I realized a few months into my marriage that I was more of a possession to Wes. One he was proud to take out and show off. He was impressed with my career and my drive, and I think part of the allure he felt was that I never was all in with him. He was used to women falling at his feet, and I'd just never done that. Maybe it was self-preservation on my part, but my heart couldn't handle any more pain. At the end of the day, I was very aware that Wes was a narcissist, and he'd always put himself first.

I nodded. I wasn't going to respond because I was here to let him say what he needed to say, and then we'd be done with it.

"I'm not a perfect man. That much is clear. And I fucked

up big time, but I still love you. You are the only woman I want."

"Your mistress is pregnant with your child. That is clearly not true." I held my hand up to stop him because I needed to get this off my chest now that he'd brought it up. "Listen, Wes, I wish things hadn't ended like this. We both know that this should have ended a long time ago. Hell, we never should have gotten married in the first place. But I was heartbroken, and you saw it as a moment to swoop in and be the hero, which I needed at the time. And I know that you tried. I do. But don't say I'm the only woman you want because that statement is clearly not true. And I won't say that to you either. We haven't had sex in over a year. I don't fault you for having needs. But I brought up divorce so many times, and you fought me hard enough that I didn't want to deal with it. You should have just taken the out."

"I didn't want to let you go."

I cleared my throat as our waiter brought our plates over and set them in front of us. Once he stepped away, I looked up to meet Wes's gaze.

"I know you didn't. But it's time now. *I need you to let me go.* And you should give things a chance with Corona. You're having a child with her."

He ran a hand through his hair. "Fuck, Pres. I have nothing in common with her."

"You have a baby in common. You need to be involved, Wes. That should be what you're putting your energy into. Not trying to save a marriage that is far beyond being salvaged."

"What if we went to therapy?" he pressed as he reached for his utensils and cut into his steak.

"Therapy can't repair this. Please. I'm asking you to give this to me without a fight. I don't have the energy with all that's going on in my life."

He nodded, his eyes welling with emotion. "Okay. Yes. If

it's what you want, I'll sign the papers tonight. I'll have the team draft up an amicable statement to send out tomorrow to the press."

"Thank you." A huge weight was lifted off my shoulders. I was ready to walk away from this part of my life and move forward.

"Tell me how your father is," he asked.

"He's okay. He's at the house with a team of fabulous healthcare providers. Barbie is off in Barbados, trying to take over the world, of course."

"And you're here."

"I'm here," I said, dabbing the napkin against my mouth.

"So, what's the story with the barbaric ex? He clearly hates me, so you must have filled him in on the details."

I glanced over, and my gaze locked with Cage's sapphire blues. I gave him a reassuring smile to let him know I was fine. The look he gave me managed to say, *I will fuck him up if you give me the go-ahead.* We'd always had this strange gift for communicating without words, and clearly, that hadn't changed. I gave the slightest shake of my head before turning back to the man in front of me.

"Really? I think the whole world knows what happened, thanks to Corona taking the story public. I'm guessing you didn't want to tell me, so she decided to take matters into her own hands."

"Correct. Can you blame me?"

"Um, yeah, I can totally blame you. She's right. I mean, I wish it hadn't come out the way it did, but you are having a child with her. You should have acknowledged it."

"I don't know if I'm ready to be a father," he said, cutting another large piece of meat and popping it into his mouth. I studied him for a moment. He had dark hair with a little gray coming in at the roots that actually complemented him. He was polished and well-spoken and generous with his money, but the man was too selfish for his own good.

"You should have thought about that before you had unprotected sex."

He raised a brow. "Well, I wasn't having any unprotected sex with my wife, or any sex at all with her, was I?"

I rolled my eyes. "I'm glad I stuck to that rule back when we were still… intimate."

It was a dig at the fact that I'd insisted on being on birth control as well as making sure he always wore a condom, even back when we were actually having occasional sex. I hadn't wanted to get pregnant, and I think a part of me always suspected he would stray. I wouldn't be surprised to learn that Corona wasn't the first. It wasn't something I even wanted to know at this point, but I was grateful that my instincts had set that precedent from the beginning. I'd used the pregnancy excuse, but truth be told, the only other man I'd been with in my life had not always worn protection.

Cage and I had a different kind of relationship. Neither ever worried about the other straying. It wasn't who we were.

"Phillip called. I know you're going to be named an official partner soon, and he's concerned about the conflict of interest with me being a client. With the magazine article coming out and the mess that I've made, I don't want to make this more difficult for you."

"It's already all out there, and I've told him there is no issue on my part." I reached for my glass and couldn't help but look over again when I felt Cage's eyes on me before quickly looking away. "I'm hoping we can just move forward in a professional and friendly manner."

"I'm proud of you, Presley. You've worked really hard. You deserve this."

"Thank you. It's been the one good thing to happen in my life at the moment."

His gaze was empathetic, but then he glanced down at his phone a few seconds later. Wes could feel things deeply in one moment, but he was always on to the next so quickly, which made it surprising that we'd stayed married for the years that we had.

"So, how long will you stay here?" he asked.

"As long as my father needs me. They built the guest-house on the property, so I have my own space. I've been able to work a few hours in the mornings, and tomorrow, I'm looking forward to taking Honey out for a ride while my dad is in physical therapy. He doesn't like me to sit in because he doesn't want me to see him struggle, so I'll go for a ride instead."

"She must be getting up there in age now, huh?" he asked.

"Yep. She's around fifteen years old, and she's looking thinner than I remember. I haven't had the time to take her out for a ride yet, so I'm looking forward to it."

"It's good for you to be here. Slow things down a little, you know?" he said.

"Yeah. I think I actually needed it."

Our waiter stopped by to ask if we wanted dessert, but we both declined. I ordered a hot tea, and Wes chose a cappuccino. We spent the next thirty minutes dividing up everything we'd shared over the last five years. He'd agreed I should keep the penthouse in the city, as I spent way more time there. He wanted the two vacation homes in Aspen and the Hamptons, and I didn't have any issue with that since I hardly ever spent time at either of them.

It was all very… civil.

Our breakup was as ill-passioned as our marriage. There were no tears or arguments. He claimed he was heartbroken, but I didn't believe Wes even knew what it meant to be heartbroken.

I knew what heartbreak felt like.

And this was not it.

He paid the bill and then smiled. "All right. You mentioned that you walked here, so how about I take you home and sign the papers in the car where we don't have an audience."

"That sounds like a plan."

When I pushed to stand, Wes did the same, and out of my peripheral, I saw Cage move to his feet.

"Do you need a ride home?" Cage asked before turning his gaze to glare at Wes.

Wes huffed several times before turning toward the much taller man standing in front of him. "Relax. I'm signing the papers and taking her home. How about you let the two of us end this alone? You've been present in our marriage enough, don't you think?"

Now it was my turn to roll my eyes. "Stop being so theatrical. You have a pregnant mistress back home. You aren't the victim in this situation."

I didn't miss the way Cage's lips twitched, and I noticed that the guys at his table used their hands to cover their mouths to keep from laughing.

"Let me know if you need anything," Cage said.

"I'm fine." It came out harsher than I meant it to. I felt like a horrible human being because I liked that Cage was being protective when I should be focused on my five-year marriage coming to an end.

Wes placed his hand on the small of my back and guided me out to the car.

The drive to my house was quiet, and when we pulled up in the driveway, he put the car in park and did exactly what he said he would do.

He signed the papers and handed them to me.

"Thank you."

"I'm sorry I let you down," he said, squeezing my hand.

"I think we both did a lot of that." I leaned forward and kissed his cheek. "I hope you step up to the plate for your child, Wes. It's the most important job in the world."

He nodded. "I know. I'll try my best."

I pushed out of the car and held up my hand to wave goodbye before walking up the path to the front door and pushing it open. I startled when I saw Lola sitting on the couch watching TV with a bottle of champagne in an ice bucket and a big bowl of popcorn.

I closed the door and chuckled. "Well, hell. What do we have here?"

"I'm watching *The Bachelor*, and damn, that man is fine." She shook her head and reached for the bottle. "And I brought some champagne so we can toast this special occasion."

"I don't know that divorce is something to celebrate." I dropped the envelope with the papers onto the breakfast nook table.

"We're not celebrating your divorce. We're celebrating this new chapter. It's time for you to start living again." She handed me a champagne flute, and I clinked it against hers and smiled.

"Fine. Cheers to new beginnings," I said, and she squealed as I tipped my head back, and the cool liquid made its way down my throat.

I did feel like something had been lifted from my shoulders.

Like a dark cloud had finally moved aside to allow some light to shine in.

Wes and I were no longer tied to one another.

Maybe this really was a new chapter.

And even with all that was going on, it was the first time in a very long time that I was excited about tomorrow.

eight

. . .

Cage

"SO WE AGREE, it's time to get Mr. Wigglestein neutered. Go ahead and make the appointment up front with Kate." I pushed to my feet because I wasn't going to spend one more minute discussing this with her.

It was ridiculous at this point.

The little horndog had the whole town in a fucking uproar, and everyone wanted to take it up with me. My phone was ringing off the hook, and the dog didn't even belong to me.

"Well," Mrs. Remington said as she stood and smiled down at the Don Juan of Cottonwood Cove. "Isn't this a little barbaric? Maybe I should do a little more research."

Really?

Your dog is the horniest fucking pug on the planet.

Remove his fucking testicles and call it a day.

"Mrs. Remington, there are *Wanted* signs hanging on posts downtown with a photo of Mr. Wigglestein's face. You've had several opportunities to keep him contained, yet you continue to let him run free. The only responsible choice at this time is to neuter him."

"You mean castrate him," she huffed.

"I mean, stop him from impregnating all the female dogs in town."

"Why don't they get their dogs fixed?" She stormed toward the front office.

It always ended the same way. We'd have a nice therapy session about the situation, and then she'd get worked up on her way out the door and change her mind in the end.

"Most of the dogs that are currently carrying little Wigglesteins aren't even of age to be fixed. You are allowing your dog to go to the dog park unleashed and mount every dog he comes into contact with. It has already been reported to animal control, and at some point, this is going to become a legal matter." There, I said it. I'd threaten her ass to get her to just agree to make the appointment before someone put a hit out on the little dude. I crossed my arms over my chest and raised a brow.

"I hope no one ever castrates you, Dr. Reynolds," she snipped.

"Well, I hope they don't either. But I'm not mounting non-consenting women in the park, am I?"

That didn't sound right. It wasn't like I was mounting consenting women *anywhere*, but that was beside the point.

"Fine. But I want *you* to do it," she said as she looked at me. "I will not allow anyone else to touch Mr. Wigglestein's testicles."

Who the fuck else would do it?

"Consider it done."

I'd take a lot of pride in ending Casanova's reign over all the bitches in Cottonwood Cove.

She made the appointment for next week, and I waved goodbye as Kate burst out in laughter once Mrs. Remington was out the door.

"The day in the life of a small-town animal doctor," she said as the office phone rang.

"Anyone calling to discuss Mr. Wigglestein is not to get

passed through to me. Tell them we have it under control. I need to go get Gracie in twenty minutes, so I'm heading out soon."

"You got it," she said as she answered the phone, and I started down the hall. "Oh, let me check with him."

I pinched the bridge of my nose because I hadn't even made it the ten feet to my office, and I wasn't in the mood for anything more today.

"Hey, Doc!" she shouted.

"I'm already gone," I grumped.

"It's Presley Duncan, and she sounds upset."

"I'll take it in my office." I sat down and picked up the phone. "Are you all right?"

"Yeah. Of course." Her voice quaked. "I, um, I hate to do this, but I need a favor."

"Tell me."

"I took Honey out this morning for the first time, and she was really off. Lethargic and tired. I've noticed she's lost some weight, but it's been a while since I've seen her, so I thought maybe it was due to her age."

"Doesn't your dad have a private equestrian doctor that he flies here from the city weekly?" I knew this because he'd come to me about working for him when I'd first moved back to town, but I couldn't run this practice and take care of his ranch. Not when I was balancing a newborn at the time, as well.

"Yeah, Dr. Flank was here, and he completely ignored my concern. He said she's old and that this happens. But I asked Butch about her, and he said she hadn't been eating or drinking much in the last two weeks. He shared it with Dr. Flank, as well. Yet the guy doesn't appear to be concerned at all!" Her voice cracked on the last word, and I could tell she was getting worked up.

Presley was always in control of her emotions, unless it involved her horses. She was fiercely protective, but she also knew a whole lot about them, and she wouldn't be concerned if there wasn't reason to be.

"Any other symptoms?" I asked as I closed my computer and reached for my keys.

"Aside from her not eating or drinking, I've noticed that she's drooling a lot, and her mucus appears to be tinged with blood."

"Stay with her and keep her comfortable until I get there. I've got to grab Gracie from school, so I'll need to bring her with me."

"You're coming here?"

"Is that not why you called?" I asked dryly.

"I thought you'd give me some medical advice. I didn't mean to pull you away from work."

"I'm done here for the day. I can't assess her over the phone. I have an idea what it is, but I can't be certain until I come and look at her for myself."

"Thank you. I can watch Gracie while you examine her."

That same sharp pain hit me square in the chest again. It was my gut warning me to back the fuck off. Seeing her with Wes the other night had me on edge. They'd left together, so who the hell knew what that meant. Maybe they were staying together.

At the end of the day, she wouldn't be here long. Whether she stayed with her asshole ex or not, her life was not here. It was important that I remembered that. And being around her again after all these years had me feeling completely out of control.

I'd been ready to knock her ex the fuck out.

I had Gracie to think about now. I couldn't act recklessly.

"I'll see you soon."

I made my way out of the office and picked up Gracie from school. She talked a mile a minute from the moment she was buckled up in the back seat, just like she always did.

"This isn't the way to our house, Daddy. Where are we going?"

"Do you remember that friend of mine that you met the other day?"

She started clapping her hands. "Presley? Of course, I remember her. She shares your heart with me."

I thought kids were supposed to be fucking forgetful. Why did mine have to be the one that remembered every single thing she'd ever heard?

"Listen, Gracie girl… *You've* got my whole heart. We've got to stop by Presley's family's ranch to check on a horse that isn't feeling well. How about we don't talk about Daddy's heart while we're there because I'm working, okay?"

"You can't talk about your heart at work?"

"I'd rather not," I said as I pulled down the long driveway and headed toward the barn.

"Because you're a doctor, and you don't want people to know you have me and Presley in your heart? It's a secret, Daddy?"

I put the truck in park. "Me loving you is never a secret. But I just don't want to be talking about it when I'm at work. Does that make sense?"

For the love of God, just let her say yes.

"Oh, so other people don't know. Okay. I promise I won't tell the other people about your heart, Daddy."

For fuck's sake, I was making this worse by the minute. I jumped out of the truck and grabbed my medical bag before coming around to get Gracie unbuckled and help her out. I pulled her hat down over her ears and kissed the tip of her nose, which made her giggle.

"I think we're going to get more snow soon, but it will be a little warmer in the barn. Keep your hat and mittens on."

"I wonder if it will snow at my Valentine's Day party in a few days. You're coming to my party, right?" she asked as her little mittened hand slipped into mine.

"Of course, I am. You know you're my valentine."

"We're at work now, so you shouldn't be saying that." She looked up at me with wide eyes.

"It's fine." I laughed.

"Can I ride a horse yet?"

"You're too young to ride horses, but maybe in a few months, we can give it a try," I said. She'd been asking about learning to ride for a while, but the whole idea scared the shit out of me.

I looked up to see Presley hurrying toward us, and her eyes landed on my little girl, her lips turning up in the corners. "Hey there, Gracie. I'm so happy you're here."

Gracie's hand slipped from mine, and she started running toward Presley, which took me by surprise. She hardly knew her, yet here she was, putting all her trust in a complete stranger as she flung her little body through the air. Presley caught her on a whoosh and settled her on her hip, pressing her lips to the very same spot I'd just kissed her.

"You kissed me on the nose just like Daddy did."

"Well, it's a cute nose, isn't it?"

I cleared my throat. "All right, do you want to show me where Honey is?"

"Yes. Of course." She carried my daughter and led us into the barn, heading for the back stall. I stopped and shook hands with Butch, whom I hadn't seen in a few months since I last ran into him at my brother's restaurant.

"Well, if it isn't Dr. Dreamy. Isn't that what the ladies call you?" he said with the laugh of a man who sounded like he'd been chain-smoking for 150 years.

"No one calls me that." I rolled my eyes.

"I'm calling you Dr. Daddy Dreamy," Gracie said over a fit of laughter.

"This just keeps getting better," I said as Butch said hi to Gracie. They'd met a couple of times.

"You're getting so big." He winked before heading out to check on the other animals.

I moved into the stall and ran my hand along Honey's face. "Hey there, pretty girl. Do you remember me?"

She was one of the prettiest horses I'd ever laid eyes on, although I'd always seen her with Presley sitting on her, smiling at me, so that was probably part of it.

"Presley?" I heard Gracie whisper from behind me as I lifted Honey's jowls to take a look inside her mouth.

"Yeah?"

"How old were you when you started riding horses?"

"I was a little younger than you," Presley said, and I turned around and shot her a warning look, which she seemed completely unfazed by.

"Maybe you could teach me?"

"I'd love to teach you while I'm home if it's okay with your daddy. Horses were my first love."

I used a light from my medical bag and investigated Honey's mouth and gums as I listened intently to the conversation going on behind me. I moved to the other side of the horse and lifted the jowls again, repeating the process on the other side of her mouth.

"Daddy, Presley wants to teach me how to ride. And horses were her first love, so she will be really safe with me."

I turned around and looked at my daughter. "I'm standing right here. I can hear just fine."

Gracie's hands flew to her mouth. "Oh. Daddy's not happy about you telling me that horses are your first love. That must be a secret, too. Daddy said it's a secret that he loves you and me and that we are in his heart. You can't talk about that at work, Presley."

This just went from bad to fucked-up in a matter of seconds.

Presley barked out a laugh as I scrubbed a hand down my face. "That's not what I said. Daddy's working right now, so I need a lot less chatter so I can figure out what's going on with Honey, okay?"

"What if I take her a few stalls down to meet Sally? She's three years old, and she's really gentle. She'd be a great starter horse." Presley's gaze locked with mine. Oddly, she was one of the few people I'd trust with my daughter around a horse. She'd grown up around them, and she wouldn't risk introducing Gracie to an animal that wasn't safe.

"Please, Daddy?" Gracie put her hands together like she was praying. The girl was a master at getting her way.

"Fine. No riding. You can just pet her."

Presley put Gracie down on her feet and took her hand before leading her out of the stall. I checked out Honey's teeth, moving from the top to the bottom to see how to go about treating her.

I was pretty surprised that it had gotten this bad, considering they had a full-time doctor caring for these horses. I stroked her head a few times.

"We're going to get you taken care of," I said.

"Is she all right?" Butch asked.

"She's got some pretty bad dental issues going on. A nasty infection on one side of her mouth. How often is Dr. Flank out here?"

"He's been coming once a week for the last six months, but honestly, the guy doesn't do much when he's here. He just does a standard check, and he doesn't stay all that long. I don't know how good he actually is."

"Yeah, I'm going to take a look at the other horses, but Honey here is going to need to get some work done because she's definitely in pain. I can come and take care of that tomorrow if they want it done quickly, which I would recommend."

"Thanks for coming by so quickly. I know Presley is pretty upset about it," he said, as he leaned against the stall. "Gracie is loving that horse a few stalls down. I think you might have a horse girl on your hands."

"I'd prefer she just stay inside and color," I grumped before moving out of the stall to check the other horses as Butch's loud laughter bellowed out behind me.

After I'd made my rounds, I paused to find Gracie brushing Sally, with Presley's hand over hers, teaching her how to do it properly. It was surreal to be here with my daughter, the place where I'd first met this woman, and my whole life had pretty much changed course. She was the reason I'd decided to pursue veterinary medicine. She'd always been so driven with school and everything that she did, and it inspired me in a lot of ways.

"Hey," she said. "How bad is it?"

"It's not great." I ran a hand down my face. "She's got some pretty bad tooth decay and a nasty infection. I don't know how often your doctor is checking their mouths, but I'd recommend getting them regularly checked. The others are okay, but Daisy needs a filling in one of her teeth, as well. Honey is going to need to get an extraction. It's the best option to provide the most relief for her. I can clear my afternoon tomorrow and come out here and sedate her and get it done if you want. But you're going to need someone to stay on top of this. I don't think they're getting regular checkups, by the looks of it."

"I knew that guy didn't know what he was doing. And my dad has him driving out to Casper Creek in two days to check on another Dutch Warmblood that he has his heart set on. She's from the same breeder where we got Honey all those years ago, and she's really beautiful. But how do we trust a guy who told me Honey was fine and that it was just part of the aging process? He was going to allow her to suffer."

"You don't." It came out harsh, but I'd learned early on that once someone shows you who they are, you may as well fucking believe them. Honey had been neglected, and that shit shouldn't be happening.

"Agreed. Well, there's someone else interested in this horse, so my dad is anxious to get someone out there. I'll just tell him that I can go handle it, and if everything looks good, I'll bring her home."

"Because you're a horse doctor now?" I asked, raising a brow.

"Daddy's the best animal doctor I know." Gracie turned and smiled at me. Her dark curls fell all around her shoulders beneath her hat, and her nose was bright pink from the temperature in the barn.

"I'm the only animal doctor you know," I teased. "Come here. Let me warm you up."

Presley's gaze tracked the movement as I scooped up my little girl and tucked her beneath my chin. Her cold nose rubbed against my neck.

"I've got Gracie's Valentine's Day party in two days, but I could drive out later that afternoon with you and check out the horse, and if all looks good, we can bring her back in the trailer. You need her to be evaluated before you just sign off. Let me just make sure my parents can keep Gracie for a few hours after school."

"That would be amazing. I'll let my dad know about Dr. Flank, and we'll try to find a replacement right away."

Gracie gasped, and her head shot up. "Presley can come to the Valentine's Day party, too. Then you can take me to Grammie and Pops and go get the new horse. All the other kids have two parents that come to the party, so this would be perfect, Daddy."

My chest clenched at her fucking words. I tried hard to soften my tone as I made sure she understood that this was different. This was exactly why I'd never brought a woman into her life. Not that there'd been anyone I'd wanted to introduce her to before now—but she got attached easily, and I was aware of that.

And this woman that she was fawning all over was not staying.

I sure as hell didn't want my daughter to misunderstand things. "Presley is not your parent; she's your friend. You know that, right?"

"Yes. But friends can come to parties. Please, Presley. Will you come? We're going to have so many treats."

Presley set the brush down and moved closer, kissing Gracie on the cheek. "I'd love to come. I haven't had any fun on Valentine's Day in years. And I could use a sweet friend like you, Gracie Reynolds."

Great.

Now I was spending Valentine's Day with the woman I should be avoiding.

I could feel her seeping beneath my skin.

Invading my thoughts.

I needed to put up some fucking boundaries where she was concerned.

And that was exactly what I intended to do.

nine

. . .

Presley

"I DON'T KNOW why you're getting such a late start. There's a big storm coming. It's all they're talking about on the news," my father said, as he sipped his water and popped a few grapes into his mouth. His words were already getting clearer with each passing day. He was making progress, which didn't surprise me at all. He was a fighter. I'd always assumed I inherited my inner badass from him. I clearly didn't get my mother's inner pageant poise that she'd so wished I'd embodied.

"Yeah, well, they've been talking about this big snowstorm since I got here, and there hasn't been one flurry yet. Don't worry. The truck has snow tires. And it's only an hour and a half drive. I'm going to the Valentine's party at the school now, and then we'll get on the road. It'll probably take around four to five hours round trip. We'll be home right before it gets dark."

"That was nice of Cage to agree to drive with you and check out the horse for us."

"Yeah, it was very nice of him," I said, clearing my throat. I hated that I was excited that he was coming with me. We'd be stuck together for five hours, and I barely slept last night thinking about it, even if he'd been cold to me when he stopped by the barn yesterday and treated me like I had the plague.

Being around Cage again after all these years reminded me why I was so hung up on the guy from the first time I'd laid eyes on him.

I mean, things were obviously different now. We were in different places. But it didn't mean I didn't miss him. It didn't mean I didn't want to know about his life. Or that I wasn't dying to ask what the story was with Gracie saying we were both in his heart. I imagined it was a misunderstanding and that Gracie had just confused my name with something else. But these questions consumed my thoughts.

And sure, I was curious if he had a girlfriend. It would be weird for me not to wonder.

We had a history.

He was making an effort to keep distance between us, stepping back every time I was around him.

Yet I only wanted to move closer to him when he was near.

I'd spent the last five years finding ways to put space and distance between me and my husband. Yet here I was, excited about a quick road trip with my ex-boyfriend.

I shook it off. This would all pass as soon as I went back home in a few weeks. At the rate my father was recovering, I'd be going home sooner than I'd planned. And I'd be a partner at the firm before I knew it.

My father cleared his throat and pulled me from my daze when he spoke. "I've got that animal doctor coming out later in the week to meet with you and Butch. I still can't believe that the fraud of a man I was paying allowed those animals to suffer. I should bring my wrath down on him."

He'd been furious to learn that two of his horses had pretty severe dental issues, and even the younger horses were in need of some dental care quickly before things got worse.

Cage had come by and sedated Honey yesterday before extracting her infected tooth. He'd had to do a filling for Daisy, as well. Both were eating and drinking normally this morning, so I felt hopeful that they were on the mend.

Cage had barely acknowledged me, almost like he couldn't stand the sight of me. I'd asked about the Valentine's party, and he'd kept his answers curt and short, making it very clear he wasn't in the mood for conversation.

You don't have to tell me twice.

I'd spent a lifetime with a mother who didn't want me around, so I was quick to flee when I felt that slight bit of rejection. I had no idea how he'd act today, seeing as we'd be trapped in the truck for several hours.

Apparently, he'd asked Butch to take him to the house to see my dad after he'd finished up. He and my dad had always gotten along, and they shared a mutual respect for the other, though I don't think they saw one another much after our breakup.

"Let's save our wrath for physical therapy, okay? You've already terminated Dr. Flank. Focus on your recovery, and I'll handle the horses." I leaned over and kissed his cheek.

"So, did Wes sign the papers?"

"He did. Everything has been filed. No more worrying, okay? I'm going to head out now." I was looking forward to seeing Gracie again. There was just something about her. She was all warmth and sweetness. Hopefully, that would balance out her father's sudden disdain for me.

"Call me when you arrive there, and let me speak to Cage about the horse."

"I will. Get some rest."

I made my way out to the driveway, where Butch had pulled up the truck with the horse trailer attached to the back. He reminded me for the hundredth time to take it slow over the pass. White Peak was on the other side of the mountain, which was a narrow road that I'd never loved driving on.

I pulled over at Cottonwood Blooms on my drive to the school to pick up the pink and white bouquet I'd ordered this morning for Gracie. I may not have been a pageant girl, but I knew that you always brought flowers to a party or a show. Janine, who owned the floral shop, was as friendly as she'd always been, and I waved goodbye before getting back into the truck.

When I pulled up and found a place to park the oversized monstrosity, I glanced in the mirror and reapplied some lipstick. I'd decided to wear my pink blouse and dark jeans with my tan knee-high boots and my camel-colored dress coat. I wasn't sure what you wore to a kindergarten Valentine's Day party, and I was suddenly more nervous than I'd been for red carpet events with my ex-husband.

I saw the text from Cage, which was very him.

CAGE

Room 1A

I laughed as I stepped inside the building and followed the crowd down the hallway. He was a man of few words, especially when his walls were up.

And they were definitely up.

When I walked into the classroom, Gracie came running toward me. I didn't know that I'd ever felt this kind of instant love for another person. Well, maybe for her father, back in the day. I bent down, and her arms settled around my neck. She smelled like strawberries, and her hair was up in two little buns, with wild curls springing free. Her cheeks were pink, and she smiled this cute, crooked smile that was absolutely adorable.

"I'm so happy you're here. Come sit with me and Daddy. We have a special spot for you."

"Thank you for having me." I pushed to stand, and she led me to the table where the sexiest man in the room was sitting on a very tiny chair, looking like an oversized grump. I didn't miss the way several women watched him, and their gaze moved to me when I sat in the chair on the other side of Gracie, who sat between us.

"These are for you," I said. She made this little gasping sound and reached for the floral arrangement, holding it to her nose, her little eyes closing, and she breathed them in.

"These are the prettiest flowers I've ever seen, Presley."

Cage huffed and glanced at the pink roses that he'd brought that were lying on the table. "You just said that to me."

"But I've never gotten flowers from Presley before. I love yours, too, but hers are extra pretty."

Gracie left to get us each a cup of juice, as all the kids were serving their parents.

Or their guests, *as I'm sure Cage had clarified many times before I'd arrived.*

I understood his need to protect her, but she'd invited me to a school Valentine's Day party. She wasn't offering me a kidney.

"Thanks for coming," he said, keeping his voice low.

"Of course. I'm happy to be here. Are you sure you're okay with the drive today? I'm hoping we're back by around seven p.m."

"Yes. It's fine. My parents are happy to have Gracie for a few hours. The truck has snow tires, right? The weather said it's going to snow, but I've been hearing it for days now."

"That's what I told my dad. If for any reason it gets bad, we'll just turn around and come home."

Gracie handed me a paper cup, her sweet smile reaching her dark brown eyes once again. Damn, she was cute. We sat there sipping our juice and eating cookies when Gracie's teacher came over to say hello.

"It's nice to see you, Mr. Reynolds."

"I keep telling you, you can call me Cage. You were my teacher back in the day," he said.

She smiled, but she didn't call him by his first name. Instead, she turned her attention to me. "I'm Mrs. Clifton. Who do we have here?"

"This is Daddy's special friend." Gracie beamed.

Cage cleared his throat. "This is Presley Duncan. She used to spend her summers here, and she just came back to town for a little bit. She's not staying long."

Well, that was kind of a dick thing to say. He didn't need to act like I was some random person he'd met on the street.

The man suddenly seemed anxious to get me out of town.

I held out my hand. "Yep. I barely know the guy. But his daughter sure is sweet. Nice to meet you."

Gracie giggled, and I had no idea if she even had a clue that we weren't being friendly. Mrs. Clifton chuckled before being pulled away when two kids started arguing over a cookie.

A little boy sauntered over, and he was glaring at Cage with his arms folded over his chest.

"Hi, Mr. Gracie's dad."

"Hello, Preston." Cage's tone was dry, lacking any emotion. "It's Mr. Reynolds."

"Like the tinfoil?" The little kid smirked, and it was hard not to laugh.

"Nope. Like the man that's about ten times your size."

"I might be as big as you when I grow up."

Gracie was gaping from her father to the little boy, and she looked at me with wide eyes.

"I guess we'll have to wait and see. I heard you weren't in school yesterday. Are you feeling all right?" Cage raised a brow. Who knew that kindergarten tension could be so riveting? I had no idea what was going on, but these two were definitely not friends.

"I got *spended* 'cause Gracie tattled on me." I imagined that was kindergarten speak for suspended. Was that a thing in kindergarten now?

"You cut my hair," Gracie said, just as a woman walked over to stand next to Preston.

She had long blonde hair, the tightest white tee that dipped inappropriately low for a school party, and cleavage for days. She stared directly at Cage and batted her lashes, and I tried not to roll my eyes at how obvious she was.

Leave a little something to the imagination, lady.

"I heard our kids had a little love squabble," she purred.

It took all I had not to wave my hands in her face. She hadn't acknowledged me. How did she know that we weren't together? What if I was his girlfriend? I scooted my chair closer to Cage, and he glanced over and smirked. It was the first friendly gesture I'd gotten from him in two days.

"My daughter is five years old. She doesn't have love squabbles, Rhonda. But I suggest you talk to your son about being careless with scissors. He cut a piece of her hair off two days ago. If he'd slipped, he could have really hurt her. And just know, if it happens again, I'll take this a lot higher than going to the principal."

"Oh, Cage, kids will be kids. How about you and I talk about it over dinner and drinks this week?"

His shoulders stiffened, and the look on his face was even more irritated than usual. I decided to throw my hand out in her direction. "Hey, I'm Presley. I think the big guy here is going to be busy with me for a while."

"Is that right? I'm not sure I understand," she said, glaring at me and completely ignoring my hand, so I pulled it away.

"I think she was pretty direct," Cage said. "And I'll say it nicely for the last time. Teach your son how to handle scissors."

Rhonda whipped around and reached for Preston's hand, and the kid stuck his tongue out at Cage. To my surprise, Cage stuck his tongue out at the little boy, which had my head falling back in laughter. Gracie had gone to get us more cookies, and I studied the man beside me.

"Did you really just stick your tongue out at a five-year-old?"

"Did you almost just throw down with his mother?" he said, unable to hide the smile on his face now. He leaned close to my ear so only I could hear. "That kid gets under my fucking skin."

Yeah? Well, you get under my skin, too. But in a very different kind of way.

Chills ran down my back, and I tried to remain composed.

"Really? I couldn't tell." My voice was all tease.

We spent the next thirty minutes watching the kids sing songs while we ate more treats. It was the most entertained I'd been in a long time. Just watching all the students clapping completely offbeat, Preston glaring at Cage as he stood in the front row, Gracie doing all the dance moves she'd been taught, even if no one else was doing them with her.

It was… refreshing.

I realized in that moment that I never just sat and enjoyed *anything*. I was always in a hurry. Researching, reading, presenting, attending events, shopping, traveling—my life was a rat race, and I couldn't remember the last time I laughed this much or smiled or just felt this at peace.

After the classroom started to empty out, Cage looked at his watch and startled. "We've got to get on the road."

I nodded, and we said our goodbyes. Cage told me to follow him over to his parents' house, where he would drop off Gracie, and then he'd leave his truck there. It brought back a lot of memories when we pulled in front of the Reynolds' home. Of the hundreds of times I'd been here. The love I'd experienced in this home.

They were everything I'd ever wished for in a family. I jumped out of the truck, and Cage turned around to look at me.

"We need to be quick. The clouds are coming in," he said, carrying Gracie up the walkway.

"I just want to say hello, and then we can go."

He pushed inside, and the next thirty minutes were spent hugging and chatting with Alana and Bradford. Gracie was telling them all about the party, and Cage kept glancing at his watch.

"All right. We need to get on the road. I'll call you when we're on our way back."

"Okay, be safe." Alana wrapped her arms around me, and I wished we weren't in such a hurry. "How long are you home for?"

"A couple of weeks," I said.

"How about you come to Sunday dinner this weekend? Everyone would love to see you."

I glanced over at the brooding giant beside me, and he scrubbed a hand down the back of his neck.

"Is that going to be a problem for you?" My gaze locked with his.

"My problem is that if we don't get on the road soon, we won't be back for Sunday dinner at this rate."

Alana rolled her eyes, Bradford barked out a laugh, and Gracie clapped her hands. "Presley's coming to dinner."

Cage kissed his daughter goodbye and thanked his parents. I hugged them both before bending down to give Gracie an extra-long hug.

And then I ran after the man who was already on his way to the truck.

ten

. . .

Cage

GOOD CHRIST. These people were going to be the death of
me. The clouds were getting darker, and we should have been
on our way an hour ago. At this rate, we weren't going to get
back until well after eight p.m.

"Keys," I grunted, holding out my hand.

"Why do you think you're driving?"

I just stared at her and held my hand still until she
relented and handed me the keys. I was about to be stuck in
the car with her for several hours, and now she was coming
to Sunday dinner.

I was doing all I could to have some clear boundaries, but
it was becoming more challenging with every family member
fawning all over her. And I was in a bad mood after my run-
in with that little fucker, Preston.

After we'd gotten home from the barn the other night,
Gracie showed me a chunk of her hair that was missing. I'd
seen red. What if he'd slipped and stabbed her in the neck
or the eye? And his mother didn't seem to give two shits
about how out of control her kid was. The woman hit on me
every time I saw her, and I'd shut her down every damn
time.

Why would I be interested in a woman who didn't give a fuck about her child hurting other kids?

My hands gripped the steering wheel as I made my way around the curve, and we climbed the mountain. We were going slower than I'd like because we were hauling this trailer behind us.

"Why do you look like you're having murderous thoughts?" Presley broke the silence.

I didn't answer at first.

I hadn't slept well.

Hell, I hadn't slept well since this woman had come back home.

I'd fucked my right hand thinking about her so many times over the last week I probably had carpal tunnel. It was more action than my dick had seen in years, so now he was on edge and reacting every single time we saw her.

"Why do you ask?" I glanced over at her before putting my eyes back on the road.

"I hate when people answer a question with a question."

"Isn't that what you do for a living?" I said, trying to hide the humor from my voice.

"You just did it again. Under the pretense of inquiring about my profession."

I let out a long breath, leaning forward to look up at the sky, seeing it darkening the further we drove. I'd driven in snow hundreds of times, so I wasn't overly concerned. I just didn't want this to turn into a ten-hour trip.

"I'm thinking about Preston. He cut a piece of Gracie's hair, and he could have really hurt her by having scissors by her neck."

"He's a little shit," she hissed. "And the apple does not fall far from the tree. His mom had zero concerns about the scissors. She was just focused on Gracie's father."

"She's looking for a husband, and she's definitely looking in the wrong place if she thinks that's going to happen here."

"Yeah? You've never hooked up with her?"

I rolled my eyes. "Give me a little credit. I have a child."

"Does that mean once you become a parent, you don't hook up with people?" She chuckled. "That's kind of ironic, really. I mean, you have to *have sex* to make a baby, right?"

"Last time I checked."

"And then what? You just stop having sex once you have the kid? That doesn't seem logical."

"What the fuck are you talking about?" I groaned. "I didn't say I didn't have sex. I said I didn't have sex with Rhonda."

"Oh. So, you do make time for yourself, huh?"

"Presley."

"Cage."

"Can we not talk about this right now?"

"We're both grown-ups. I don't know why you have to make it so weird. There's no shame in talking about it. All the kids are doing it." She sang out the last line and then laughed hysterically.

I didn't comment. I was too focused on the raging erection growing behind my zipper now that she'd brought up sex, and it was making things very uncomfortable for me.

"Fine. I'll DJ." She turned on the radio and found a country station. It was one thing we'd always agreed on.

Country music.

She sang along like she always did.

I focused on the road and tried not to think about my dick for the next hour or so, and the snow started to fall and turn into a full-on blizzard. I didn't miss the way Presley kept looking out the window and then biting down on her bottom lip, which again led to me having an issue down south.

We'd just made it to the pass, and I couldn't see two feet in front of me anymore. The roads were getting slicker by the minute.

The car in front of us was barely moving.

"See if you can find a weather station," I said.

She flipped around, trying a few channels before she found what we were looking for. The sky was growing dark already as the storm moved overhead. I glanced in my rearview mirror, and there was no one coming from behind us, which was a little alarming. No one was coming from the other side of the road, either.

"Should we turn around?" she asked.

"I don't think we can at this point. There's no place to turn around, not with this giant trailer on the back. And I'm guessing going back the other way isn't much better anyway."

"Shit," she whispered.

I turned up the volume just as the weatherman said they'd closed the pass ten minutes ago. We must have been the last ones through. This was a bad fucking idea. I should have known better. But how many times had they claimed we were getting a storm, and it hadn't been a big deal at all?

We were almost at a complete stop as the car in front of us caught up to the one in front of them as we edged further up the mountain.

I glanced over to see Presley staring out the window as she fidgeted with her hands in her lap.

"Hey, it'll be fine," I said, but the car in front of us skidded out, and Presley shrieked. The car straightened, and I weighed our options. Going forward was really the only choice we had. "Do you have reception on your phone?"

She looked down and shook her head. "No. There's no service."

Fuck.

We continued driving, and Presley's voice shook as she spoke, and her hands started flailing around. "I'm so sorry I dragged you out here. Now you're not with Gracie, and this was—this was a huge mistake."

The snow was coming down so hard I could barely see out

the front windshield as the wipers moved rapidly back and forth. We'd been on the road for four hours now, and we weren't even halfway to where we were supposed to be going. Clearly, we weren't getting there tonight. But I wanted to reach my parents to let them know we were all right, and I'd need them to keep Gracie overnight.

"Presley," I said, my voice even. "We're fine. Nothing bad is going to happen. We just aren't going to make it there today. There's a small motel up ahead where we can wait it out. At the rate we're going, we wouldn't be there till morning anyway, so we may as well pull over and get some sleep."

"Oh my gosh," she groaned. "I'm really sorry that I'm keeping you from Gracie and that I ruined your night. And it's freaking Valentine's Day."

"This is how you're spending Valentine's Day, too, right?"

"I'm in the process of getting a divorce; it's not like I have a hot date lined up. And I usually spend Valentine's Day alone anyway." She paused, as if she'd said too much, and my gaze locked with hers as the car was at a complete stop now. "Wes traveled a lot, and I never minded being by myself, if I'm being honest."

It was clear that her marriage had been over for a long time. But I hated hearing the loneliness in her voice.

And I heard it loud and clear, without her actually saying the words.

I knew her.

I still fucking knew her as well as I did all those years ago.

I didn't want to dig any deeper. We'd just be asking for trouble. The timing had always been a struggle for us, and now we lived on different coasts.

We were different people than we were all those years ago.

I leaned forward as we started driving again. It was slow, but at least we were moving. The snow continued to fall harder the further we drove.

"I'm fucking starving. Tell me you brought snacks. You always liked road trip food," I said, refusing to look over at her, even though I felt her eyes on me.

"It was only supposed to be an hour and a half each way," she said.

"Fuck. You didn't bring anything?"

"I didn't say that. I just wanted to hear you beg."

"I've never been above begging, have I?"

Fuck. Why did talking about snacks make me hard?

"Fine. But admit that when you mix M&M's with popcorn, you get the best snack ever invented." She unbuckled her seat belt and reached behind her seat for a shopping bag that she pulled up front.

"Get that damn buckle back on now," I demanded, my voice coming out harsher than I meant it to. But who knew what could happen in this storm. I was trying to keep her calm, but we were in one of the worst storms I'd ever experienced, and I'd seen my fair share.

She snapped her seat belt back into place, pulled out a ziplock bag, and shook it around. "Relax. I'm buckled. Now say it, Reynolds."

"Is it the only option you brought?" I asked, looking up ahead and seeing lights off to the side of the road. I knew that motel should be coming up soon, and we didn't want to miss it, or we'd be at risk of running out of gas and sleeping in the car soon.

She huffed and reached into the bag. "I'm not an asshole. I brought another option. Popcorn and Hot Tamales. But come on, the chocolate mixed with the popcorn makes a sugary, salty snack that is absolute perfection. Yours is just... like having toothpaste with your popcorn."

The years of debate over this was still fresh in my mind, but my chest squeezed that she'd remembered and brought my favorite snack.

"What can I say? I like a little spice with my snack."

Motherfucker. I did it again.

My dick was raging with rebellion over fucking talk about Hot Tamales. Even the fear of being near death didn't have him keeping a low profile. I shifted in my seat a bit, trying to get things under control.

"Is your back hurting?" she asked, and I could hear the concern in her voice.

"Yeah. Just getting a little stiff." Well, the stiff part was true. I just wasn't going to tell her it was my dick that was stiff all because she'd pulled out some fucking popcorn and candy. Before I knew what was happening, she unbuckled and scooted closer, and her hand slipped between the seat and my back.

I nearly jerked off the road when her hands pressed against my lower back.

"Jesus, Presley. Get fucking buckled," I hissed.

"Stop being a stubborn ass and let me help you. I'm the one who got you into this mess. Let me try to give you some relief."

She didn't have a fucking clue how badly I wanted to be relieved.

"Presley." My voice was firm, and there was no sign of humor.

"Yes?" she asked, as her fingers worked into my lower back, and damn, did it feel good, aside from the fact that my erection would require medical attention if she didn't move the fuck away from me.

"I need you to slide over and buckle yourself into your seat," I hissed. "Now."

"I'm sorry. I thought it would help." I didn't miss the hurt in her voice.

She buckled herself back up and set the bag of popcorn and Hot Tamales beside me before turning her head to stare out the window.

"It wasn't that it didn't help. It's not a *you thing*. It's a me thing."

"Oh, don't offend me with the, *it's not you, it's me* speech. It's clearly me. You've been cold to me since that day at the barn. You're so freaking hot and cold you're going to give me whiplash." Now she was shouting. Clearly, I wasn't the only one who was all over the place.

"How exactly can't you keep up? I'm here, aren't I?"

"Well, let's see. You gave me a ride home the first night and acted perfectly pleasant. Well, as pleasant as you are capable of being. And then, Wes came to town, and you threatened to fight him. You wanted to take me home that night because you didn't trust him. Then you came to the barn and couldn't stand the sight of me. You agreed to come on the trip, but you barely looked at me when I got to the school. You are all over the fucking place, Cage Reynolds."

There she is.

Full of life and fury.

I looked up to see the gas station and the motel a hundred feet ahead. Thank fucking God. I was starting to panic that we'd missed it because there was hardly any visibility at this point.

I pulled in, and Presley fell back in a fit of laughter as she looked at the huge sign lit up in red lights.

DIE.

"Who's all over the place now?" I asked, throwing the truck in park.

"Did you seriously pull into a motel next to a gas station with a red, murderous sign that says *die*?"

"It's supposed to say diesel. Clearly, the last three letters burned out." I'd admit it was a little creepy that the snow was falling so hard it was a complete whiteout, aside from the red letters of death that lit up the sky.

I wasn't ready to have the conversation she was trying to have. I had been hot and cold with her. Worried about her ex hurting her one minute and not wanting to get too close the next.

It was fucked up.

I was fucked up.

But right now, we needed to find a place to sleep for a few hours and stay warm until this storm died down.

I turned off the ignition. "Let's bring the food. I doubt this place has room service."

"You think? The welcome sign at the neighboring gas station looks like the entrance to hell. I doubt we're getting a burger and fries here."

"Lose the attitude. We're alive. It's a win," I snapped at her and reached over the seat to get my coat before grabbing the ziplock baggy and tossing it into the shopping bag. I watched as she zipped her tall boots on her feet over her jeans before she leaned forward to pull her dress coat on.

Not the wisest clothing options for the blizzard from hell.

She pushed her door open, and I jumped out, as well. My legs and back were stiff, but at least my dick had calmed his ass down.

"I knew you blamed me for bringing you on this trip!" she yelled as she slung her purse over her shoulder and held onto the side of the truck.

"Yeah, you're probably wishing you wore better footwear about now, huh?"

"You just can't wait to stick it to me, can you?" she snipped as she let go of the truck and stomped toward the motel. We'd parked fifty feet away because we had the trailer on the back, and I didn't want to block anyone in.

"Slow down. It's pure ice."

"I'm fine! I live in New York!" She turned around, anger radiating from her hot little body, and it all happened in slow motion. Her purse flew from her shoulder as her legs went up in the air, and she came straight down on her back, landing on the snow-covered parking lot.

Fuck.

I hurried over to help her up and reached for her hand, but of course, her stubborn ass refused the help.

"I don't need your help," she said, and her voice wobbled.

"Take my goddamn hand."

I attempted to set the bag down, blinking as the snow soaked us both, making it difficult to see anything other than her. I tugged hard as I pulled her to her feet, just as my boot lost traction, and I went backward, with Presley falling forward. Her body was limp as she landed completely on top of me, and hysterical laughter left her lips.

And just like that, my legs and back weren't the only things that were stiff.

eleven

. . .

Presley

I COULD NOT REMEMBER the last time I'd laughed this hard. I'd been scared for my life just a few minutes earlier. Worried that I'd put Cage in danger. Frustrated that the man was friendly one minute and appeared to hate me the next. Yet, here I was, sprawled out on top of him, with the snow coming down hard as he blinked up at me. Popcorn and Hot Tamales covered the snow like confetti, as he'd clearly forgotten to zip up his treat bag.

And all I could do was laugh.

"Is this funny to you?" he asked, but the softness in his gaze made my chest squeeze.

"It's a little funny." I shifted to get up, and something hard poked me in my lower belly.

Oh. My. God.

My eyes met his, and I tried hard not to laugh some more.

He gripped my shoulders and easily lifted me before he moved to his feet. "Laughing at a man's dick is not cool."

I covered my face with my hands and shook my head. This whole day had just been… unexpected.

I bent down and tried to pick up the splattered treats

decorating the snow, and he grabbed the bag. "Leave it for the animals. Let's get inside."

"I wasn't laughing at your dick, by the way." I hurried behind him, trying to keep up, but he came to an abrupt stop, and I slammed into his back before he whipped around to face me.

"Stop talking about my dick. Stop touching me and taunting me with your hot little body. I'm fucking done. Do you hear me?"

I bit down on my bottom lip because he looked damn good, acting all angry and pissed off. I'd always loved how worked up he got.

With me in particular.

"Got it, Cowboy."

He urged me in front of him, and we walked toward the door. This motel looked like a scene from a horror flick, but it was better than being out on the road any longer. Cage pulled the door open, and I stepped inside.

"Hey, y'all. Looks like you took a tumble out there. I'm Margo, by the way," a woman in her mid-fifties said with a whole lot of enthusiasm. She wore glasses, and her brown hair was pulled back in a ponytail.

"Hi, Margo," I said. "We're okay, just happy to be out of the cold."

"We need two rooms if you've got them available."

"Let me check on that." She typed on her keyboard for the longest time. Like she was booking us a trip to the moon. The place was small and couldn't have more than ten rooms, so I wasn't sure what she was searching for. She stopped and glanced up at us with a weak smile and then went back to typing manically on the keyboard once again.

I glanced over at Cage, who appeared highly annoyed, with his stiff shoulders and a prominent crease between his eyebrows as he tapped his fingers against the counter impatiently. I reached forward to grab a piece of soggy popcorn that was stuck to his shoulder and tossed it into the trash can. There was a door with a sign that read *Gift Shop*.

"Well, folks, I'm sorry to tell you that, due to the storm, we've had a few people come in over the last two hours. We've got one room available, but it's the smallest room we have, and the heat's a bit faulty in there."

"Fuck," Cage grumbled under his breath as he ran a hand through his damp hair.

"It's not the end of the world. We're grown-ups, after all. At least one of us is," I snipped because the man acted like he was being forced to share a room with a serial killer. "And it's better than sleeping out in the truck."

"So, you'll take it?" Margo asked.

"Yes, it's fine." He pulled out his credit card, just as I did the same.

"This whole thing is my fault. The least I can do is pay for the room."

"Put it away." his voice commanded, and Margo looked up at him with puppy dog eyes, like she'd never seen a more beautiful man. Hell, I got it. It was hard to look away for me, too. Even when he was being a complete jackass.

"I noticed that door led to a gift shop. Do you have any warm clothes in there by any chance? Or maybe some snacks?"

"Oh, yes. We carry long underwear, toiletries, and groceries."

"Great. I'll go stock up." I hurried inside and grabbed two pairs of the one-size-fits-most long johns and some fuzzy socks for both of us. There were packages of mini donuts, Pop-Tarts, chips, and, of course, the ever-trustworthy M&M's.

I swiped my card, and the woman loaded everything into two bags, and I met Cage near the front desk. He was using the motel phone, and I assumed he was talking to his mom as he explained that we'd had to stop for the night.

I pulled out a powdered sugar donut as I watched him

talk, and I groaned when I took the first bite. I was starving. Cage's gaze landed on mine, and there was a mix of heat and anger, but he held his hand out, and I placed a donut there.

"All right. Thanks again. I'll see you tomorrow."

He ended the call, thanked Margo for the phone, and guided me toward the elevator. Once we stepped inside, he stood on the other side of me, but he didn't take his eyes off me. We were both soaked, and I was trying hard not to shake from being so cold.

"What's in the bag?"

I told him the list of sinful goodies I'd purchased, and he raised a brow. "No Hot Tamales?"

"No. What a shocker that they don't carry them. They had long underwear and fuzzy socks, but not *your* favorite candy. And do you know why that is?" I tried to hide my smile as the elevator doors opened, and I stepped off with him right behind me.

"I can't wait for you to tell me."

"Because no one eats Hot Tamales. It's an endangered candy. But the M&M... that delectable treat has held its own since the beginning of time, or at least since candy was invented. It's tried and true—the superior snack."

He paused at the door and pulled out the key. "Maybe you just didn't look that hard for them because you enjoy acting like your candy is better than mine."

When I flipped on the light, I cringed at the orange and mustard floral bedspread that matched the curtains. Margo wasn't kidding about the faulty heat as the room was not warm. It was better than being outside, but it was a far cry from comfortable.

"Jesus. This is a shit hole," Cage grumped as he pushed the door closed. "I bet there have been murders in this room."

"Don't worry. I promise not to murder you, for Gracie's sake."

"How do you know I won't murder you?" His voice was

deep and gruff, and it had me squeezing my thighs together, even while I trembled from being wet and cold.

His gaze softened again as he clearly noticed, and I dropped the bags onto the chair by the door before handing him a pair of long underwear. "Here you go."

"You go change first. I know you're cold. I'll try to see if I can get this heat to turn up a little bit."

I walked into the bathroom and was grateful that I had a brush in my purse and some lotion. I tugged off all my wet clothing and hung them over the shower curtain in hopes that it would all be dry by morning. I slipped off my bra and panties because they were soaked, as well, and slung them over the tub. I used the towel to dry myself off and pulled on the dry clothing, which already felt much better. I looked in the mirror, brushed my hair, and washed my face with warm water before applying a little lotion.

I made my way out to the room, where Cage was playing with the buttons on the thermostat.

"Hopefully that works," he said, as his gaze traveled the length of my body, from my face down to my toes, before snapping back up and grabbing his clothing. "I'll be right out."

I set the bag on the bed and then laid out all the snacks as I popped another donut into my mouth before guzzling some water. When the door opened, I had to cover my mouth to muffle my laughter.

Cage Reynolds. Six foot three inches of manliness, standing there in what looked like a painted-on crop top and capri leggings.

Tears streamed down my cheeks as my entire body shook. He looked ridiculous, yet still managed to be sexy as hell with his six-pack on full display. The bottoms were so small that the waistband sat below his deep V, and my gaze followed the light dusting of hair down to the clear outline of his still-erect penis.

"Can you stop staring at it like that? It's not helping matters."

My teeth sank into my bottom lip. I was pleased that I still had an effect on the man, just like he still had an effect on me.

"Sorry. They only had the one size."

He moved to the bed and sat beside me, stretching out his legs and reaching for the Pop-Tarts. He tore the foil packet open and took a bite.

Yes, my mind wandered to thoughts of him tearing the foil packet of a condom. And what would follow.

And yeah, the heat must be working because I wasn't that cold anymore.

"I saw that. *One size fits most.* Are most people unusually small? It's a bit biased, kind of like your whole M&M-Hot Tamale theory."

"I'm not unusually small, and they fit me just fine. And don't shame me for having great taste in candy."

"And what am I? A giant?" he asked as he leaned back on the bed and devoured the strawberry Pop-Tart. My gaze moved to the elephant in the room… his dick that was practically bared to me behind the thin fabric.

Giant was a fitting word.

My God. When was the last time I'd even been turned on?

I cleared my throat and moved to my feet, finding my phone charger and plugging it in.

"I have service in here, so I sent a text to my dad and let him know what was going on. He asked me to apologize to you, and he's just glad that we're okay. So, if you need my phone, feel free to use it."

"Nah. I already spoke to Gracie. I asked my mom to let Kate, my receptionist, know to reschedule my appointments for tomorrow. Hopefully, we can make it to White Peak and bring that horse home with us if the roads have cleared."

I sat back down and tore open the package of M&M's, not even caring that I'd probably have a terrible stomachache by morning. I was hungry, and donuts and candy were better than nothing.

"You still want to go?"

"We're here, right?" he asked as he ate a few handfuls of chips.

"Yeah. We're here."

"I hope you won't be missing any important appointments tomorrow. You'll be able to reschedule them?" I sat back down beside him.

"It's not a problem. Mr. Wigglestein is scheduled to be neutered in the morning so that everyone in Cottonwood Cove can sleep better. But one more day won't matter. Although Mrs. Remington is so hell-bent against doing it, she'll probably take this as a sign."

My head fell back in laughter. "I heard about this scandal. He's impregnated quite a few ladies, right?"

"He sure has. She lets him run all over the place, humping everyone in sight. But the women have spoken, and they've had enough." He smirked, and damn, the man was sexy.

"Hey, it's a bitch's world. Let them reign. I should offer my legal assistance to the female dogs in town if she doesn't go through with it."

"Trust me. If she doesn't go through with it, I'll hire you myself."

He pushed to his feet and brushed off his hands before rolling up the bag of chips and setting it on the dresser.

There was no TV in the room, and I cleared off the wrappers from the bed while Cage closed the curtains.

"I can sleep on the floor," he said, reaching for a pillow.

"Don't be ridiculous. We've been through hell tonight. I think we're mature enough to share a bed, right? Plus, it's freezing in here. I'm counting on your body heat to keep me from getting pneumonia." I tried to make a joke, but I was just as nervous as he was about sharing a bed.

And this was not a big bed. This was a poor excuse for a full-sized bed.

I moved to the bathroom to wash my hands, and I brushed my teeth with my finger and some water.

Cage was already beneath the ugly comforter when I stepped out, his back resting against the dingy headboard, and I walked across the room and flipped off the light. I tiptoed to the other side of the bed and slipped beneath the scratchy covers. I rubbed my hands together and covered my mouth as I blew a few breaths in an attempt to provide some heat.

"You cold?" he asked.

"It's okay. I'm always cold. I'll warm up soon."

Before I knew what was happening, he pulled me closer to him, his chest to mine, as my head settled beneath his chin. The man radiated heat and smelled like mint and Hot Tamales, which someone should bottle up and sell because it was my new favorite scent. I closed my eyes as I listened to the sound of his heartbeat.

"I'm sorry I've been hot and cold with you, Pres," he said, his deep voice breaking the silence.

I'd figured he was done talking for the night.

"It's okay. You don't owe me an explanation."

"Well, I think the big guy already outed me." He chuckled. "I was… a little uncomfortable when you had your hand on my back. It's been a while for me, so sometimes that just happens."

I processed his words, and I tried to steady my voice.

"It's been a while for me, too, so I get it."

We lay there in silence again, but now I could hear the sound of my heartbeat right along with his. It was pounding in my ears.

"How long has it been for you?" he asked, catching me by surprise. I didn't think he'd go there.

"I can't remember, honestly. More than a year. How about you?"

More silence.

"Maybe eight months. I'm busy with work and Gracie, so that's sort of my last priority at the moment."

His fingers grazed along the back of my neck in the most soothing way. Every inch of my body was touching his.

"That has to be hard," I whispered. "No pun intended."

His body shook, and I knew he was trying to keep from laughing.

"Sure."

"I'm sorry for making you uncomfortable."

"Don't worry about me. I have my ways of relieving myself," he said, his tone light and flirty.

Oh. My. God.

"I guess we have something in common, then." I knew I was playing with fire, but I was so painfully attracted to this man I could barely stand it.

He pressed his hips forward, letting me feel just how much he wanted me. "Here's some motivation for you next time you're alone."

My breaths were coming faster now, and I made a conscious effort to keep it under control, but it was a challenge.

"You've always provided all the motivation that I need, if I'm being honest." He'd been who I saw every single time I fantasized about a man. I wasn't proud that it was always Cage that I thought of.

His breaths halted, and his hand found my chin, and he tipped it back so my gaze would meet his. There was just a bit of moonlight coming in through the opening of the curtains, forming a halo of light around his handsome face.

"So have you. I still think about you, you know."

"Me, too." A single tear rolled down my cheek, and he

swiped it away with the pad of his thumb. "But you seem determined to keep this distance between us."

"I can't go there with you. Not again. Not when we both know that you're leaving soon. And it's not because I don't want you. Fuck, Presley. I want you so fucking bad I can't see straight. But I can't do halfway with you. We tried that once before, and look at the mess we made. Losing you once wrecked me. Losing you twice would be the end of me. I've got Gracie to think about now."

His words weighed heavy on my chest. Losing him had wrecked me, too. In the worst way. I'd been destructive and spent the years after I'd lost him making things worse. And now I was picking up the pieces and trying to put my life back together.

He was right. We lived on opposite sides of the country. This couldn't go anywhere. We'd be playing with fire if we crossed the line.

Temporary had never worked for us.

We'd always been all or nothing.

"I get it. And my life is a mess right now. It would be a mistake to act on anything."

"So, we agree. No crossing the line. But we can be friends, and that's better than nothing."

"Look at us. We finally agree on something besides horses and country music."

"Horses, country music, and friendship. It's a start. Even if your favorite candy sucks."

I chuckled, but my body was burning at the moment, so I was doing all that I could not to press harder against him. His erection rested on my lower belly, and I squeezed my eyes shut, willing myself to go to sleep. His breathing slowed, but his arms tightened around me.

And even in this dingy, cold room, I felt more comfortable in my own skin than I'd felt in years.

"Can I ask you something?" I whispered.

"Yes."

"What did Gracie mean about me being in your heart with her? It sounded like it was written somewhere?"

He was quiet for the longest time. "Kids just say things, and half the time, they don't make sense. I don't know what she was talking about."

I shouldn't have been disappointed. I'd figured as much. But for whatever reason, I liked the idea of him being forever marked by me.

"I thought so."

"What's that little bird tattoo on your wrist about?" he asked.

"It's a raven. I did that right before my wedding so I wouldn't completely lose myself. So I'd remember who I was. The way that you saw me, soaring and flying and free. Which had always been the best version of myself."

"That had nothing to do with me and everything to do with you."

I closed my eyes and remembered a time when I thought I'd spend the rest of my life right here. With this man.

"Cage?"

"Yeah."

"I missed you."

"Missed you, too, Raven."

My chest squeezed as he whispered my nickname, and I nuzzled closer.

It might not be forever, but at least we had right now.

And at the moment, that was enough.

twelve

· · ·

Cage

MY FUCKING dick woke me from a sound sleep, and it took me a minute to process where I was. Presley was pressed against me, and my erection was hard enough to tear through the flimsy fabric of these ridiculous long johns. I pulled away slowly, not wanting to wake her. I took a moment to just take her in while she slept.

Her long black lashes rested against the top of her cheeks. Her skin was flawless, slightly flushed, lips plump.

Fuck. This wasn't helping.

I closed my eyes and thought about the last documentary I watched about germs. Anything to stop my cock from throbbing.

But nothing was working.

I needed a release, or I'd never survive the drive with her today.

I tiptoed to the bathroom and closed the door. I glanced down to see my dick so hard that the tip was sticking out of the top of my long johns.

I turned the water on and tugged my clothes off because I couldn't get into that shower quickly enough.

This place was a dump, and the water pressure was shit,

but none of it mattered. My head fell against the wall, and I wrapped my hand around my dick, gripping it like my life depended on it.

I squeezed my eyes closed as I imagined my mouth crashing into hers with the force I felt in this moment. We were both desperate to taste and touch and explore.

Fuck. I missed everything about her.

Her smart mouth. Her perfect tits.

I pumped harder. I was so close it wouldn't take much.

My breaths were already labored.

I imagined my hands moving down her lush curves as I gripped her hips. I knew the sounds that she made for me. Hell, I'd memorized every last one.

Every fucking gasp.

Every fucking moan of pleasure.

She jumped up and wrapped her long legs around my waist.

"I need you inside me right now, Cowboy," she purred.

I thrust into her, burying myself so deep that I hoped I could stay there forever.

I pumped my hand up and down my cock, faster now.

And I fucked her in my dreams the way I wanted to fuck her in this moment.

The buildup had me on edge as bright lights exploded behind my eyes, and the most powerful orgasm tore through my body.

"Presley! Fuck!" The words were out before I could stop them.

I hadn't come that hard in years.

I hoped like hell that she was still asleep and hadn't heard me. But at the same time, I had no shame in my game.

We'd both admitted that it had been a while.

I'd never stood on ceremony with this woman.

I reached for the soap and cleaned myself up before climbing out of the shower, feeling a hell of a lot better than I did when I stepped into it.

I dried off my body and my hair and pulled on yesterday's clothes, grateful to be out of the ridiculous pajamas. I used my finger to brush my teeth with some water before stepping out of the bathroom.

She was sitting up, staring at me, when I entered the room, and she tucked her hair behind her ears. How did she manage to look so fucking pretty without any effort?

"Good morning," I said, making my way over to the dresser to check my phone.

"It certainly is for one of us." She smirked before moving to her feet with a devious grin on her face.

"Hey, you've clearly never woken up with a bad case of morning wood because someone's tight little body was rubbing against you all night."

Her head tilted to the side, and she smiled. "Way to give a girl a confidence boost first thing in the morning."

"I'm glad you're taking pleasure in my discomfort," I said as I pulled the curtains open and looked outside to see that the snow had stopped falling.

"I'm guessing you're more comfortable now?" she asked with a chuckle.

"I'm actually feeling fucking fantastic now. Thanks for asking. Let's get dressed and get on the road."

"Okay. I hope there's a pancake house in our future. I'm starving for real food," she said, making her way to the bathroom.

"Me, too." I dialed my mom, and she put Gracie on the phone as my gaze followed Presley when she stepped back into the room wearing her jeans and boots but leaving on the long underwear top beneath her coat.

"I miss you, Daddy."

"I miss you, too, Gracie girl. I'll see you after school today."

And just like that, I was brought back into the reality that was my life now.

I had a little girl waiting for me at home.

My life was there.

And as much as I wanted to get wrapped up in this woman, I knew I couldn't go there.

So, our next chapter would have to be a friendship.

And I'd have to learn to deal with it.

Regardless of how badly I wanted her.

———

BRINKLEY

Mom just told me that Presley is coming to Sunday dinner. Why have you failed to mention this?

GEORGIA

What? She's still in town? Have you been talking to her?

FINN

Did you not know that they got snowed in on their little road trip? And what are the chances that there was only one motel… with one room… and one bed? Cue the dramatic music.

What are the chances that you just won dick of the year, you asshat? So much for bro code.

HUGH

I'm glad I'm not dick of the year. But the whole thing is… interesting.

BRINKLEY

I'm still processing Sunday dinner, and now we find out that you went on a romantic vacation with your ex-girlfriend, who you're still clearly in love with.

GEORGIA

This has the makings of an epic second-chance romance. I'm telling Ashlan to use this for inspiration for her next book.

Ashlan was our cousin, who was a bestselling romance author. Georgia and her husband owned a publishing house, so, in Georgia's mind, everything had the potential to be a book these days.

For fuck's sake. Her dad needed me to check out a horse. There is no romance here. She's leaving. She lives in New York. I live here. I have a child and responsibilities. Nothing happened in that motel room, aside from me wearing long johns that were clearly not made for a normal-sized human.

HUGH

I've never seen long underwear that wasn't made for small humans. It's like trying to fit a five-pound sausage into a two-pound bag. That shit doesn't work.

BRINKLEY

I can already tell that Hugh knows more… He's diverting the conversation and trying to focus on the ridiculous fashion you're referencing. And Finny didn't reply and make a sausage-penis joke, which means he's afraid to say the wrong thing.

GEORGIA

How did you get that from their response?

BRINKLEY

I'm a reporter. I can see through bullshit a mile away.

FINN

I was getting my pregnant wife a glass of water. I'm the one who mentioned their blizzard-of-the-year staycation.

If any of you bring this up at dinner, I will blurt out every skeleton in your closet and torture you for the rest of your lives.

HUGH

Another sweet family Sunday night dinner with the Reynolds.

BRINKLEY

"Ahhh… hello deflection, nice to see you again." You're making threats now? This is an obvious attempt to take the attention off yourself. This tells me everything I need to know. Dinner can't come soon enough.

Fuck. My siblings weren't going to make this easy.

"Grammie and Pops said we could bring Maxine and Bob Picklepants to dinner tonight," Gracie said, with her little hand in mine, as we walked home from the park.

Of course, she asked them, and they said yes.

Because why not? They'd invited my ex-girlfriend to dinner, so what's the difference if a pig and a dog join us, too?

It'll be one big fucked-up evening.

"That's fine."

"And Presley's coming. I really like her."

"You know she's just an old friend, right? Someone I used to know. She doesn't live here, and she'll be going home soon." We stepped into the house, and I dropped the keys onto the entryway table.

"But you can still be friends with someone who doesn't live here, Daddy. All my cousins live in Honey Mountain. We're still a family, even if I don't see them every day."

"Yes. That's true. Go get washed up and changed, and I'll get Maxine and Bob ready to go."

She squealed as she ran down the hallway toward her bedroom, and I rubbed my temples. My phone vibrated, and I glanced down to see a text from Presley. We'd messaged about the horse we'd brought back with us after we got home a few days ago. And then I'd texted her congratulations when Finn had sent me the article with her interview about becoming the first female partner at her firm. So we'd been texting a bit. It was not a big deal.

Friends were allowed to text.

RAVEN

Hey. Are you sure you're all right with me coming to dinner tonight? I can make up an excuse and say I'm sick if you'd rather I not be there.

Yeah. Why wouldn't I be?

RAVEN

Let's just say that I know you well, and I'm guessing you're not thrilled because you've got these boundaries in place, and you don't like to cross them.

Well, I'd say sleeping with you in a bed with my dick out of control has already crossed most of the boundaries, right? We agreed to be friends. I'm good with that.

RAVEN

Wow. Way to bring the dirty talk to the text chain. I didn't see that <eggplant emoji> coming.

That's what she said.

> RAVEN
>
> Ahhh… so he does still have a sense of humor.

We're both going to need one tonight. Brinkley is trying to sniff out what's going on. She just heard about the road trip, so she's going to be nosy as hell.

> RAVEN
>
> Well, she'll see that there's nothing going on, and then we can just have a good time. I'm looking forward to seeing everyone and to meeting Lincoln and Maddox.

I'd updated her on all that had happened in the family during the last six years on our road trip from hell.

Although, I'd be lying if I didn't say I was bummed when it came to an end. She'd shared a lot about her life in New York. She loved it there. About how making partner at her law firm was everything she'd worked for since the day she started law school.

Just be ready to be in the hot seat tonight.

> RAVEN
>
> You worry too much, Cowboy. You know I can handle myself.

You always could. I'll see you soon.

Gracie came out of her bedroom wearing her favorite flower girl dress that Lincoln had bought her, with cowboy boots and a ski jacket. My daughter had her own sense of fashion, and as long as she wore her coat, I'd let it go.

I loaded the animals into my truck. Maxine sat up front in the passenger seat, while Bob sat in the back with Gracie.

When we arrived at my parents' house, Gracie led

Maxine inside, and I had to carry Bob because he'd fallen asleep on the four-minute drive over, and he refused to walk inside.

We were the last to arrive, and Presley was already there. She appeared completely comfortable as she laughed at something Georgia had just said.

I set Bob down on the kitchen floor, and he finally got his second wind and wiggled his way over to my mother, who had a treat waiting for him.

Gracie was introducing Presley to Maxine, and I looked up to see Brinkley watching me with that devious look on her face.

"Good to see you, brother," she said, and I didn't miss the smirk.

I gave her a warning look as I made my rounds and gave everyone a hug. I kissed my mom on the cheek, pulling my dad in for a big bear hug before he guided everyone to the table.

Gracie had her hand in Presley's as they walked to the dining room.

My chest squeezed.

Boundaries.

How do I keep my daughter from falling for this woman when I can't control myself around her? Gracie had no clue about self-preservation.

My mother could clearly read my mind because her gaze locked with mine, and she gave me that look, the one that told me to relax.

Always the therapist.

We took our usual seats, with Presley taking the chair beside me that my mother had added to the table. Gracie sat on the other side of me but leaned forward to continue telling Presley about Maxine.

"And she really loves Daddy. Maxine thinks she's his girlfriend."

"Well, Maxine is easy on the eyes. He could do worse." Presley smiled, and everyone chuckled.

"Yeah. Yeah. Yeah. Let's eat." I placed some vegetables on Gracie's plate before piling some on my own and handing the platter to Presley.

"Your daddy gets so uncomfortable when you talk about that kind of stuff, doesn't he?" Brinkley said with a wicked grin on her face, and I glared at her. She loved to put me on the hot seat.

"Not if we aren't at work. He doesn't like to talk about those kinds of things at work. Right, Daddy?" Gracie asked, and I knew exactly where she was going.

"It's fine. Let's eat our dinner," I said, trying to stop the train wreck before it happened. "So, Reese, how is the pregnancy going?" I asked.

Reese chuckled at the shift in conversation and smiled. "I feel just as good as I did yesterday when I saw you. It's going well."

But everyone else was smiling at Brinkley, who looked like she was up to no good, as usual.

"Well, I'm glad you're feeling good, Reese," Brinkley said as she reached for her wineglass. "But, Gracie, what things doesn't Daddy like to talk about at work?"

Fucking Brinks. The little deviant.

Hugh barked out a laugh, and Finn was smiling as Georgia looked at me with empathy. She knew what was coming. Brinkley could sniff out a body of water in the middle of the desert, and Gracie just made it clear she was keeping a secret.

"Badgering a child is beneath you," I hissed.

Presley's head fell back in laughter. Even though she had no clue what was happening, she knew my family well enough to know that they were giving me shit.

Gracie leaned forward and smiled as she watched Presley on the other side of me. "It's not a secret here because we're a family. Daddy doesn't want the work people to know that me and Presley are inked on his heart and that he loves us." She shrugged, all that innocence making it hard not to want to scold her for outing me to the nosiest fucking people on the planet. They would have a field day with this.

I groaned. "I'll explain this later. Mom, how's work going?"

"Nice try," Brinkley said over her laughter.

Presley put her hand on my forearm as if she wanted to help. "It's not literally *inked*. She's confusing something from a story he must have shared."

She was trying to make it better, but I was fairly certain that she'd just made it worse.

"Can you pass the chicken please?" I asked, and my father handed me the platter with a ridiculous smile on his face, and I desperately wanted to change the subject. "Is this a new marinade, Mom? It's really good."

"It's barbecue sauce in a bottle," Finn said over his laughter. "The kind we have every week."

"What story did Daddy tell you that made you think you and Presley were *inked on his heart*?" Brinkley asked my daughter, with the widest grin spread across her face.

She was like a motherfucking dog with a bone.

Like Mr. Wigglestein if a bitch was in heat a block away.

"I don't know. Daddy tells me lots of stories."

Ahhh… good answer, kid. That ought to stop the feeding frenzy for a minute or two.

"Ink is kind of a strange word to take from a story. What was it about?" Georgia asked, completely clueless that she'd just asked the worst question possible.

"I don't know a story about ink. I just know Daddy calls the writing on his heart his ink. And his heart says Gracie and Presley with my birthday. We're his heart, and we're there forever. Right, Daddy?"

I closed my eyes for a second and waited for it.

Three.
Two.
One.

"That's why you wear a T-shirt at the lake now? I thought you were sensitive to the sun! Tattoos are works of art. Show that shit off, man," Hugh said over a mouthful of potato salad.

"Don't talk with your mouth full," I hissed. "And I am prone to burning."

"And let's try to get through a dinner with our granddaughter without anyone swearing, all right?" my mother said, and Hugh laughed louder.

I couldn't help it if I'd walked around with my shirt off at home and I had the most observant five-year-old on the planet. The tattoo wasn't even that big. I'd gotten it shortly after Gracie was born. She'd noticed it over a year ago and had barely mentioned it after I said it was inked there on my heart forever.

They both were.

It was supposed to be just for me and no one else.

But now it would be the topic of conversation for years to come.

Long after the woman beside me left town.

Which she would be doing very soon.

thirteen

. . .

Presley

WELL, this was an unexpected turn of events. I felt a little dumb for coming to his defense, seeing as he was not telling the truth when he'd told me Gracie was just confused.

I wanted to be irritated, but honestly, I was honored to be tattooed on the man's body for life—I just wasn't sure how to feel about it.

"My work here is done," Brinkley said, dropping a dinner roll onto her plate like it was a microphone. The entire table erupted in laughter, aside from the big grump sitting next to me.

I covered my mouth with my hand. It wasn't that big of a deal. He was being a bit dramatic.

"Sleep with one eye open, Brinks," Cage grumped.

"I look forward to it." His sister waggled her brows and then turned her attention to me. "So, how long are you stay-ing, Presley?"

"Probably a couple more weeks. My dad is on the mend, but I want to stay until he's fully recovered, or at least well enough to be without the full-time nurses at the house."

"I've missed you. I'm glad you're home. Don't stay away

so long next time." Georgia smiled at me, and that heavy weight settled on my chest again.

I'd always loved his family, and when I lost Cage, I lost all of them.

"I won't." I shrugged. "And at least the big guy here has me inked on his heart forever, so I'm kind of with you all in spirit, right?"

It was silent at first, and then laughter bellowed around the room from everyone, including Cage.

"Relax," he said once they all pulled themselves together. "I'm probably going to ink Maxine there next."

Gracie was clapping, and I spent the next hour laughing and talking and catching up with this family, whom I'd missed so much.

After we ate dessert and had some coffee, we all moved to the family room, and I sat on the floor with my back to the couch as Bob Picklepants, the cutest dog on the planet, sprawled across my legs. I still couldn't believe that Cage had agreed to keep Maxine at his house. Being a dad had softened him in a way.

Although that was probably the only thing soft about him.

Damn. Why did my mind keep going there?

It had been so long since I'd felt anything physically. Of course, this would be the one man who had to make me feel all the things.

My phone vibrated, and I glanced down to see a text from Lola.

LO

Hey, girl. How's it going with Dr. Dreamy?

I quickly responded.

Stop. All good. Are we meeting for brunch tomorrow? I can meet you at Cottonwood Café after I take Honey out and spend a little time with my dad.

LO

Yes. But don't avoid the question. I know you're still thinking about your night spent spooning him and his giant <eggplant emoji>.

<middle finger emoji>

I tucked my phone away and looked up to see Cage watching me intently. Almost like he knew that I was texting my bestie about him.

I should go. I'd been here a long time.

"Well, thank you so much for having me. Nothing has ever compared to a Reynolds family dinner."

"Are you heading out?" Alana asked as I gently slipped Bob off my lap and kissed the top of his head. I pushed to my feet, and she wrapped me up in a hug.

This was what I'd always wanted.

A mother who loved me the way that Alana loved her kids. I'd always thought I'd be that kind of mother someday, but clearly, that hadn't happened.

Work had become my life, and I didn't mind it when I was there. But being here made me look at life a little differently.

I didn't have casual dinners on a Sunday night with friends. I worked long hours. My dinners were normally work related, or we'd do a fancy dinner out in the city with clients. There was nothing casual about it.

And when Wes and I did get together with other couples we'd socialized with over the years, conversations were more about what fancy vacation you were taking next or what second home you were considering buying. I wasn't around people who just laughed a lot and asked how you were doing and how you were feeling.

People who really cared, I guess.

Aside from Lola. She was the one person who'd kept me grounded. I'd need to find that kind of normalcy and comfort when I got back home. I was going to make it a priority to spend time with people outside of work.

"Daddy, please?" Gracie had her hands together like she was praying, and her fancy dress swooshed around her ankles.

There was nothing that I loved more than a girl who could rock a dress fit for a wedding, with a pair of cowboy boots. Throw in a pig and a dog and a father who adored her, and she was winning at life.

"Come on," Brinkley said. "Lincoln and I haven't gotten to have Gracie spend the night in a while. And I was already set to pick her up in the morning, but this way we can just wake up there."

I'd heard Cage mention earlier that she didn't have school tomorrow due to a teacher's in-service day, or something like that.

"All right. I'll pick her up after work tomorrow." He scooped up his little girl and rubbed his scruff on her neck. "You need a break from Daddy, huh?"

"Never!" Her head fell back in a fit of giggles. I couldn't look away. There was something about seeing them together. I'd always been so devastated that he'd had a baby with someone else, but seeing it was different. It didn't hurt me. It made me happy. He'd done exactly what he should have done all those years ago. I was the one who'd made all the mistakes, wasn't I?

I felt a hand in mine and looked up to see that Alana had caught me staring at them.

"They're sweet together, aren't they?"

The lump in my throat was so thick that I couldn't speak. I nodded and smiled.

I gave her another hug and made my way around the group. I agreed to meet Brinkley, Georgia, Lila, and Reese for dinner next week at Cottonwood Café, and they told me to bring Lola. I was looking forward to it.

Cage said his goodbyes, as well. He had Maxine on a leash and Bob in his arms as we both walked toward the door.

I grabbed my coat and zipped it all the way up for the short walk home. I loved that I could walk everywhere here, and it was peaceful and quiet.

Once we were outside, we paused in front of his truck.

"Well, that was painful." He opened the back door and set Bob down before lifting up Maxine and placing her beside the dog, who was already lying down.

"That was fun." I chuckled.

"Brinkley wasn't going to let that tattoo go." He scrubbed his hand down the back of his neck. "I'm sorry I wasn't honest with you about it. I did it a long time ago, and I just thought it would make the situation uncomfortable."

His heated gaze locked with mine, and my stomach fluttered. I wasn't that girl who got butterflies over all the boys when I was young. It had always been this one boy that gave me every flutter and nervous moment I'd ever had. And that clearly hadn't changed.

"It's okay that you missed me, too."

His gaze narrowed as if my words surprised him, and then he looked away for a few seconds.

"Where's your car?"

"I walked." I shrugged. "Being out of the city has been a nice break. It's so peaceful here."

"You're not walking home. It's late. Get in the truck." He pulled the door open.

"You're ridiculous."

"I've been called worse. You going to make me pick you up and put you in the truck, or are you going to do it yourself?"

I rolled my eyes and climbed in. He stared at me before reaching for the seat belt, and I slapped his hand away. "I can buckle myself, Reynolds."

"Then do it now."

"So bossy." I rolled my eyes and reached for the seat belt.

He closed the door and went around to the driver's seat before pulling out of the driveway.

What was his problem? One minute he was being sweet and the next, he was being an ass.

"I'll show you something peaceful if you don't mind taking a pit stop."

"That's fine. I planned to walk home, so clearly, I wasn't in a hurry," I said, not hiding the irritation from my voice, even though I was not upset about getting a ride home from him.

He pulled into his driveway at his house and put the truck in park.

"This is where you're taking me?"

"Yep."

He jumped out of the truck and opened the back door to get Maxine as I helped Bob out, who trotted next to me toward the front door.

"That bastard never walks for me," Cage said as he glanced over his shoulder at me.

"Maybe you could soften your delivery?"

He laughed. "Maybe you're right."

He pushed the door open and flipped on a light as I stepped inside. "Wow. It's gorgeous."

"Yeah? I had a lot of help from my mom and my sisters. Clearly, they can't stay out of my business." He tossed the keys onto the little table in the entryway, and I took in the dark, wide-plank floors that ran through the house. It wasn't cluttered or busy, but it was warm. We moved to the family room, and Bob jumped up onto the couch and curled up on the blanket. Cage lifted Maxine into what looked like a playpen for kids, and she started playing with some sort of ball. There were pictures of Gracie on the built-in bookshelves, and a few paintings hung on the walls, which I took my time admiring.

"Do you still paint?" he asked.

I had thought about majoring in art for a hot minute because, aside from riding horses, I'd always loved to paint. My mother was mortified that I'd wanted to pursue a career that would make me one of many struggling artists in her mind. My father had encouraged me to keep it as a hobby, and he'd never taken it seriously.

But Cage had always thought I was talented. My eye caught on a frame on the bookshelves, and I moved closer. It was the sketch I'd done of this house and then painted when we were maybe sixteen or seventeen years old. I'd given it to him for Christmas as a gift that year, and it was the day that he'd promised that he'd build me that house someday.

"You saved it?" Every detail, from the wraparound porch to the red door and the Adirondack chairs, was there.

"Of course I did. It was a gift. What did you think I'd do? Set it on fire when you married someone else?"

"I don't know, Cage. Things ended kind of abruptly, wouldn't you say?" I turned around to face him, not hiding the sarcasm from my tone. "There were a lot of things said, so I sure as hell didn't think you'd be tattooing my name on your heart or saving a picture that I made you all these years later."

"You want to do this? I mean, do you really want to open that can of shitty worms and dissect it?"

I swiped at the single tear falling down my face. I'd never been a crier, but I'd cried more since I'd come home than I'd cried in my entire life combined. "How can I turn down a shitty can of worms?"

"Come on. Let me show you my favorite place, and then we can make one another miserable if you still want to."

I followed him through the gorgeous kitchen, with black cabinets and a grand island in the center, to a set of French doors that led to the backyard. He turned on the outdoor lights and held out his arm for me to sit on the couch, and he reached for a long lighter and turned on the firepit that was in front of the couch. The water wasn't too far off in the distance, and he had a dock with a boat parked there.

He had an outdoor kitchen area, and he pulled open the refrigerator and grabbed two bottles of water before sitting down next to me.

"Thank you," I said, setting the water down on the side table. The warmth from the fire made it comfortable to sit outside, though most of the snow had melted over the last few days since we'd returned home.

"This is probably the most peaceful place I've found yet," he said.

The sound of the water splashing against the shore and the leaves rustling in the wind had my body relaxing as I sank into the couch.

"This is hard to beat."

"I'm sorry I lied about the tattoo." He cleared his throat, and when I looked up, my gaze locked with his.

"I'm not mad that you didn't tell me about it."

"All right. What are you mad about?"

"I don't know. Maybe I'm mad at the world." I shrugged with a forced chuckle before continuing. "Mad that our timing was just never right. And I guess in my mind, I'd imagined that you got back together with Gracie's mom or met someone else and that you were living this perfect life. And the thought used to haunt me so badly that I couldn't come back here. I couldn't stand the idea of you with someone else." My voice cracked on the last word, and the sound itself was heartbreaking, let alone the words that I'd just admitted.

He reached for my hands. "I told you back then that what I had with Gracie's mother was a one-night stand. One drunken night when I was angry and jealous because you had started dating Wes, and it was eating me alive. I didn't know her all that well. We met at a bar. I didn't see her again until eight and a half months later when she showed up on my doorstep, about to give birth. She was going to give Gracie up for adoption, and her parents convinced her that I should have the first right to keep her before she gave her away. So, I'd been there in the delivery room, and she gave birth, and I only saw her one more time after that."

"She had no second thoughts?"

"No, she had to go before a judge to relinquish all rights to our daughter. Her name was on the birth certificate, and she was terrified of having any legal recourse as far as child support. I never wanted any of that, so I was relieved that she'd signed over her rights. There was no romance or love there. Nothing at all. But I'm grateful for the gift that she gave me. I'm grateful that she had the decency to come and find me and give me the option to raise my little girl."

"Where is she now?"

"I don't know. She was a successful model, and she wanted to travel the world, which I hope she's doing. We obviously hadn't planned to have a child. I'd used protection, so I don't know what the fuck happened. But I wouldn't change a thing now. At the time, I was pretty fucking terrified."

"It's like the universe never wanted us to be together, huh? Things just kept happening to keep us apart," I said as I looked out at the water.

"Well, we had a pretty epic couple of years, though, didn't we?"

"We did." I moved closer to him. I never could stay away when he was near. From the moment I met him, it had been that way. "I remember counting down the days until summer so I could be with you in Cottonwood Cove."

"Summers were pretty damn good. And once I got a car, I was able to come see you in San Francisco. We made it work, right?"

"Remember that Valentine's Day when we were seniors in high school, and you drove to the city and surprised me? You stood outside my window with a boom box, trying to be all romantic." I fell back laughing, but I kept a hold of his hand because I imagined this would be the last time that I held it.

God, I loved his hands. They were large and strong. Just like him.

"Getting through your guard gate was a goddamn miracle in itself. Your mom refused to put me on the permanent list." He chuckled. "She always wanted you to go to Harvard and find your husband there."

"Barbie is an asshole. That hasn't changed." I shrugged, and my teeth sank into my bottom lip. "She found my dad there, and she was hell-bent on me doing the same. I'd let her down so many times that I guess she had that one coming."

"I'm sure she was thrilled that you married a Wellington."

"She was. I think the fact that you and I found a way to go to college together actually freaked her out. She actually thought I might not go to Harvard."

"You went to undergrad with your boyfriend and attended a California state school. You were such a fucking rebel, Raven." His smile was so big, and the flames from the firepit shone in his gorgeous sapphire blues.

"Can I tell you something?" I asked.

"Yes."

"Those four years… they were the best of my whole life."

We'd found a way to go to undergrad together. Everyone said that we wouldn't last because we'd been dating long-distance all through high school. But our bond had only grown stronger once we got to see each other every day.

Cage was like a drug to me back then. The more of him I got, the more of him I wanted.

He was my whole world.

And then life threw us a curveball.

fourteen

. . .

Cage

"YEAH. We'd finally gotten a break, right?" Hell, we'd practically lived together for four years. We spent every night together. I was fairly certain that Presley Duncan was the only person on the planet that didn't annoy me back then, and considering how much time we'd spent together, she should have gotten some sort of fucking medal.

She unzipped her coat, as the heat from the fire had warmed the space. When her hand slipped from mine, I missed it the second it was gone. This wasn't smart, bringing her here. Talking about this shit. The past was in the past. It couldn't be changed. The damage was done.

Not everyone got a happy ending.

I'd accepted that.

But sitting here with her, getting a taste of everything I didn't have…

Everything I wanted…

It was like a sober guy planting his ass in an open bar.

It was a dumb fucking thing to do.

Once her coat was off, her fingers found my hand, tracing along my knuckles as if she'd missed the contact as much as I had.

"And then we didn't get into one single grad school together." She shook her head at the memory, which was still pretty raw in my mind. "I swear my mother somehow rigged it so that I miraculously got into Harvard, yet I didn't get into one California law school, even though I was a damn resident of that state."

I chuckled. She'd been convinced her mother had that kind of reach, but I knew she didn't. She might have pulled some strings, getting letters of recommendation from senators and powerful people for her Harvard application, but they didn't have the power to keep people from accepting her. Not that it mattered. We both got into impressive programs. We should have been adults about it.

"I didn't know it would be as tough as it was," I admitted, my gaze moving out to the water. I remember being exhausted with my class load, and the time change and the distance was hard. We were flying back and forth whenever we could, and it was fucking tiring.

"I think your dad getting sick changed things, you know? We were already struggling, and then when we weren't able to visit as often anymore, it all just felt impossible. Especially with you being a jealous ass," she said.

"Oh, really? You scared the shit out of my lab partner my second year of vet school. I believe you threatened her." I laughed, and it echoed around the yard.

"Please. She was asking for it," Presley said, changing her voice to this dramatic high pitch. *"Cage, I was hoping we could study later."*

"Nothing ever happened with Carmie Carson."

"Yes. *Carmie.* I wanted to scratch her eyes out when I saw the way she hung all over you when we went to that happy hour that time I visited."

"You were sitting on my lap at that happy hour. She just asked if I wanted to join her study group."

"Whatever. I got a vibe from her. I trust my instincts. And

you're not one to talk. You scared the living shit out of poor Leo Wilson when you came charging at him like a freaking caveman."

I winced at the memory. "I actually liked Leo, but I saw his hands on you, and I guess I just saw red. It was a bad time, you know? I was exhausted from school, and my dad's prognosis didn't look great when he first started chemo, and I felt like I was losing my girl, I guess."

Her gaze softened as her fingers interlocked with mine. "You were never losing me. And Leo's hands were not on me. I'd just slipped on the ice when you happened to come charging out of nowhere with your surprise visit. And you were the one that thought we should take a step back from our relationship."

"We were fighting all the time. I was in a really dark place and struggling, and you were trying everything you could to keep us together. Flying to see me all the time when you were completely exhausted from school. Dealing with my moods and my jealousy because I couldn't handle being away from you. And then you started that fucking internship, and Wes was having you travel with him. It just felt like too much at the time. My family was struggling, and my dad's treatment took a toll on him. We were all a mess. I know I did a lot of things wrong; I own that. And I thought taking the pressure off would help, but it just made things worse. The longer we went without seeing one another, the harder it was. So, I ended it because I thought it would be for the best at the time."

Tears streamed down her pretty face. "I felt like you completely pulled away. Like I'd lost my best friend. We were barely talking anymore, and Wes was always there, you know? Waiting in the wings, I guess. And when you finally called after weeks and asked, I said that I was seeing him. We'd gone to dinner a few times, but it was nothing serious. I hadn't even kissed him at that point. But I wanted you to be jealous and fight for me. It was childish and stupid. I know that now." She shook her head and swiped at her cheeks.

"And I went the other way, didn't I?"

"You said you were happy for me. You said you were just having fun and dating different women, and you thought this was better for us. And it hurt in a way I can't even put into words. So, I just focused on school and let myself pretend to be happy with Wes, and the relationship progressed. But it was never like ours. It was different. It looked good on paper, I guess." A sarcastic laugh left her lips. "He wined and dined me, but there wasn't a friendship or any kind of passion because I'd already given my heart away."

"And then I called you on a drunken bender and broke down," I said, closing my eyes at the memory.

"It had been months since I'd heard from you. I'd called and texted, but you'd stopped responding."

"I thought you were happy. I thought he was better for you than I was at the time. I was fucked up over it. I tried to go on a few dates, but no one was you. No one compared."

"What a mess we made of everything. Was that the night you met Gracie's mother? I've done the math a million times in my head, and I feel like that phone call was when everything changed."

I nodded and looked out at the water. "You said that things had gotten serious with Wes over the last few months. You told me that he'd just told you that he loved you, and you weren't sure how you felt about it. I asked if you were sleeping with him, and you said you'd slept with him for the first time the night before I called, and I knew I had no right to be mad. I'd slept with two other women by that time. Numbing myself and trying to forget you. But I was so fucking crushed because I knew I'd fucked everything up."

"So you went out and met her that night, didn't you?"

I nodded. "I'm not proud of how I handled things. I pushed you away and then blamed you for leaving."

"I was miserable. I was trying to make myself love a man who was really good to me at that time. He wasn't rejecting me the way you were. He was older, and he felt like a safe place to land, I guess. But the first time I slept with Wes, I locked myself in a bathroom afterward and cried for hours. I missed you so much that it physically hurt."

"Fuck. We can't change the past, and I wouldn't change anything now because Gracie is the light of my life. I know I was meant to be her father. I just always thought I was meant to be the man who'd grow old with you, too."

"I did, too. But I'm glad that you have your beautiful daughter, Cage. It used to devastate me—thoughts of you with a child that wasn't ours—but seeing you with her is the most beautiful thing I've ever witnessed. It makes me think that all we've been through was worth it. And I'd go through all of it again if it meant you got to be Gracie's daddy."

Fuck me.

This woman.

She'd been the only woman who'd ever really understood me. The one I'd bared my soul to, and that hadn't changed, had it?

"I would do it all again, too, but I'd do everything in my power not to hurt you. It's my one regret in life. Hurting you. Losing you. I'll never forgive myself for it, because in a way, I guess I don't want to. I know I lost the only woman I'll ever love, and I accept it. I own it. But I'll carry it with me. Hell, that's why you're inked on my heart with my daughter. Do you remember the day that we met? I mean, the actual date?"

"June 23." She shrugged as her bottom lip trembled. "It hits me hard every year because it's still the day that goes down as the best day of my life."

"It's Gracie's birthday. It's the day my daughter was fucking born. The day the two most important girls came into my life. That's why it's inked beneath your names."

"She was born on June 23?" Her voice shook, and a sob escaped her throat.

"Come here," I commanded before pulling her onto my lap and wrapping my arms around her. Needing to feel her warmth. Needing to hold her and tell her how sorry I was for destroying us.

For all the pain I'd caused.

She settled against my chest and cried.

And I just sat there holding her.

Wishing I could turn back time.

Wishing things could be different.

She pulled back and looked up at me. "I shouldn't have given up on you. I shouldn't have married Wes or turned my back on you when you told me you were having a baby. I blamed you all these years, but I was the one who should have fought harder."

I stroked her face. "You didn't do anything wrong. It was all me. And I'm so fucking glad you're here and that I can tell you everything. I hate that all these years have gone by without speaking to you because I've missed you, Raven."

"I've missed you, too, Cowboy," she whispered.

"Did I tell you the divorce is final?" she whispered. "I heard from Stew today. It's all done."

I pulled her hand to my lips, opening her palm and kissing her there. "How do you feel? It's okay if you're sad about it. You can talk to me."

"I'm not sad about it. I'm relieved, which probably makes me a horrible person."

"You don't have a horrible bone in your body, Presley Duncan."

"Thank you. I feel like I can finally move forward with my life in a way," she said.

"You sure you don't want to live a simpler life? Move back to Cottonwood Cove and do pro bono law for a living?" I asked with a chuckle, trying to keep my voice light when nothing about the question was light. I wanted to know if she'd consider uprooting her life for me. The guy who'd broken her heart all those years ago and didn't deserve a second fucking chance.

But it didn't stop me from wanting it.

She pushed up, settling one knee on each side of me as her dark gaze searched mine.

"I've got so many people relying on me now. I've let my work become my sole purpose in life in a way, and it's gotten me through the last few years when I didn't want to see that my marriage was fractured. And I never thought they'd make me partner this quickly. It's everything I've worked for." She looked away for a few seconds before returning her gaze to me, a playful look taking over her face now. "You know, New York City has some of the best schools in the country. Gracie would love it there. There's so much to do. And they need veterinarians in the city, too."

She was doing what I was doing. Trying to act like it was just a silly suggestion, having me and Gracie move out there, but I saw the way her breath hitched when the words left her mouth. I saw the way she swallowed as she waited for a response, and fuck me if I didn't want to give her what she was asking for.

Because she deserved everything she ever wanted.

But I had a child to think about. And our life was here.

"If I could, I would do it for you. But I have a practice, and my daughter has a life that I've worked hard to build for her here. She's settled and happy, and she's surrounded by family. I can't just uproot her the way I wish I could if it meant being near you again."

She bit down on her bottom lip, with that worry line prominent between her brows. "It's ironic, really. We're exactly where we were all those years ago, right?"

I sighed. "I guess we are. Living different lives on different sides of the country. But we're smarter now. We aren't going to mess things up the way we did back then. We won't make promises that we can't keep."

"Agreed. But I'm here now. And what if we just enjoy this time together, knowing that it will come to an end when I leave? There won't be any hurt feelings or unfulfilled expectations."

My large hands covered each side of her face as I pulled her closer. "How would that work?"

"Well, we're friends, right? I love spending time with you and Gracie, and I'd like to continue seeing both of you while I'm here. I want to know her, Cage. *I need to know her.*"

The sharpest pain hit my chest at her words. "I want you to know her, too."

"Okay. Then I want to spend as much time with you both while I'm here as you're willing to give me. And we can stay in touch when I leave."

"Because we're friends now." My voice was gruff. Her mouth was so close that I could just lean forward the slightest bit and devour her.

"Cage," she whispered as her gaze searched mine. "I need…"

"Tell me what you need."

"I haven't felt anything in so long, and I feel all of it with you. I know I'm leaving. I know this can't go anywhere. But I just want one night with you. One night to feel good. To feel alive. To feel… you."

Her words hit me hard.

Denying this woman had never come easy for me.

But this was different. Something inside me snapped.

And I was going to give her everything that she wanted.

Because this was something I could give her.

I could give her tonight.

fifteen

. . .

Presley

IT WAS INDESCRIBABLE. The pull I felt toward this man.

The need.

The desire.

All of it.

His hands were on me as he pulled me closer.

One hand wrapped around the side of my neck, angling my mouth just where he wanted me. The other hand tangled in my hair.

It was a frenzy.

His mouth crashed into mine. Years of pent-up desire and passion exploded as my lips parted, and his tongue slipped inside and tangled with mine.

I pressed harder against him, needing to be closer, needing more. He groaned into my mouth, and a whimper escaped my lips. I was feverish and turned on, desperate for this to last forever.

No one had ever kissed me the way that Cage Reynolds did, but this kiss...

It was next level.

It was both of us finally giving in to what we wanted so

badly. My hands tugged at his hair, wanting to hold him close and keep him here.

Everything we'd shared tonight… Confessions and truths and all the hurt…

It all led to this moment.

Our kiss slowed. His tongue began to slide in and out as he teased me wickedly. He nipped at my lips and groaned before his tongue slipped back in. My head fell back as my body reacted to the delicious torture of his mouth and his hands. He kissed his way down my jaw and neck as he tilted me back further, cupping the back of my head in the palm of his hand before he claimed my mouth again.

We kissed for so long that my lips ached, but we never came up for air.

I loved the way his desire pressed between my thighs as he thrust forward the slightest bit. Loved feeling how badly he wanted me, too.

"Cage, please," I said, my voice barely recognizable, hoarse and laced with need.

His hands moved to my hips, and he guided me against his hard cock as his lips and tongue continued their sweet torture on my mouth. It was the most erotic thing I'd ever experienced, and I was losing my freaking mind. I ground against him faster and faster, moaning into his mouth as stars exploded behind my eyes, and I went right over the edge. I cried out his name with no shame, and I rode out every last bit of pleasure.

When was the last time I'd come with a man?

It had definitely been many years ago—with the same man who'd just taken me there once again.

He'd always known my body.

Always knew what I needed.

Our kiss slowed, and my hips stopped moving, and I pulled back to look at him. My teeth sank into my bottom lip, and I smiled. Normally, I'd be mortified that I'd just had the best orgasm of my life while making out with my ex-boyfriend, but I wasn't embarrassed.

Because he was looking at me like I was the most beautiful woman in the world.

"Raven." His voice was deep and low. "My favorite thing in the world is seeing you come undone. The only thing better is if you had done it with my cock inside you. But beggars can't be choosers."

I'd almost forgotten how much I loved his filthy mouth. He'd always been a man of few words, until he had me naked, and then he'd had a lot to say.

"You don't need to beg, Cowboy. I want to feel everything tonight. Don't pull away from me now. Let's give each other this one night. No holding back."

"One night, huh? And then what? We just go to Sunday dinner at my parents' house, and you come over and play with Gracie like nothing happened between us?" He smirked.

"I guess so. I mean, I'm not the one making all the rules. I want to be with you. If it's just for one night, I'll take it. If you want to be with me every day until I leave, I'll take that, too." I couldn't believe how bold I was being. But I'd always been comfortable telling Cage what I wanted.

His gaze softened, and he ran his big hand through my hair, tucking it behind my ear. "I can't afford to be broken when you leave. I'm trying to be realistic. I need to have some boundaries in place."

"I get that. So, if you want this to stop right now, I'll go home, and we'll pretend it never happened."

"We'll pretend you didn't just cry out my name while you rocked yourself against my cock and I fucked your mouth with my tongue? Is that what you're referring to?"

"Oh my gosh," I said, fanning my face. "You haven't lost your dirty mouth, have you?"

"I've never used it on anyone but you, so consider yourself the lucky one." He smirked and then nipped at my mouth when I started to talk. "I'm not done."

My eyes widened when he pulled back.

"We're giving ourselves tonight because one night can't do that much harm. We'll get whatever this is out of our system, and then we'll go back to being friends until you leave."

"Okay. That works for me."

"Yeah?" he asked, his voice softer now. His hand settled on the side of my neck, and his thumb traced along my jaw. "I don't want to make it hard for you to leave. I know you've worked really hard, and believe it or not, your happiness has always been more important to me than my own, even if that seems unbelievable after some of the things I did. But I always thought I was doing what was best for you."

"I believe that. I promise that if you rock my world tonight, I'll still go back to my kick-ass job in New York. You aren't derailing any dreams by giving me pleasure that I'm in desperate need of."

"Ravens were always meant to fly. I'd never want to clip your wings."

"My wings are firmly intact. It's my vagina that's slowly been dying all these years." I chuckled. "Now, stop getting all sappy and have your way with me."

His heated gaze locked with mine, and before I could process what was happening, he was on his feet with me in his arms. My legs wrapped around his waist, and he leaned forward and turned off the firepit before one hand moved to my ass and the other rested on my cheek.

"You don't have to ask me twice." He carried me inside and down the hallway before he dropped me onto a very comfortable bed. I glanced around the space, which was very fitting.

Very Cage Reynolds.

It was dark and moody. Gray bedding that was notably

soft, and a black modern light fixture hung overhead, providing dim lighting that set the mood perfectly.

Although my body was currently on fire, it wouldn't take much to set the mood.

Nothing would calm down this building anticipation that I was finally going to be with this man again. The one I'd thought about every day for six years.

"Do you know how many times I thought about you being in this bed? Dreamt about it so many fucking times," he said, his voice painfully sexy as he reached for my sweater and pulled me forward so he could tug it off of me and toss it onto the floor.

"Tell me," I whispered as he laid me back on the bed, and his mouth came over the pink, lacy bra covering my breast. His tongue flicked at my nipple, which was painfully hard, before he pulled the lace to the side and blew lightly, causing an embarrassing groan to escape my lips.

"I've thought about it a lot. In the shower. In bed at night. And every fucking second since you arrived back in town." He reached behind my back and unsnapped my bra before tossing it on the floor. "I love your fucking body. Every goddamn inch of it."

His fingers trailed down my stomach as his tongue swirled around my breast, circling my nipple, and the sensation was overwhelming. He switched sides and chuckled against my skin when I squirmed beneath him.

"Stop torturing me," I said, tugging at his hair and pulling him up so I could look at him.

"Is someone anxious, even though you've already come once just a few minutes ago? You always were a greedy girl."

"Are you not anxious?" I asked, suddenly feeling self-conscious about how desperate I was. He was the man, after all. Shouldn't he be in a hurry?

He studied me for a few seconds before reaching for my

hand, placing it over his erection, and running my hand up and down its length.

Jesus.

It was like running my hand up and down a baseball bat.

Large and thick and hard.

"I'm anxious, but I want to savor every minute I get to have with you. I want to taste you and touch you and make you come so many times that it will keep me going for another decade without you."

Oh. My. God.

"Great freaking answer," I said as I continued to stroke him over his jeans. "But I want to do the same to you. So how about you start taking some clothing off."

His tongue peeked out and slid along his lower lip as his heated gaze studied me.

"All right, but first, I want to undress you." He moved down and pulled off my booties one at a time before pushing my legs apart, and I squeezed my eyes closed because it had been so long since anyone had touched me.

Since this man had touched me.

He unbuttoned my jeans before stopping on the zipper. "Open your eyes."

My eyes sprung open, and I tried desperately to calm my breathing.

"Your eyes stay on me. If we get one night together, I want to see you. I want to watch as you come apart. I want to remember every fucking thing, and I want you to do the same."

Damn. I forgot how demanding he was. I nodded as he pulled the zipper down painfully slowly. He tugged my jeans down but left my panties on and threw the denim on the floor with the rest of my clothing.

He stood over me, staring down, his eyes scanning my entire body as his fingers trailed between my breasts, over my stomach, and to the edge of my pink panties. I sucked in a breath, my entire body shaking with anticipation.

His eyes were hooded as his fingers slipped beneath the thin lace and dipped inside.

"You're so fucking wet. So fucking ready." He swiped along my most sensitive area before pulling his hand away, dipping his fingers into his mouth, and groaning. "So fucking sweet."

I was ready to combust right there. I pushed forward and sat up, reaching for the button on his jeans. "Let's see if you're ready."

This wickedly sexy grin spread across his face as he reached behind his back and tugged the sweater over his head. I pushed his zipper down while he used his feet to kick off his shoes, and I shoved his jeans along with his boxer briefs down in one aggressive move because I had no patience left.

His dick sprung free, and I couldn't help the gasp that escaped my lips.

He'd always been large and thick and impressive.

But it had been so long since I'd seen him. I wrapped my hand around his shaft and moved up and down a few times as my gaze traveled over his impressive abs before stopping at the ink on his chest.

I was a weird mix of overly emotional and ridiculously turned on. I pulled my hand away and traced my fingers over the writing that had so much meaning that he'd marked himself forever with it in beautiful script.

Presley.

Gracie.

June 23.

I pushed up on my knees as the mattress dipped low because I needed his mouth on mine right now. I tugged his head down and kissed him.

I kissed him for all that we had.

For all that we lost.

And for all that I wanted tonight to be.

He scooped me up, his mouth never losing contact with mine, as he crawled onto the bed and moved us back toward the headboard. We were both on our knees now, with his hand covering the side of my neck.

"I need to taste you. Right. Fucking. Now," he growled.

"I need to taste you, too."

He moved so fast that I barely processed what was happening. He was on his back, and his hands were on my hips. "I'm not waiting, so we'll do it together. Sit on my face, beautiful."

He shifted me so my back was to the headboard, settling me so that his mouth was exactly where I wanted it. A whoosh of air left my lungs as his tongue swiped along my center. I leaned forward, my hand wrapped around his erection, and I lowered my mouth over him. He groaned against my core, and I loved that I was having the same effect on him as he had on me. I lowered my head, taking him as deep as I could, while my hand stayed at the base as I moved up and down his engorged shaft. The sensation of his mouth on me was overwhelming.

But he gripped my hips and held me there as his tongue slipped inside, and I moved faster, circling the tip of his dick with my tongue before I slid back down and felt him in the back of my throat.

His hips bucked against me as we found our rhythm, and I tried to stop myself from the building need that was taking over.

I took him in further as I pressed harder against his magical mouth, and he continued to push me to the edge with his tongue.

I couldn't hold on any longer, and I wrapped my lips tighter around his cock, working him faster, just as my entire body started to shake, and a burst of lights went off behind my eyelids. I groaned with him in my mouth as he went right over the edge with me. I stayed right there, riding out every last bit of pleasure as he came just as hard. I could tell he was trying to shift my mouth away from him in warning, all while holding my hips still until I was done, but I wanted to taste him the way he was tasting me.

And nothing had ever been better.

sixteen

. . .

Cage

WE BOTH FELL BACK on the bed, and I rolled on my side to look at her as our breaths were still coming hard and fast. Hell, I hadn't even been inside her yet, and it was the best sex of my life. Our bodies had always been in sync, but this was even more intense than I'd remembered. Maybe it was because we both hadn't been with anyone in a long time.

Maybe it was just because it was us.

I pushed the hair away from her beautiful face and stared at her, wanting to memorize every line and every curve.

And she stared right back.

"You're fucking perfect," I said.

"So are you. That was—amazing."

"It was." I pulled her closer, and for a brief moment, this panic settled in my chest that I'd fucked up by allowing myself to go here. Because this connection was too strong. Too real. And even if it was just for one night, it was going to hurt like hell when it ended.

Again.

"Are you panicking a little bit?" she whispered.

Goddamn. How did she always know what I was thinking?

"Why do you say that?"

"Because it makes me nervous, too."

I kissed the top of her head. "Maybe we're both afraid to feel good because it's been so long."

"Yeah. That's true. But at the same time, I like feeling good, and I wouldn't mind feeling good a few more times before we pretend it didn't happen." She chuckled.

"Well, good. Because I plan to make you feel good as many times as possible before the sun comes up." I rolled her onto her back and settled between her thighs as I hovered above her.

She bit down on her bottom lip. "I'm on the pill. And I was never with Wes without using a condom. So, I'd love our one night together to be the way I remembered it. With nothing between us."

Fuck. My gaze locked with hers. "You were never with your husband without a condom?"

"No. I didn't want to get pregnant, and for whatever reason, I didn't fully trust him."

"I've never been with anyone but you without wearing one either. But it's always been different with you and me, hasn't it?"

"It has," she whispered.

"It's always just been you and me." I was already hard again, and she noticed because she widened her legs for me, and I teased her entrance.

"You and me, Cowboy."

I pushed inside her slowly. So fucking slow at first, and she squeezed my dick like a fucking vise. I moved a little further, waiting for her to adjust to my size. I knew it had been a while for her, and I didn't want to hurt her. But my dick was on the verge of exploding, and I wasn't even all the way in.

"I don't know how long I'll last. It's been a while." I

pressed my forehead to hers as I pushed forward a little bit further, testing every bit of restraint that I had.

Slow.

Once I was all the way in, I stayed perfectly still, savoring and enjoying the feel of her while fighting the urge to pull out and thrust into her hard and fast.

I wanted to own her. Possess her. Make her mine. Mark her the way she'd marked me.

All these thoughts were spinning through my mind when she startled me by shoving against me, rolling me over so she could be on top.

I gripped her hips as she looked down at me.

"No holding back, remember?" she said as she started moving. Steady at first, finding her rhythm. My hands moved to her gorgeous tits, which fit perfectly there.

Like they were fucking made for me.

Like she was fucking made for me.

And she rode me up and down, her eyes never leaving mine.

Faster and harder as I moved my hand down between us, knowing exactly what she needed. It was so fucking good I didn't know how much longer I could hold on.

My eyes closed, and I concentrated on her.

On waiting for her to come.

Because pleasing her was all I wanted in this moment, even if my dick had a mind of his own.

"Open your eyes," her voice said around her frantic breaths, and I looked up to see her watching me. "If we get one night together, I want to see you. I want to watch as you come apart. I want to remember every fucking thing, and I want you to do the same."

She repeated my words to me, and it was the sexiest fucking thing I'd ever heard.

Making her demands just the way that I had.

I bucked up against her with a fury.

Desperate and needy.

Again and again.

And just when I thought I couldn't hold on one second longer, she exploded around me. Squeezing my cock until I followed her right over the edge.

Her head fell back, and she met me thrust for thrust.

She cried out my name as a guttural sound left my throat.

And I just watched her in all her beauty.

My fucking perfect raven.

Flying free just like she always did.

———

It had been two days since I'd seen Presley.

Two days since I'd dropped her at her house the morning after our night together.

And I was in hell. I couldn't stop thinking about her, and we were texting all day, every day because we were giving this new friendship idea a try.

I pulled down the long driveway toward Duncan Ranch and put the truck in park. I'd just dropped Gracie at school, where she asked me no less than five hundred times if Presley could teach her to ride a horse. I'd agreed to come check on the horses a couple of days a week until Frank found a replacement to work here full time.

And I was just trying to hold on to my sanity. Keep some bit of distance there, as our night together was a one-and-done deal.

But I couldn't think of anything else.

"Hey," Presley said as she came walking out of the barn in a long cream-colored skirt with her boots peeking out at the ankle. Her sweater hung off one shoulder, making my mouth water, and it pissed me the hell off. "I didn't think you were coming until tomorrow."

She'd stuck to the plan and hadn't made any attempt to

see me again, so I wondered if I was the only one who was struggling.

"I didn't have anything on the schedule this morning, so I thought I'd run over and check on Honey." I shoved my hands into my pockets because we both knew I was lying. Honey was doing well, and there were no concerns at the moment. "What are you up to?"

"I was just going to go for a ride. Why don't you ride with me?"

I cleared my throat and thought it over. It had been a while since I'd found the time to take a ride. I was in the middle of building a barn, and I planned to eventually get a horse or two. "I guess I can go for a quick ride before I take a look in her mouth and then make a quick round to see the others."

"Great. I want to get back in an hour so I can meet with Baxter to get an update on my dad's physical therapy."

She walked in front of me. The fabric of her skirt hugged her ass perfectly while it swooshed around freely at her ankles.

"I don't know if that skirt is the best idea for riding," I grumped, and it came out harsher than I meant it to.

But fuck that skirt.

It was putting all sorts of visuals in my head that I shouldn't be thinking about.

She glanced over her shoulder and smiled like she was enjoying seeing me agitated.

We saddled up, and she climbed onto Honey, her skirt riding up as she draped it over her thighs effortlessly. I took Duke, the six-year-old stallion, who was one of my favorites.

We trotted out of the barn and took off once we were in the pasture.

I glanced over to see the wind catching her hair as it blew all around her, and she had a big smile on her face. We rode for a few miles before she pointed over to the trees, where we used to come and hang out when we were teenagers. The Duncans had one of the most gorgeous properties in Cottonwood Cove, as their ranch was set up high with impressive views of the cove. We tied the horses to the tree, and she pulled a blanket out of her saddlebag and shook it out before setting it down on the grass.

I sat down beside her, keeping a little distance between us, even though her citrus scent was already flooding my senses.

"What's going on? You seem a little tense." She raised a brow as she leaned back on her elbows.

"Your skirt just kind of pisses me off."

There, I said it. I was an asshole, and I wouldn't argue that.

"My skirt pisses you off?" She smirked. "The color or just the style in general?"

"The way it hugs your perfect ass."

She nodded and picked at a piece of grass before turning to look at me. "Are you struggling, Cowboy? Thinking about the other night? Because I am."

I looked out at the water. "Something like that. We probably fucked up doing that, huh?"

"I don't think so. We know what this is. There are no expectations this time around. And we have a history. I can't speak for you, but I needed to feel something. I'm not ashamed to admit that being with you, even if just for a few weeks, has given me a new perspective."

"How so?" I asked, narrowing my gaze as I studied her.

"Well, I don't feel this overwhelming sadness anymore when I think about you. Meeting your daughter has been really special to me. I adore her, and I'm grateful that I get to spend time with her. That I get to know the little girl you're raising. I guess it's shown me that I am capable of being happy again. I thought I lost the ability to feel that, you know?"

I let her words sink in. Hell, I was feeling things I hadn't felt in a very long time. Things that I knew were dangerous to be feeling. That was what had me on edge. But I wasn't going to say that to her.

"Gracie's nagging the shit out of me about letting you teach her to ride."

"Let me do this. I promise you I won't let her do anything dangerous. She loves horses, and you know it's my passion. Let me give this to her. And you're coming by and checking on the horses a couple of days a week now. It's the least I can do to thank you."

"Fine. I can't argue with that. She'll be excited. Just take it easy, okay? Nothing too fast. She's got big ideas, but she's young and clueless about all that can happen with an animal that size."

"I give you my word. I'll take it slow, and we won't do anything remotely reckless."

"All right. How about tomorrow after school?" What the fuck was I doing? I was clearly finding a way to see her every day until she left.

"Sounds good. I'm looking forward to it."

We sat in silence for a little bit, and I glanced over at her as she looked out at the water.

"I thought I lost the ability to feel, too. You aren't alone in that. And you definitely showed me I was wrong," I said, keeping my voice low.

She turned to look at me as her lips turned up in the corners. Her honey-brown eyes appeared lighter with the sun shining down on her.

"I'm glad to hear that."

"So that rule we have seems fucking stupid now, doesn't it?"

"The one where we gave ourselves one night together and nothing more? Is that the one you're referring to?" She moved closer and chuckled.

"Yeah. Who's fucked-up idea was that?"

"I'm pretty sure it was yours." She reached for my hand,

turning it over and tracing the lines in my palm. I closed my eyes at how fucking good it felt when she touched me.

How good it felt when she was even in my vicinity.

"Well, I have a lot of idiotic ideas, don't I?"

"You've had your fair share." She leaned against me, resting her cheek against my chest, and I opened my eyes to look down at her.

"What if we enjoy this time together as friends, with a few perks involved?"

"I believe that's called friends with benefits." She tipped her head back to look up at me.

"We've just got to be okay when it comes to an end. And Gracie can't know this is anything more than a friendship, or she'll get all sorts of ideas."

"So, you don't want me to tell your daughter that I'm having sex with you? Hmmm… that's going to be so difficult." She oozed sarcasm before laughing a soft, melodic sound that moved around us.

"Don't be a smartass. You know… the more people that know what's going on, the more complicated this gets."

"How about we keep this just for me and you? It's no one else's business. Maybe it'll help us both in the end."

"How so?" I tugged her onto my lap and wrapped my arms around her.

"Well, for me, I thought I'd just grown to hate sex. But after the other night, I realized I really, really like it. So maybe I'll go back home, get back to my real life, and be open to meeting someone."

I flipped her on her back so fast that she gasped. I hovered above her. "New rule. We don't talk about you fucking anyone else while we're together."

"Fine. But you know what I mean. It gives us hope that we can both be happy again."

"You know what would make me happy right now?" I asked as I pushed the hair away from her stunning face.

"What?" she whispered.

"If I could bury myself deep inside you right here and every day until you leave."

She smiled. "Good thing I'm wearing this skirt that pisses you off so much, huh?"

My mouth crashed into hers, and I kissed her hard.

I lifted her skirt, and she fumbled with the button on my jeans. My pants were pulled down, and I slid her panties to the side as I continued kissing her like I'd die if I stopped.

Hell, maybe I would.

She gripped my ass and urged me forward. I pressed into her inch by inch until I was buried deep, and nothing had ever felt better.

I knew I was fucking up by letting myself go here.

But I didn't even care.

I couldn't walk away now if I wanted to.

And I definitely didn't want to.

seventeen

. . .

Presley

"I CAN'T BELIEVE this is really happening," Lola said when we met Brax at his office and signed the agreement for the building that the spa would be going into. "I can't believe you're actually buying the whole building."

My father and I had discussed it, and we'd decided to go in as partners on the building and purchase it instead of renting the space. It was a wise investment, and I had 100 percent faith in my best friend.

"Who better to invest in than you?" I signed the contract, and Brax was going to take the contract over to my father at the ranch to sign the other docs.

"Damn. I hope I can pull this off." Lola had a wicked grin on her face. "It would help if I had a partner."

"You do have a partner. I'm here, aren't I? I'm just not going to be working the day-to-day side of the business. But I'm involved. I'm invested. I believe," I sang out.

Brax laughed and pushed to his feet as we said our good-byes and left with the keys in hand.

"You sure have been in a good mood lately. Acting all happy and light."

"As opposed to what?" I laughed as we walked the short distance to the new building.

"Well, come on. You know you've had that whole Wednesday Addams vibe going these last few years. Dressing in black and not smiling a whole lot." She smirked because she was full of shit. But I was willing to admit that I felt lighter than I had in a very long time.

Plus, I *was* having all the orgasms a girl could ask for these last two weeks. I just wasn't telling her about it. I kind of liked having this secret with Cage. Something that was just for me and him.

This morning he'd dropped to his knees in one of the empty stalls in the barn and buried his head between my legs until I could barely contain my cries. Hell, the horses had started making noises as if they knew what was going on.

"Well, my divorce went through. Isn't that reason enough to be happy?" The judge had approved our wishes to dissolve our marriage, as we'd both signed and agreed to the terms.

"It doesn't explain the fact that you're glowing. You have that whole *I'm having multiple orgasms a day* look. Are you going to tell me I'm wrong?"

"I'm going to tell you that it's been good to be back here. My dad is making progress. I'm seeing old friends." I shrugged as we paused in front of the building, and I handed her the keys.

"Old friends, huh? It sure seems like Cage is over at that barn of yours an awful lot. And Gracie's taking riding lessons a couple of days a week. Are you still going to tell me that nothing is going on?"

Cage, Gracie, and I had fallen into a routine, and I'd be lying if I didn't say it was the reason I had a permanent smile on my face.

I'd get up and work for a few hours in the morning, then join my father for breakfast, just in time to meet Cage in the barn. He came by almost daily now to check on the horses.

We'd go for rides and sneak in a little time together under the trees out in the middle of nowhere, where it was just us.

I most definitely have that I'm having multiple orgasms a day *glow.*

And I was going to enjoy it while it lasted.

My father had made so much progress that Baxter and Louie were blown away. It was inspiring to see how hard he was working, and the fact that it was paying off was a bonus.

Most afternoons, Gracie would come by for a riding lesson, and the three of us even had dinner together a few nights this week.

"I'm just saying that I'm happy, Lo."

"I know you are. It looks good on you," she said as she pushed open the door.

"Don't bring any of this up when we go to dinner tonight, okay?"

"You think Brinkley Reynolds isn't going to sniff this shit out? I'm not even observant, and I know something's going on." She laughed as we both walked through the space and brainstormed ideas.

"I can handle Brinkley. Just don't add fuel to the fire. What are your plans for design? Have you thought about it?"

"Well, my bestie is an investor in the business, and she's also a talented painter. I thought maybe she could paint a mural in the meditation room."

"Really? You don't want to do swanky wallpaper?"

"I don't. I want it to be earthy and cool and vibey." She chuckled.

"All right. I'd be happy to paint a mural when the time comes." When was the last time that I'd painted? It had always been therapeutic to me to paint, but I'd stopped after Wes and I got married. He'd been very particular about the art in our home, and he knew painting was a hobby of mine, but it wasn't something I'd ever shared with him.

"Great. I'll send you some photos of what I have in mind.

Hopefully, we can get construction going sooner rather than later." She glanced down at her phone. "Oh, we're going to be late. It's already time to meet the girls for dinner."

It was the first afternoon in two weeks that I hadn't seen Cage and Gracie, and he'd already pouted about it this morning, which made me laugh. We'd kept things very private, only meeting at the barn, but we'd have dinner at his house, and we'd even started venturing out with the three of us. We'd been to Reynolds' a few times, but Gracie was with us, and Cage explained that we'd just finished riding, so Hugh and Lila hadn't questioned it.

Brinkley would be another story.

———

After some inappropriate yet completely typical conversation with Mrs. Runither, she led us to our table in the back.

"I love bringing Lincoln here because he gets so awkward with how touchy Mrs. Runither is." Brinkley had a wicked smirk on her face.

"Well, Finn loves it. He eggs her on," Reese said as she opened the menu. "And have I mentioned that this baby has an appetite because I'm always starving."

We all laughed, and Georgia told us how Maddox refused to come to Cottonwood Café because he felt like he was being violated. She shook her head with a big smile on her face. Lila told us that Hugh always wraps his arms around her when they walk in, so it sort of wards old Mrs. Runither off.

"Damn. You all have these hot men, and I'm still single. How is that fair?" Lola asked.

"Maddox's brother is single," Georgia said with her eyes wide. "You would love Wyle."

Lola put her hands up. "I've heard about him from Madison and Felicia, who told me he's charming and gorgeous and completely unattainable. I've had plenty of that, thank you. I'm over the good-looking playboys. Been there. Done that."

"Well, if he met the right woman, I think he'd settle down," Georgia said. We paused to place our orders quickly and then jumped right back into the conversation.

"I totally agree. He just hasn't met the right woman," Lila said.

"Any time you start a sentence with *If he met the right woman*, it's a huge red flag for me. That's just asking for a lot of heartache."

"Speaking of unattainable men… You and my brother seem to be spending a lot of time together," Brinkley said, her gaze finding mine.

"Yeah. It's been nice catching up after all these years. He's helping a ton at the barn right now, but I think my dad found someone who can start in a few weeks."

I cleared my throat and reached for my glass of wine, trying to act completely at ease while Lola squeezed my hand beneath the table.

"Interesting." Brinkley reached for her glass. "I stopped by to see Gracie on my way over here, and she went on and on about how much she loves riding with you *every day*. And apparently, she loves it when she and her daddy have dinner with you, which is almost every night." She raised a brow as a wide grin spread across her face.

The server set our food down, and I thanked her before looking up to see everyone gaping at me, waiting for an answer. "I love riding with her, too. And it's been nice to spend time with her and Cage. I know you all have questions, but can you give me a pass on this one? I don't want to analyze it. I just want to just enjoy the time I have with them."

Georgia's eyes watered, Lola smiled like she was proud that I hadn't denied it, Reese had her hands on her heart like I'd just said I was pregnant with twins, Lila was nodding in agreement, and Brinkley's gaze completely softened.

"I love that you didn't make up some crazy story. You're clearly a gifted lawyer. And that's a fair request. Listen, we all want you to enjoy the time you have here because I haven't seen my brother this happy in a long time. So, even if it's just for a few weeks, I'll take it." Brinkley picked up a chicken finger and took a bite.

That was easy. I didn't have to admit to anything, yet I'd found a way not to answer the questions.

"Can't you be a lawyer in Cottonwood Cove?" Georgia asked as she leaned her head on my shoulder.

"Trust me, I've tried to talk her into it. But she's really good at what she does for a living, and all those rich fuckers depend on her in New York. Plus, that whole magazine article has gone viral, so she's like the face of the modern woman back there right now." Lola bit off the top of a french fry. "But when she gets tired of the rat race, she can come run the spa with me."

"I cannot wait for you to open the doors. And you're right down the street from my office," Reese said. "We can have lunch all the time."

"Consider it done."

"Hey, my office isn't too far. Don't forget to text me when you meet up." Georgia threw her hands in the air.

"I'll meet you guys when we're here in town. And, Presley, I'm in the city now half the year, so you'll have to come over and see the house," Brinkley said. Her husband was a famous quarterback for the New York Thunderbirds.

"I'd love that."

My phone vibrated, and I looked down to see a text from Cage.

COWBOY

Hey. How's dinner?

Good. Miss me?

I tucked my phone back into my purse and looked up to see Lola watching me.

"It was Phillip. They have a new potential client they want me to try to close," I said. It wasn't a complete lie. I did have an appointment tomorrow with a huge production company at a major network. They were looking for new representation after a change in ownership. And Phillip thought I should take the lead on the account and convince them to sign with us. I'd heard about it this morning, not tonight, but at least it wasn't a complete lie.

"That's exciting," Georgia, Reese, and Lila said at the same time, but Brinkley and Lola shared a look that I didn't miss.

"It is." I smiled, but my mind was already wondering when I could get out of here and sneak over to see Cage.

I felt like I was in high school again.

And it was nice to be excited about something. Even if I should be excited about leading the meeting with A.R.C. Network, and not the fact that my ex-boyfriend couldn't go a few hours without seeing me, it still felt damn good.

I couldn't hide the smile on my face as we spent the next two hours talking about Brinkley's wedding plans, Lola sharing her ideas for the spa, Georgia telling us about a new author they signed at the publishing company, Lila sharing that she and Hugh were ready to start trying for a baby, and Reese getting excited about the idea of them raising their kids together. Lola ordered several desserts, and we all shared them and laughed some more until we made our way outside.

We said our goodbyes and hugged one another, and then Lola and I started walking together. Reese was the designated driver, and she took the girls home. She'd offered us a ride, but we both wanted to walk off our dinner. And I wasn't planning to go home, but I wasn't about to tell anyone that.

We stopped in front of Lola's little cottage, and I hugged her goodbye. She'd had a few glasses of wine, and she was getting all sappy.

"I'm happy for you," she said, squeezing my hands. "And I'm not going to ask any questions about why we passed your house and you kept walking with me. Have fun."

I didn't think she was paying attention, but I wasn't going to deny it.

"Love you. I'll call you in the morning."

I waved goodbye and walked two more blocks before turning down Cage's street. I went to the back door and knocked lightly. It opened so fast it startled me, and he reached for my arm and pulled me inside.

"It's about time, woman." Then his mouth was on mine.

eighteen

. . .

Cage

I'D JUST HAD the best sex of my life… for the second time today. I couldn't get enough of this woman. I'd all but begged her to come over after her girls' night. I'd never had a woman at the house while Gracie was home. Hell, the only woman who'd ever been in my bed was Presley. But the one time I'd brought her here, Gracie had been with my parents.

She was lying in my arms, completely naked, and I wanted to keep her right here. I pushed the thought out of my head.

"So, tell me about this meeting tomorrow," I said, as she intertwined her fingers with mine.

"It's the first step, you know? I've never been the lead with a potential client, and certainly not one of this magnitude. I'm sure Ben and Grant are having a meltdown over it, but Phillip has the final say."

"Fuck those two. If they give you any shit, you just call me."

She rolled onto her stomach and smiled. "Are you going to beat up everyone who gives me a hard time?"

"If you let me, yes. I still wish I would have punched Wes

in the face. The dude just bugs me with his preppy-ass tweed coat."

She put a hand over her mouth, more than aware that my little girl was in the house right now. "You want to punch him for wearing a fancy sports coat?"

"I want to punch him because he was the lucky bastard who got to marry you. You're the best person I know, so I envy him that he got his shot with you." I caught myself off guard as the words left my mouth.

But fuck it.

It was the truth.

"Yeah? Well, my mom's due back from Barbados in a few days, and I think she'd beg to differ on that."

"I think your mom is jealous of you. I've always thought that," I said, tucking her hair behind her ear.

"Barbie Duncan is not jealous of me. She can't stand me most of the time."

"Not true," I said, tipping her chin up so she was looking at me. "You've always beat to your own drum. You didn't want to do pageants, so you put your foot down. She was the one who'd followed in her mother's footsteps and didn't choose for herself. You loved horses, and you followed that passion and became a national champ. You love to paint, and you had several teachers tell you that you could have pursued it professionally. She envies your independence."

"Yet I went to Harvard Law and became an attorney because I didn't want to disappoint them."

"There's no shame in loving your family," I said, putting my finger to her lips when she started to argue. "You love your mother whether you want to admit it or not. And you do love law; you're a natural at winning arguments. And if you want to paint, there is nothing stopping you from doing it as a hobby. It doesn't have to be your profession to start doing it again. Hell, Georgia plays more pickleball than most professional players."

She chuckled. "Did I tell you that Lola wants me to paint a mural at the spa? It's just been so long since I've painted, I don't know if I'm any good anymore. Remember how I used to dream about having a room that looked out at the water where I'd spend my free time painting? Apparently, my younger self thought I'd be living this life of leisure." She chuckled.

"I do. You talked about it for years." I pushed up to sit and reached for her hand. "I want to show you something."

I pulled on a pair of joggers, grabbed a white button-up from my closet, and helped her slip her arms into the sleeves, buttoning just a few center buttons. My dick was already hard again at the sight of her in my dress shirt.

I held my finger to my lips to remind her to keep it down, as Gracie was sleeping down the hall, and I reached for her hand. Presley hadn't spent much time at my house, and I'd never taken her upstairs. Gracie and I had bedrooms on the main floor, along with her playroom and a guest room, but I'd built a loft upstairs. We tiptoed up the stairs, and the light from the moon illuminated the room.

"What is this?" she whispered as she took in the grand space with nothing more than a wood table that I'd used as a desk a few times.

"I don't know. You told me to build it, and I did. I've used it as an office before, but I usually do all my paperwork in the kitchen. So, I haven't decided what this is. I guess, in a way, this is your painting room."

Her eyes were wet with emotion as she walked across the room to the row of windows looking out at the water. There were French doors that led to a little balcony.

"Cage," she whispered as she stared out at the dark water in the distance. "I can't believe you did this."

"Hey, I didn't break every promise I made to you. It might not have led us to where we wanted to go, but I'll tell you what…" I pulled her into my arms. "If you want to paint and look out at the water, this room will be here for you any time."

A tear ran down her cheek. "Thank you."

My hands moved to the spot where the shirt dipped low, and my fingers traced along her breast as her head fell back. I moved my free hand between her legs to find her soaked.

Jesus. We were both insatiable. My hands found her ass, lifting her up before setting her on the desk. She tugged my head down to kiss her as our hands explored one another the way they always did. She found the waistband of my joggers and dipped her hand inside, wrapping her fingers around my throbbing cock as she spread her legs wider.

The light from the moon provided a halo around her, and her gaze locked with mine as I pushed inside. I sealed my lips to hers to keep from making any noise, and I thrust into her warmth, over and over. She pulled back, her hooded gaze telling me she was close, and my hand moved between us. Her breaths were coming faster, and her head fell forward, biting down on my shoulder to keep from crying out my name. I pumped into her a few more times before burying my face in her neck and groaning as I came so hard I couldn't see straight.

What the fuck was she doing to me?

We continued moving, riding out every last bit of pleasure, before I leaned back to look at her. I pulled out and grabbed a few tissues from the box on the desk and cleaned her up. She just sat there, all sated and sexy, as she watched me. I tossed the tissue into the garbage and helped her to her feet.

"I'm starving. How about you?"

"I could eat," she whispered as we tiptoed back downstairs.

I held up a box of cereal, and she gave me a thumbs-up as I reached for two bowls.

I turned around to see her looking in the refrigerator for

the milk, and for whatever fucked-up reason, it took my breath away. Just seeing her in the middle of my kitchen in nothing but a white, oversized shirt… It hit me hard.

How badly I wanted this.

Her.

A little whimper came from the hallway just as a voice broke through my thoughts.

"Daddy," Gracie's voice cracked, and it had me turning in panic just as she entered the kitchen. "You weren't in your room."

Her whole body shook, and I rushed toward her, bending down to meet her eyes. "I'm right here. What happened, Gracie girl?"

"I had a bad dream." She blinked several times as I ran my hands through her wild mane of hair, doing anything I could to comfort her. Her gaze moved behind me. "Presley? Is that you?"

Fuck.

I was the fucking worst guy on the planet.

This would confuse the shit out of her.

"Um, hey, sweetie. Yes, I just stopped by to, um…" Presley stumbled over her words.

"She stopped by to borrow some milk. She was all out." My words came out rushed, but I was pretty impressed with myself for thinking that up so quickly.

"We always have milk. Right, Daddy?"

"We do, yes. I was just loaning her some milk, and then I was going to head back to bed by myself." What the fuck? Why did I say that? "Why don't I heat you up a warm glass of milk? It will help you sleep."

"Okay. Can you stay for a little bit and sit with me, Presley?"

Jesus. She was wearing my shirt, and she had no panties on under it, and my mind was in full panic mode.

"Of course. Do you mind if I use the restroom real quick?"

"Okay," Gracie said, and Presley winked at me as she walked down the hallway.

She came back quickly, wearing the jeans she had on when she arrived. She was still wearing my white shirt, though she'd buttoned a few more buttons to cover herself up.

I was warming some milk on the stovetop, and Gracie led Presley to the couch, where she proceeded to climb onto her lap.

This ought to have Presley running for the hills really quickly. The reality of my life wasn't quite as sexy as it appeared.

Thankfully, the pig was still asleep in the laundry room, and Bob was on the couch, snoring beside the girls.

"Tell me what your bad dream was about," Presley said, her voice soft and soothing. Were we supposed to ask that? Gracie had only had bad dreams a few times in her life, but she hadn't had one for a while. I'd never asked what they were about; I'd just tried to comfort her. I probably should have asked, though.

"I think I was chasing after Sally so that I could ride her, but I couldn't catch her."

"Ah, you had your first horse dream. You know what that means, don't you?" Presley asked as she stroked Gracie's hair, and my daughter melted against her chest. I set the warm mug of milk on the coffee table and dropped to sit in the leather chair beside them.

Gracie's eyes were closed, and her voice was quiet. "What does it mean, Presley?"

"It means you're a real horse girl now. You only have those dreams once you have horses in your heart," Presley said, kissing the top of Gracie's hair.

"Like you and me are in Daddy's heart?" my daughter asked, her voice sleepy now.

Presley looked up at me, her eyes locked with mine.

"Exactly. Once you're in someone's heart, you never really leave."

"But you're leaving soon. Right, Presley?"

"I'm here for a few more weeks. But I'll be back to visit, and you know that you can still ride Sally any time you want after I leave. I think she belongs to you, too, now."

"Will you stay with me until I fall asleep?" Gracie asked.

"Of course I will, baby girl. I'm not going anywhere right now."

I picked up the mug of warm milk because clearly, Gracie had found comfort elsewhere, and now I was a fucking mess. I took a sip of milk as I watched Presley continue running her fingers through Gracie's hair, as my daughter dozed off.

And I just sat there watching them.

My girls.

Watching the way my woman comforted my little girl.

The guilt that I felt that Gracie didn't have this whenever she wanted it. She didn't have a mother who knew to ask about her bad dreams. She was stuck with a father who didn't have a fucking clue how to raise a little girl on his own.

And now, I'd brought a woman into her life that she was growing attached to, knowing that she'd be leaving her.

Leaving me.

I set the mug down, and Presley's voice broke through the silence.

"Cage," she whispered.

"Yeah?"

"Stop overthinking it. It's just a bad dream. We all have them. She runs to you because you're her safe place. Stop doubting yourself."

Fuck me. How does she always do that? Always know what I'm thinking.

"All right. I know you have that meeting in the morning. Should I take her off your lap?"

"Nope. I'm going to stay right here and hold her for as long as she needs me, if that's okay?"

I nodded, even though she wasn't looking at me, and I leaned back in the chair. "It's okay with me."

And I sat there watching them until my eyes grew heavy and I dozed off.

I didn't wake until the sun came through the windows, which had my eyes blinking open.

And my daughter lay sound asleep in Presley's arms in the exact same place they'd been a few hours ago.

nineteen

· · ·

Presley

I'D hurried home to catch a shower and change as quickly as I could for my meeting. This was a big one, and I hadn't slept a whole lot, but I didn't care. Normally before a meeting of this magnitude, I would have gone to bed early and laid out my clothes the night before.

But none of that seemed all that important in the grand scheme of things.

Gracie had had a nightmare, and she'd wanted me to comfort her.

Had anything ever felt that damn good before?

Being needed by that little angel kind of trumped everything. What I wore to this meeting seemed less important this morning, but maybe it was because I hadn't slept much.

I pulled out my cream business suit and chuckled when I thought of what Lola said. I normally would choose my black suit, but that just felt boring this morning. I slipped on the cream silk shell before pulling up the skirt and pushing my arms through the sleeves of my blazer. I'd usually wear heels, even though no one could see my feet, just because it made me feel more put together. But today, I slipped on my scuffed-up cowboy booties, which were far more comfortable and gave me a different kind of confidence.

I wore my hair in loose waves and applied my makeup, keeping things light and natural, before setting up my laptop at the little nook table. I set my coffee mug and a large glass of water on the table so they'd be there if needed.

I yawned a few times as I looked over my notes and saw the text from Phillip come through.

> **PHILLIP**
>
> Good morning. I'm going to be on the call, but I won't be speaking unless you need me to. This is your meeting. You're about to be an official partner at this firm. Take the reins and work your magic and close this deal.

I blew out a long breath and shook off the nerves.

> Don't worry one bit. I've got this.

> **PHILLIP**
>
> I don't have a doubt in the world. See you soon.

I cleared my throat and used the camera as a mirror to make sure my hair and makeup were okay before joining the meeting room.

One by one, different faces came into view as they introduced themselves. Phillip was there, and I was actually relieved that Grant and Ben weren't attending, as they would just be looking for areas to criticize me.

Dan Walker, the president of A.R.C. Network, was in his mid-fifties, with silver hair and a friendly smile. Margo Linsworth was the vice president of the company, and there were two other men, John Windsor and Pete Harlow, who were members of the board.

"Thank you all for being here. I'd like to tell you a bit about our firm and share all the reasons why we'd be your best choice for your legal representation," I said.

Margo was the first to speak. "I recently read the article in *New York Law* magazine about you becoming the first female partner of the firm. That was quite a spread they did on you. Happy to see it. You've got one impressive résumé."

"Thank you," I said, grateful that they'd done their research. "I've worked at Harper, Wallace, and Beezley since I graduated from law school, and actually even before that, as I interned for Phillip Harper while I was still a student."

"May I just add that she graduated from *Harvard Law School* at the top of her class? She's a bit humble, if you haven't noticed. I think Presley is one of the great legal minds of our future."

They all smiled and nodded, and I felt my cheeks heat at the compliment. Phillip was a very well-known and respected attorney, and getting praise from him was as good as it gets.

"Thank you for the kind words. So, let's get down to business, shall we?" I reached for my coffee, acting like I was completely at ease when inside, my heart was racing so fast that I feared they would hear it. "If you're looking for a firm that will make you their priority and always be one step ahead of any fires coming your way, then you've come to the right place. And let me tell you why," I said, as I started my PowerPoint presentation.

I shared our background, several cases we'd won, different examples of situations that had been handled with the utmost discretion, and our track record for being the best in the business.

It was an easy case to plead because I truly believed it was true.

I wouldn't want to be a partner at a firm I didn't believe in.

We went back and forth for the next hour, with them asking questions that were easy to answer. Phillip never had to interject even once. I didn't miss the smile on his face every time I glanced at him.

And it felt damn good.

I'd proven that I was more than ready for this next step.

"Well, I've got to tell you, this was impressive, Presley. We've met with three other firms, and none of them made me feel certain that they were the right fit. You've managed to do that today. I think I speak for everyone when I say that you can go ahead and send over the contracts," Dan Walker said, and his team nodded in agreement.

"What he's basically saying is that he makes the final decision, so he doesn't really care what we think," Margo said as they all erupted in laughter. "But lucky for Dan, I think we're all on board. Very impressive presentation. I know everyone is making a big deal about you being the first female partner at the firm, but I'm here to say that I think they're the lucky ones."

"I couldn't agree more. I pride myself on recognizing talent. I'm guessing we have that in common, Dan." Phillip folded his hands and smiled.

"Agreed. You've got to surround yourself with the best, and that's always been the key to my success. We look forward to working with the best, and we're happy to have you join the A.R.C. family."

My hands were shaking as I smiled at the camera. I hadn't expected a decision today, but to say this had gone better than I'd imagined was a massive understatement.

Grant and Ben were going to shit themselves when they heard that we'd signed them. Maybe now they'd get on board with my name being on the outside of the building along with theirs.

We said our goodbyes, and Phillip and I stayed on the call while he gushed about how well it all went.

"Proud of you. It was your first major test, and you killed it just as I expected you would."

"Thank you. That means a lot," I said, reaching for my coffee, in desperate need of a caffeine boost.

"So, you think two weeks is enough? We're ready to have you back, but I don't want to rush you."

I cleared my throat, as thoughts of leaving had my chest feeling heavy. My dad was making a miraculous recovery, and I was thrilled about it, but I wasn't quite ready to go back to the madness of my life.

"Do you think you can give me three weeks? I'd like to make sure Dad is settled after the nurses leave and keep an eye on him." I knew that wasn't the reason I was asking for the extension. My father was doing so well that the nurses were planning to leave earlier than expected. He'd have more than enough time to adjust to the change with the date we'd planned for. But here I was, buying a little more time.

It didn't mean anything. I was enjoying myself. It was just like extending a vacation that you were enjoying. There was no shame in that. Then you return to your regular life, and you forget about the vacation because you're back to doing what you love.

"I can absolutely work with that. I've got to say, small-town life agrees with you. You seem more relaxed and lighter. I thought being there and dealing with all of this was going to be stressful for you."

"Well, don't get too excited. Barbie's coming home this week. Let the stress begin." I chuckled.

"You'll be fine. I could only hope Brianna would want to be there for me if I were in this situation, but I think we both know that won't be happening. You might need to be the one that comes and takes care of me when I'm too old to take care of myself." He chuckled, but there was a sadness there. Phillip had traded his relationship with his daughter for his relationship with the firm. He'd been married three times, and I hoped that Veronica would be the one to stay. She didn't love the hours he worked, but I knew she loved him. I'd always put him on a pedestal for his work ethic, but for the first time, I wondered if Phillip had missed out. Thinking about the concern I'd seen on Cage's face when Gracie stumbled into the kitchen last night. He was an amazing father. Phillip hadn't had that presence in his daughter's life. He'd dedicated his time and energy to the firm.

And was there anything better in life than his little girl clinging to him the way she did?

If you'd asked me a few weeks ago, I'd have said that Phillip's legal accolades were the greatest gift one could ever receive.

But today, I was looking at life a little differently.

"You know I'd be there in a heartbeat. But you're not quite that old just yet," I teased.

"Damn straight. I've got another decade to conquer the world. I'll keep you posted on the contract, and I'll see you at the team Zoom meeting tomorrow. I think you'll be seeing a different side of Ben and Grant after this meeting." He smirked.

"One can hope. I'll see you tomorrow," I said before waving goodbye and ending the call.

I spent the rest of the day at the house with my father. He was fully walking on his own now, no more wheelchair. Carol had been relieved, and only Lexi was on duty now, and the night nurses were no longer necessary.

My mother would be thrilled that he was going to be back to business as usual. She hated when people struggled or were anything less than perfect.

We were having dinner in the dining room together, and he finished chewing. "Mom will be back at the end of the week."

"Yes. That's what she said. She'll be happy to see your progress." I popped a bite of pasta into my mouth.

He chuckled. "Yes. Having deficits doesn't really work well for her."

We'd never had a deep discussion about their marriage, and he never got involved in the arguments between my mother and me.

"Does that bother you? Her lack of tolerance for imperfection?"

He took a sip of his water before setting the glass back down. "I believe that most people's strengths and weaknesses are one and the same. I was drawn to your mother for her drive and her demand for perfection, so I can't fault her for it when it doesn't fare well for me."

"Sure, you can," I said, as I used my hand to cover my laugh, and he smiled. "I mean, it's okay for you to call her out when she's acting irrationally."

"Your mother makes no apologies for who she is. I knew it the day I married her, and I've known it every day since. We built a life together that I'm grateful for."

"Really, Dad? You never wanted… more?"

His eyes widened. "More? We've got six homes, three companies, and more money than you or any of your future offspring you may or may not ever have will know what to do with. What more could I ask for?"

I dabbed at my mouth with my napkin before dropping it back into my lap. "There is more to life than material things. I'm not taking away from all you've built, because it's amazing. But when I say more, I'm referring to love. An actual loving relationship."

He studied me for the longest time before speaking. "You're more than aware that I grew up in a trailer park with an alcoholic mother and no father, Presley. I earned a scholarship to Harvard, where I was suddenly surrounded by people who had a lot more than I'd grown up with. I remember being fascinated by how relaxed they were with the daily things that had always caused me stress. Like making sure I had a warm meal or gas in the car. And I decided at that time that I was never going to be in a situation where I was hungry or cold. I was going to work hard to make sure I accomplished that."

I knew all of this. My father was a self-made man, and that was the reason I'd wanted so desperately to make him proud. But that wasn't what I was talking about.

"I love that you built all of this by working hard. But that's not what I mean. I'm talking about a happy, healthy relationship. A home filled with love." A lump formed in my throat because it made me feel ungrateful that I'd had so much growing up, yet there'd been something major missing from my perfect life. And it made me feel and sound like a brat because I'd never known what it meant to be hungry or to be without a roof over my head... I wanted for nothing materially.

And I'd learned that it was easy to be annoyed by people with money who weren't overflowing with joy. But the truth is, money didn't buy happiness.

Only people who didn't have money believed that was true.

Money only bought stuff, and sure, that was wonderful not to ever have to stress about finances. But it certainly didn't mean that life was without hardships or sadness.

Money certainly didn't fix loneliness either.

"I suppose it's all about what's important to you. For me, this life, it's what I'm most proud of. Your mother is the reason that most of this was possible." He held his hands up to stop me from arguing. "Your mother came from a wealthy family, you know that. And she saw something in me. Trust me when I tell you, she had every guy on campus chasing after her. But she saw this kid from the trailer park as more than he was. She believed in me when no one else did. She encouraged me to go on to law school when we first got married, and she encouraged me to start my investment business on the side. And on top of that, she gave me the greatest gift of all."

My eyes watered as I listened because he'd never shared this with me, and I didn't know why she should be getting so much praise for seeing what a great man he was, but it made me realize how much he truly loved her.

"What was that? When she encouraged you to buy this ranch?" I knew this was his happy place, and it wasn't her favorite home to spend time in. It was the one thing I'd noticed that she did for him. She spent months here at a time because he loved it here.

His gaze softened, and he reached for my hand. "No, Presley. She gave me you. I wanted a child, and she didn't think she was cut out for motherhood. But I knew I was meant to have a child, and I actually dreamed of you many times before you came into the world. I would tell her about this little girl with blonde hair and dark eyes and big dreams."

Tears slipped down my cheeks. It should sting hearing him say that she didn't want me, but it didn't. I knew my mother well enough to know she wasn't someone with a burning desire to experience motherhood.

"So you forced her to have a baby?" I said as a sad laugh left my lips.

"No. She came to me one night and said she dreamed of you, as well. But she said she knew she wouldn't be any good at it, so as long as I agreed to let her have help, she would agree to be a mother."

I shook my head and smiled. It was *so* like my parents to discuss having a child as if it were a business decision. "It's not like buying a car or a house, Dad. I'm an actual human being, and I know she can't stand the woman I've become."

His brows shot up with surprise.

Was he seriously surprised to hear this?

"I know who your mother is, Presley. She can be cold, and she's stubborn and strong and set in her ways. But when she looks at you… she is ridiculously proud of you. She wishes she had the confidence to do exactly what she wanted. Your mother didn't love pageants at first; she just accepted it, as it was what her family expected of her. But you… you have always beat to your own drum. And I promise you on all that I know to be true—she admires you more than you know. She once came to our bedroom after you two had argued when you refused to wear a dress and go to that last pageant she'd signed you up for, and she said these words to me…" He paused to take a sip of water, and I waited for him to finish like he was going to tell me the secret to life.

"I'm sort of dying here. What did she say?"

"She said," his voice softened, "'our daughter has your ability to stand up for what she believes in. I may not agree with her choices, but I wish I had a little bit of that in me. But if you ever tell her I said that, I'll deny it until my dying day.'"

"Why? Why deny it? Why not tell me that she admires it? Why not tell me that she doesn't despise me?" I asked, my voice shaking as the words left my mouth.

"Because she is stoic and proud, and like I said, her strengths are her weaknesses. Just like all of us, right?"

I shrugged. "I don't know about that. I don't think your strengths are your weaknesses."

"Sure, they are. I'm driven to a fault. I worked long after a doctor told me that I was at risk of a stroke. I ignored him. I thought I was bigger than any health scare. Being driven can be both a positive and a negative."

I thought about his words. I could be stubborn when I wanted to be. I was prideful to a fault, always trying to prove myself to my mother and to everyone around me. Hell, I'd married a man I didn't love because I wanted everyone to think I was okay after Cage and I had ended things. I was guilty of trying to look perfect to everyone around me. I'd been desperate to make partner at the firm so everyone would think I was smart enough, good enough.

"I'm glad you got a second chance to learn that you aren't untouchable, Dad. That you have to take care of yourself, because I need you." My voice cracked.

He squeezed my hand. "There are different types of happiness for each of us. I found mine. Your mother found hers. The question is, have you found yours?"

"I'm getting there. I'm glad to be out of a loveless marriage, and I'm going to find my new normal when I get back to New York. I know I'm damn good at my job, and I'm really proud of that."

"I'm proud of you. You have nothing left to prove. All I want for you now is to be happy."

"I'm working on it," I said as I moved to my feet and wrapped my arms around his neck.

"What in the world is going on? Who died?" My mother's voice startled me, and I turned around to see her standing in the dining room in a lavender skirt and suit jacket, looking at us like we were doing something completely inappropriate by hugging.

My father barked out a laugh. "We're having a heart-to-heart. Didn't your alien leaders teach you that that's what humans do?"

"Are you drunk?" she asked, but her lips turned up the slightest bit in the corners. Was this their idea of flirty banter?

"Had I known you were coming home early, I might have had a cocktail." He smirked.

"I thought you weren't due back for a few days?" I asked as I took my seat again.

"Well, I heard your divorce was final, and I had to make sure you were keeping it together. I didn't need you to distract your father from his treatment with all your drama." She waved her hand around, and I saw it there in her eyes.

She was here because she wanted to make sure that I was okay.

That we were all okay.

And for the first time in my life, I saw my mother through a new lens.

And she wasn't the devil from this view.

She was just an imperfect human, like the rest of us.

twenty

. . .

Cage

BRINKLEY

Does anyone want a fun fact?

GEORGIA

Ooohhh, I love fun facts.

FINN

I feel like there is always a life lesson in your fun facts.

HUGH

Let's hear it.

I'll pass.

BRINKLEY

Of course, you will. Mom and I took Gracie to try on her flower girl dress for the wedding yesterday.

Fun fact. You picked her up from my house, so I'm more than aware.

BRINKLEY

Fun fact. She told us about a bad dream she
had a few nights ago.

HERE WE FUCKING GO. It was only a matter of time
before my sister figured out everything. And I didn't even
fucking care who knew anymore. It would be over before it
got started, so they could say all they wanted. None of it
mattered. I was doing what I wanted to do, which was to find
a way to stop by the barn every fucking morning. Go for a
ride with Presley before we'd fuck like bunnies and talk about
life. I talked to her about things I didn't even allow myself to
think about most of the time. We had dinner with Gracie
almost every night, and then she'd go home, and I'd put my
daughter to bed, and then Presley and I would talk on the
phone all night until we fell asleep. So, fuck anyone who
wanted to say anything about what we were doing. I would
neither confirm nor deny. This would be my shit show to
clean up in a couple of weeks when she left. It was no one's
fucking business.

Again. I was there. And it wasn't a fun fact. It
was a fucking nightmare about a horse.

GEORGIA

Oh, she loves Sally so much. She's dreaming
about her.

HUGH

Damn. I'd have bought her a horse years ago
if I'd known how much she'd love riding.

FINN

I tried. The OLD ball and chain shut me
down.

Am I the fucking ball and chain? That makes no sense. And stop calling me old, asshole.

BRINKLEY

Back to the point. She told us every detail about the field she was running through. The way she chased after her horse but couldn't catch her.

GEORGIA

I'm literally crying right now. This is so sweet.

Thanks for this wonderful retelling about my daughter's bad dream, but I've got to make a house call for Mr. Wigglestein. He's chewed through his stitches, and Mrs. Remington thinks it might be infected.

FINN

You took his testicles, man. He's just trying to find them.

HUGH

God rest Mr. Wigglestein's balls. <praying hands emoji>

BRINKLEY

Hello? I wasn't finished.

Is there a point to this story? If so, go ahead and make it sometime today.

BRINKLEY

Well, Gracie shared how she came running out to find her daddy, but he wasn't in his bedroom. But she was thrilled to see Presley in the kitchen in the middle of the night. IN THE MIDDLE OF THE NIGHT!

She'd stopped by to borrow something.

HUGH

Night goggles?

FINN

Your penis? <eggplant emoji>

Fuck off.

BRINKLEY

Gracie said it was two o'clock in the morning, and she knew that because she has a clock in her bedroom.

HUGH

Damn. That kid is a freaking genius. I couldn't tell time in kindergarten. Clocks are fucking confusing.

FINN

I learned to tell time unusually young. She gets her smarts from me.

We have a digital clock, dickweiners. She knows her numbers. What's your point, Brinks?

BRINKLEY

My point is that I find it interesting that Presley Duncan needed to borrow a cup of freaking milk at two o'clock in the morning. Gracie said she came by to borrow milk. <head exploding emoji>

Why is that surprising? She lives in New York. It was 5:00 a.m. there. Time for breakfast.

GEORGIA

I love that you're having slumber parties with Presley. This makes me so happy.

Listen. It was a onetime thing. She's never borrowed milk in the middle of the night again.

GEORGIA

Bummer. It's been so nice getting to spend time with her after all these years. I wish we could keep her.

BRINKLEY

She's not a dog, for God's sake.

HUGH

Well, Cage does have a thing for strays.

FINN

Move over, Maxine… Daddy's got a new honey in town!

If you ever call me Daddy again or refer to a woman as a honey, I will throat punch you so hard you won't ever regain consciousness.

BRINKLEY

Just admit you're in love with her, and we'll call it a day.

There was nothing to admit. I'd never *not* been in love with Presley. It would be like admitting that I didn't need air to breathe. But loving her didn't mean anything all those years ago, and it didn't mean anything now. At the end of the day, love had never been our problem.

> Stay out of my business and act normal tonight.

FINN

Sounds like Daddy's bringing his honey to Sunday dinner.

BRINKLEY

I'll bring the milk, just in case she needs a cup for later.

HUGH

<glass of milk emoji> <honey jar emoji>

> <middle finger emoji>

GEORGIA

<heart eyes emoji>

———

Presley was leaving in a few weeks, so I was getting in as much time with her as I could. I'd survived another Sunday night dinner with endless jokes about milk and all of them giving me a hard time.

I'd taken on a new attitude about the whole thing. I was going to enjoy it while it lasted, and I'd deal with the ramifications later.

I was still being careful where Gracie was concerned, though we spent a lot of time together with all three of us. Presley didn't spend the night at my home with my daughter there, and we weren't affectionate in front of her either.

As far as Gracie knew, Presley was a friend who was visiting. I'd made it very clear that she'd be leaving.

We pulled up to Georgia and Maddox's house, as they'd invited Gracie over to teach her how to play pickleball. That was much safer than horse jumping, which was her new obsession, so I would push pickleball even if Georgia was crazed over the sport.

"Daddy, can I still ride Sally after Presley goes back to her home?" my daughter asked as we pulled into the long driveway in front of their house. I still had a headache from this morning, as Maxine had been escaping from her playpen lately, and she'd made a mess in Gracie's bedroom. It was time for her to go back home, but the Langleys were avoiding my calls. I'd deal with that this week.

"We'll see. I'll talk to Presley and ask if she has anyone she can recommend to continue your lessons."

"I want to be a real horse girl like Presley. I want to learn how to jump with Sally."

I pinched the bridge of my nose at the thought. It was difficult enough for me to see her on top of an animal that had the capacity to throw her off and hurt her. But I trusted Presley. And the truth was, I didn't think there was anyone else that I'd be comfortable with to continue her lessons. Reese had offered, and of course, I trusted her, but she was pregnant, and Finn was a ridiculously protective dude when it came to his wife. He didn't want her riding right now, and I knew they'd argued over it many times, so I wasn't going to push it.

"Maybe when you are a lot older. Jumping over things on horses is for much bigger people. But I think you're going to love pickleball."

"But Presley could teach me." Her little hand was in mine as we walked up the path to the front door.

I turned around and looked at her. "She's not going to be here that much longer. Let's just stick with the lessons that we have left and get used to sitting on a horse before we start jumping over things, all right?"

"Okay. I'm going to be the bestest at pickleball, Daddy. I promise."

Jesus. Now I felt like a total ass cracker. I didn't give a shit if she was good at pickleball. I just didn't want her sitting on a horse and jumping over things. No fucking thank you. I'd prefer if she just stayed home and colored, if I was being honest. I'd been working on something for Presley that I knew Gracie would enjoy, as well. So, in a way, it was for the two of them.

When the door opened, Georgia was wearing a pink tennis skirt and a white sweater, and she held up a matching outfit for a child, which was clearly for Gracie.

"Are you ready to learn from the best?" my sister asked, and I rolled my eyes as Maddox barked out a laugh.

"I love it!" Gracie squealed and took off with my sister down the hall.

"Does she need an outfit for everything?" I asked, as I followed Maddox into the kitchen and set her backpack on the counter.

"I think your sister has had baby fever ever since Reese got pregnant," he said with a laugh. "And damn if I don't want to put a bunch of babies in her."

"Dude. No. This is not a conversation I'm having with you." I gave him a warning look. "Sex with my sister is never a conversation we're going to have."

He put his hands up and laughed before moving to the refrigerator and grabbing two bottles of water. He set one in front of me as I dropped onto the barstool.

"What are you going to do with the afternoon off?"

"I've got to run by Duncan Ranch. Presley and I will take the horses out for a ride and give them some exercise." I didn't look at him because I could feel him assessing me.

"You going to be okay when she leaves?"

"Jesus. Not you, too?"

He chuckled. "I'm not getting into your business, and I won't share what you tell me with anyone. I just know you, brother. And I can tell that she's different, you know? And when that happened to me, I was freaked the fuck out. And I got to keep her, so I can't imagine if that hadn't been an option."

"Well, I knew that going in. I live here. She lives there. So, we're just having a little fun, you know?"

He studied me for a long moment. "Could she practice law here?"

"I'd never ask her to do that. She just made partner at some big, fancy firm. She loves her life there. We don't talk about it because we're both settled in our lives. I've got Gracie to think about."

"You're still allowed to live and have a life. You know that, don't you?"

"She's got one parent. The least I can do is give my little girl a stable life, and that life is here."

Georgia and Gracie sauntered into the kitchen wearing matching outfits, and as much as I wanted to be annoyed, it was cute as hell.

"You're ridiculous," I said, kissing my sister on top of her head before scooping up Gracie. "All right, Gracie girl. Don't let Auntie Georgie get crazy out there on the court. I'm going to head out. I'll pick you up in a few hours."

"Love you, Daddy."

"I love you." I set her down and made my way outside to my truck and drove the short distance to Duncan Ranch. I hadn't seen Presley since last night, and I was anxious to see her.

She was waiting for me when I pulled up, and I pulled her close and kissed her right there in front of the barn. I didn't bother to look around and see if anyone was there. We'd been keeping things on the down-low, as we both knew it was temporary.

When she pulled back, a little breathless, she smiled. "Wow, Cowboy. Kissing me in public. What's gotten into you?"

"I guess I just don't give a fuck what anyone thinks."

"As if you ever really did," she said. Her voice was all tease as she led me into the barn.

"How about I just check the horses, and we head over to my house instead of going for a ride today? I have something I want to show you."

"I'll bet you do." She waggled her brows, and I laughed as she followed me from one stall to the next, and I took a look at each of the horses.

We were walking toward my truck, her fingers intertwined with mine, because apparently, neither of us gave a fuck anymore.

"Presley, are you leaving?" Barbie Duncan walked toward us. Her gaze moved from our joined hands to my face. "Oh, hello, Kale. It's nice to see you."

I'd dated her daughter for many years, and she'd always made a point of letting me know she didn't know my name.

It was a game, making sure that I was aware that I wasn't important enough to get it right. I truly didn't give a shit because she'd treated her daughter like shit, and I didn't have a whole lot of respect for the woman.

Just as Presley was about to correct her, I squeezed her hand and spoke first. "*Hey, Bernese,* it's lovely to see you, as well."

She raised a brow before turning back to her daughter, who had let out a burst of laughter at our pissing match. "I checked my schedule, and I'm good to go see the spa with you tomorrow. I'm looking forward to it. God knows they need one in this town. It will make it more tolerable to be here."

The woman had one of the largest homes in Cottonwood Cove, surrounded by beautiful land with views of the ocean, and she couldn't find a way to enjoy it.

"All right. I'd like that, and Lola would love to show it off."

"Well, seeing as you and your father invested in the place, I may as well see where my money is going."

Presley's shoulders stiffened, and she nodded. "I'll see you later. I told Dad I'll be back to join you for dinner."

"Good. Time is running out before you go back to your real life," she said, raising a brow at me.

What the fuck was she talking about? I was more than aware that this was temporary. I didn't need a reminder.

"See you later, Mother," Presley said as we walked toward the truck.

I opened her door, and she slipped inside, and I came around the driver's side and got behind the wheel before pulling down the driveway.

"Sorry about that." She looked out the window as the words left her mouth.

"You don't need to apologize to me. I know it's not personal. She doesn't appear to like anyone."

She laughed. "My dad and I had this heart-to-heart about her, and I'm trying to see things through her eyes, but it's not easy."

Presley proceeded to tell me about how her mother hadn't wanted kids, and she didn't think she'd be a good mother, but she knew how much Frank wanted a child. I listened as she filled me in on all that he'd shared.

"Well, I have to say, she raised one hell of a daughter, and regardless of the way she has behaved most of the time, she brought you into the world. For that alone, I can't dislike her."

"Wow, that's quite possibly the sweetest thing you've ever said to me." She winked, and I helped her out of the truck before she followed me to the front door.

"Then you better buckle up, because I'm about to top it."

We stepped inside, and she tugged at my hand until I turned around to face her. "Does this surprise involve you being naked?"

"You can't get enough of me, can you, baby?" I leaned down and kissed her forehead. "Trust me. I want you naked really badly, but I want to show you something first."

"Fine. I'll have my way with you later."

I took her hand and led her up the stairs to the loft.

"What is this?" she asked, as she gaped at the room.

"It's a place for a raven to spread her wings and fly."

twenty-one

. . .

Presley

MY EX-HUSBAND HAD a lot of money. I'd grown up in a family that had a lot of money. My parents had bought me cars and clothing and fancy trips around the world. Wes had gifted me art that I didn't really care for and jewelry that was not even my style but had cost a fortune.

But this.

I had no words.

This was by far the most thoughtful gift I'd ever received.

I shook my head as I looked around. There was an easel with a large canvas resting there and a table beside it with every color paint imaginable. Several brushes sat beside the paint, and there was a painter's smock sitting on the stool in front of the easel. There was a smaller easel beside it, with a matching table and some finger paints and watercolors on that one. A matching smock rested on the chair there, as well. There were a few packages of M&M's sitting beside the paints. He'd thought of everything.

Cage moved to open the French doors that were directly in front of the setup, and a light breeze bustled in as I looked out at the cove in the distance.

There were tall trees in every color and shade of green.

213

The sky was a perfect turquoise blue today with swirls of white clouds, and the sun was a gorgeous mix of yellow and orange.

"I can't believe you did this. It's stunning."

"Yeah? I thought maybe you could spend your last few weeks here. You can come and paint whenever you want to. Hell, you can be here when I'm at work and Gracie's at school. Maybe this will help you get inspired to paint that mural for Lola."

A lump so thick formed in my throat, making it difficult to breathe.

"And I can teach Gracie to paint."

"I sure as fuck hope so, because you've got that girl dreaming of horses and talking about becoming a jumper. Let's push the paints, all right?"

This man. He was all tough on the exterior and soft beneath that hard shell.

"You know why I think I like M&M's so much?" I moved to the little table and grabbed a package before tearing off the top.

"Because they're better than Hot Tamales?"

"Because they remind me of you." I held one up, and he let his mouth fall open so I could set the candy on his tongue.

"Do M&M's have big dicks and do romantic gestures?"

"They're hard on the outside and soft on the inside." I smiled up at him as I popped a few pieces into my mouth before offering him some more. This time, he held my wrist and pulled my fingers into his mouth.

"I'm definitely hard on the outside."

"That you are," I said, as my free hand reached between us and stroked his erection through his jeans.

He groaned. "I want to let you paint, but I also want to fuck you really badly."

My head fell back in laughter at his words and his

honesty. I loved that he just said what he thought. Always had.

"How about I slip into that painter's smock with nothing beneath, and you can have your way with me? I've never painted in the nude."

"Jesus. It's like I gave us both a gift." He reached down and tugged my sweater over my head before dropping to his knees to help me out of my boots and then removing my jeans and my panties. I stood there in nothing but a bra, and he pushed to stand, reaching behind me and unsnapping my bra, letting it drop to the floor.

"Am I the only one that's going to stand here naked?"

"Fuck, Presley. I wish I could paint because I'd paint you. You're fucking perfect. So goddamn pretty I can't see straight when I'm with you." His large hand covered one side of my neck as his thumb grazed my jaw. His words were overwhelming me because he wasn't big on sharing a lot. So, when Cage Reynolds paid you a compliment, you knew he meant it.

"Damn, Cowboy. You know I'm already a sure thing. But you just sealed the deal."

He smiled and stepped back, reaching for the smock and pulling the top strap over my head. The front barely covered my boobs, and he moved around to my backside and tied it at the waist.

My entire ass was bare to him, and he kissed my neck as I walked forward a few steps and rested my hands on the stool. I glanced over my shoulder, and my teeth sank into my bottom lip.

"You want me to fuck you from back here, my wild raven?"

I nodded. "It would be a shame to waste the view, wouldn't it?"

"I have the best view in the house," he said, as his fingers ran down my back and over my ass.

He surprised me when he dropped to his knees and gripped my hips as his tongue swiped across my pussy. I gasped at the feel of him, his tongue and his lips on me.

I pushed back against him just as he moved to his feet, and I heard the zipper of his pants moving down.

"I love that you're already soaked and ready for me."

"Always," I whispered. It was the truth.

He teased my entrance with the tip of his dick before pushing inside me, and I fell forward on a gasp. The sensation was so overwhelming I felt tears prick my eyes. I was overcome with emotion.

Feeling connected to this man.

Like I belonged here.

Like I belonged to him.

I pushed back, wanting more. Wanting all of him.

For as long as I could have him.

He gripped my hip with one hand before his other hand slipped in the front of the painter's smock, and his hand covered my breast as he pulled me up, my back against his front. And he thrust into me, over and over.

Faster.

Harder.

My head fell back against his chest, and his fingers moved around my hip to find my clit.

Exactly where I needed him.

My eyes closed as my body started to shake. My breaths were coming hard and fast, and I gasped as the strongest orgasm of my life tore through me.

"Cage," I cried out, as he continued to drive into me one more time before his grip tightened and he buried his face in my neck, a guttural sound escaping his lips.

He continued rocking into me as we both rode out every last bit of sensation.

"You okay?" he whispered as his fingers moved beneath

my chin to turn my face in his direction. I could taste the salty tears on my lips. "Did I hurt you?"

I chuckled. "No. You gave me the best orgasm of my life, and it actually brought me to tears."

"You sure?" he asked, and I didn't miss the concern.

I wasn't about to admit that it was a mix of feeling overwhelmingly good and overwhelmingly sad that this was all coming to an end soon.

That I'd never been this happy, and I feared I never would be again.

But maybe that was the fun of it… that we knew it was ending.

Maybe it was just a fairy tale, a few short weeks of magic. It wouldn't stay like this if this were our real lives. I'd be working. He'd be working. This was just a fantasy.

Like being on a romantic vacation that came to an end.

He pulled out slowly and moved across the room to get some tissue before dropping down to his knees to clean me up. My fingers found his hair, and I tipped his head back so he was looking up at me.

"Why don't you let the rest of the world know how sweet you are?"

"Because I don't like the rest of the world." He pushed to his feet, tossed the tissue into the trash can, tucked himself into his briefs, and zipped up his pants.

I turned toward the canvas as he pulled up a stool that was in the corner of the room.

"Am I really going to stand here painting in the nude?"

"I sure as fuck hope so." He smirked and asked me to toss him the open pack of M&M's. He sat there eating chocolate and watching me as I dipped the brush into the paint and swirled it on the paper.

I forgot how much I loved this.

Letting my imagination run wild as I created something

beautiful. I glanced over my shoulder a few times, and my gaze locked with Cage's sapphire blues.

He just smiled, as if he were enjoying this as much as I was.

———

"You two couldn't come up with a more creative name than The Cove Spa?" my mother chirped as she walked through the space. Walls were already down, and we were moving full steam ahead. I was bummed I wouldn't be here to see the daily progress, but Lola promised that she would FaceTime me every day to show me what was happening.

A.R.C. Network had signed the contracts, and Phillip was suddenly anxious for me to get back and have our first in-person meeting. I knew once I returned home, life would get really busy again. So, I was going to enjoy this time here. I went for a ride as often as possible.

On both my horse and the man who was consuming my every thought.

"It's not set in stone. Do you have a better name?" Lola asked as she raised her brow at my mother.

"Well, maybe something a bit more creative," she said.

I laughed and shook my head. "You hate creativity. You like research and numbers and facts."

"Not for a day spa," she snipped. "Let me think about it. I can be creative when I want to be. I gave birth to you, after all, and you're quite the free spirit."

Lola and I both laughed harder now as we continued the tour. My mother made a few snide comments about our ideas, but for the most part, she was fairly supportive.

Shocker.

Lola's phone rang, and she said it was the contractor, so she stepped away. My mom and I stood in one of the only spaces that wasn't currently occupied by workers, which would be the yoga room.

"So, you're going to paint a mural in here, is that right?"

I studied her, waiting for her to tell me all the reasons it was a bad idea. For starters, I didn't live here.

"Yeah. I'll fly back the week before the opening, and I can paint the mural then. I just have to decide what I want it to be."

She brushed some nonexistent dust from her powder-blue blazer, and her dark gaze met mine. "Haven't you been painting lately? I noticed it on your hands the other night at dinner."

"Yes. I've been coming up with some ideas."

"Well, I'm a fan of the arts. Why don't you run them by me?"

My eyes widened, and instead of insisting she would hate them, I reached into my back pocket for my phone. I'd painted a few things at Cage's over the last few days. Gracie and I had painted for a bit after her riding lesson yesterday. All she ever wanted to paint was Sally, so Cage would need to get on board. His daughter was definitely a *horse girl*, as she liked to call herself.

I showed my mother the painting of the trees and the water in the distance. It was earthy and soothing, which might be a nice fit.

"That's… lovely. Did you paint that?"

"Thank you. I did." I scrolled to the next photo and held it up for her to see, and she took the phone from my hand. It was a layered sunset, with a large raven soaring through the sky and a second raven in the distance. There were mountains in the background, and the wingspan of the bird was open and wide. It needed more work, but it was just an idea to give Lola a few choices. Even if she said she wanted me to decide, I thought it should be a group decision.

"It's a raven, isn't it?"

"Yes."

"That's beautiful. It's tranquil. That's what you should name the spa. Tranquility. It's what we're all searching for," she said.

"Well, thank you. I'll take that as a compliment. And I'll run the name by Lola, but it's ultimately her decision."

"Fair enough. Didn't Casey call you Raven back in the day?"

I rolled my eyes. "Mom. We dated for years. His name is Cage, and you know that."

She didn't deny it. She just smirked like she was having fun. I didn't know my mother knew how to have fun or how to be funny. I could count on one hand how many times I'd heard her laugh in my entire life.

"Fine. Isn't that the name that *Cage* called you?"

"Yes. He said it was because they don't really fly the way other birds do. Ravens soar and glide through the sky, and that's how he thought I looked when I was at my horse jumping competitions."

She pursed her lips. "Oh, I always figured it was because they are wild and do acrobatics in the air. They don't follow the rules or do what's expected of them, you know?"

What the hell was she talking about?

"Did you research the raven?"

"Of course I did. He was the first boy you ever dated, and you stayed together so long. He always called you Raven, and I figured there was a reason. And then you put that tattoo on your wrist, so I've read pretty much everything there is to read about the damn bird."

I shook my head in disbelief. "You pretend that you can't even remember his name, yet you're researching the nickname he called me in private all of these years?"

"We all have our own way of doing things, Presley."

"That's true. Well, what else did you learn about the

raven, since you're such an expert?" I crossed my arms over my chest.

"Well, I hate to tell you, but they usually mate for life. I assume that's why you put a second bird in the background of your painting. They prefer one partner, and they stay together for the span of their lives. So, I'm guessing that other bird is not Wes."

I sighed. Of course, this was a dig about me getting divorced.

"Luckily, I'm not an actual raven. I'm a human being. With real feelings. And I wasn't happy in my marriage, so I made a change."

She narrowed her gaze and shocked the shit out of me when she reached for my hand. "I think you are a raven in spirit. I think you just settled for the wrong partner, so maybe that means your soulmate is out there waiting for you. You're still young, Presley. There's still time for you to be happy."

My jaw dropped as I gaped at her.

Who the hell is this woman and what has she done with my mother?

Lola came walking back into the room and gave us a curious look. "What did I miss?"

"Nothing. And close your mouth, Presley. It's very unbecoming to gape at people," my mother quipped.

There she is.

But it didn't even matter because she'd shown me a bit of compassion at a time in my life when I needed it desperately.

I leaned forward and hugged her.

She was completely stiff, but then her body relaxed, and her hand came up to pat me on the shoulder.

It wasn't the most natural hug, and we might not be perfect, but this was a start.

twenty-two

. . .

Cage

"I HAVEN'T SEEN your cousins in years," Presley said as we drove toward the city.

I had the afternoon cleared on my schedule so I could head to the city to meet Dylan and Wolf, who were having a disagreement over a dog, of all things. She'd sounded frantic on the phone, so of course, I said I'd get there as soon as I could. Gracie was in school, and I'd invited Presley along because our time was winding down, and I thought she might want to take a drive.

"She'll be happy to see you. She has a little boy now, so you'll get to meet the baby. And you remember my uncle Jack. He's staying with them right now, so he'll be there, as well."

"I can't wait to meet the man who got Dilly to settle down," Presley said with a laugh. "She was always so much fun."

I spent the next forty minutes filling her in on all the cousins and their husbands and babies. Presley had spent a lot of time with them when they'd come to visit in the summers.

We pulled up to the fancy high-rise and parked in the spot

underground where Dylan's husband, Wolf, had told me to park my truck. As we took the elevator up to the penthouse, it dawned on me that this was probably similar to the kind of place where Presley lived.

"Is this what your building is like in New York?"

"Yeah, pretty much. It's on the top floor. Underground parking. Nice views of the city." She studied me. "You and Gracie should come visit sometime."

We hadn't discussed seeing each other after she left, but I knew better than to pretend I could handle seeing her once a year when she flew back to visit. I had my practice, and Gracie had school, and I knew it wasn't realistic to fly across the country for a weekend.

"We tried that once before and made a mess of things, didn't we?" I said, waiting for her to give me a reason why this time would be different.

"Yeah. But we can still keep in touch, right?"

Keep in fucking touch, my ass. How would that work? I couldn't be friends with this woman from a distance. Look what happened when we tried being friends here.

We were all or nothing—always had been.

I didn't want to hear about her going on dates with other men.

I was a selfish man.

I wanted her all to myself.

"We can figure that out when the time comes," I said, and her shoulders stiffened a bit at my words. But this time, I wasn't making promises neither of us could keep. Presley's life was on the other side of the country, where she lived in a penthouse.

I was living in a small town on a ranch, raising my daughter with a bunch of misfit animals. And I fucking loved it. This was my life, and I couldn't change that.

Not even for her.

Hell, I knew her well enough to know that she wouldn't let me do it anyway.

The elevator doors opened to the penthouse, as this was their private elevator.

"Hello? Dilly? Wolf? Uncle Jack?" I called out, and my cousin came flying around the corner and lunged herself at me.

"Thank God you're here. Thanks for coming." She kissed my cheek and then turned toward the woman beside me. "Say it isn't freaking so. Presley Duncan? This is the best surprise!"

Dylan hugged Presley just as my uncle Jack and Wolf came around the corner, and the hugs continued.

We made our way into the living room of the expansive apartment, and Dylan offered us some sun tea. I chuckled at seeing her in this new light, as a wife and mother, and the way she was enjoying it. We made some small talk. They asked Presley a bunch of questions about living in New York, and then my cousin turned to me.

"Thanks for dropping everything and showing up. It's a bit of an emergency, and I'm hoping you can talk some sense into my overprotective, overbearing, bossy husband." Dylan shot a look at Wolf before turning her attention back to me.

I barked out a laugh, as did everyone else aside from my cousin, who didn't seem to think any of this was funny.

"Overbearing is a bit much, yeah?" Wolf said, raising a brow and looking at her.

"We'll see about that. My husband has bought a killer dog to be my shadow because he doesn't think that I can take care of myself and our child on my own," she said, making no attempt to hide her irritation.

"Baby, that's not what's happening here." Wolf reached for her hand, and she pulled it away and crossed her arms over her chest.

"Okay, I'm going to need more information. Where does

one get a 'killer dog'? Did something happen that you now need protection?" I asked.

"Yes, I'm going to need more information, too. I just got here an hour ago, and there's been a lot of yelling from this one," my uncle said, flicking his thumb at his daughter.

"Oh, I'm sorry that I have a voice, and I'm not afraid to use it. I'm not some weak damsel in distress, Wolf. Cage, you need to tell him that we don't need a vicious animal living in our home."

I turned my attention to Wolf because, clearly, Dylan was not going to give me answers to my questions.

He blew out a breath. "Obviously, it's no secret that we have a lot of money. We own a goddamn hockey team; it's public knowledge."

"And it's been that way since we met," Dylan hissed.

"Correct. But now I have to travel with the team without you because you're staying home with the baby."

"Do not use our son as your scapegoat." She threw her hands in the air. "You don't trust me. You think I can't protect myself and our child? We live in a goddamn penthouse with security downstairs."

I glanced over at Presley, who looked as enthralled with the conversation as my uncle was. Dylan had always been passionate and reactive, and I loved her for it. Wolf was also strong and determined, and though I thought they were a perfect match for one another, they were both stubborn and not willing to back down at times.

"This is fucking ridiculous." He pushed to his feet. "Cage, come on, man, talk some sense into her."

"I don't know what we're talking about. Where is this dog?" I said, glancing between them.

"First off, it's called an executive protection dog. And if I'm being honest, I put a deposit down long before baby Hugh came into the world. This dog has been being trained for the last two years to be a member of the family, as well as to do what is needed to keep you safe. You're overreacting, baby." He placed his hands on his hips and stared at her.

"I'm overreacting? *I'm* overreacting?" She repeated her words before pushing to her feet and squaring her shoulders at her husband. I reached for my tea at the same time Presley did, and the corners of her lips turned up the slightest bit because she found the whole thing very entertaining.

"You are. These are dogs that become members of the family. They are companions. They are not trained to kill. They are trained to stop the threat."

"I have heard about these dogs, and they have phenomenal reputations," I said. "They're trained to be compliant and calm under pressure."

"Not helping, Cage," Dylan snapped at me, and Uncle Jack laughed.

Wolf just stood there staring at his wife, as if he was waiting for her to calm down and get on board.

That wasn't really Dylan's style.

She'd have to work this out in her own way.

"Fine. If you all think I need protecting, you'll have to prove it to me," she said.

"Don't do this." Wolf dipped his head so he was at eye level with her. "Don't make it harder than it has to be. You wanted a family dog anyway. No one has to know that he's also a protector."

Dylan stepped back, moving around the coffee table to the big open space. She bent her knees and got into a fighter's stance, and I nearly spewed tea all over the couch.

"Prove to me that I need protection."

"I'm a fucking Navy SEAL. Are you serious?" He glanced over at us on the couch.

"Damn. I wish I had some popcorn right now," Uncle Jack said, and Dylan shot her father a warning look.

"Come on, tough guy. I'm about to make you my bitch." Dylan kept her eyes on Wolf as she circled him.

Presley covered her mouth to keep from laughing, and I shook my head in disbelief that she was going to try to fight a man who was twice her size, who was trained to kill, and also madly in love with her.

"You're being stubborn, Minx," Wolf said, his voice even as he turned in a circle, and she moved around him.

"Don't Minx me and try to distract me. If someone breaks into the apartment, they will have to get through me first," she said, as her arm made a karate chop at her husband's chest, and he took the hit and chuckled.

"Baby. That's the whole point. I don't want anyone to get near you," he said, and she did some sort of awkward double karate chop that didn't appear to make a dent in him. Her eyebrows pinched together, and I could see the frustration.

Without warning, she spun around quickly, and her leg came up in a high kick, aiming for what looked to be his head, but he was too fast. He caught her by the ankle and then somehow managed to spin her around, with her back to his chest, as he wrapped both arms around her body, holding her still.

"Let me take care of you, Minx," he whispered, but we all heard him. I didn't miss the way Presley sighed beside me. "I can't live in a world that you aren't in. Can you give me this win?"

Dylan's stance relaxed, and she turned around in his arms. "Fine. But Cage needs to check out the dog and make sure he's safe to have around the baby."

"Can you fly out to the training facility with me next month and meet him?" Wolf asked me as he tucked her hair behind her ear.

"Of course. Does this mean the show is over, though? It was just getting good."

Presley smacked me on the arm, and Dylan flashed me the bird.

"I agree. I thought you could take him, Dilly." Uncle Jack chuckled.

A little cry came over the baby monitor, and Dylan asked Presley if she wanted to go with her to see the nursery and meet the baby.

Presley jumped up and left the room with my cousin.

"So, this is the girl you dated for years, yeah?" Uncle Jack asked, keeping his voice low. "The only girlfriend I've ever met."

"Because she's the only one I've ever had." I shrugged, and Wolf sat down beside me.

"I take it you're back together?"

"No. She's just back home for a few weeks. Her dad had a stroke. I hadn't seen her in years, so we're just catching up."

"Catching up, my ass. You sure don't look at her like it's nothing." Wolf smirked, the cocky bastard.

"Well, you would know, wouldn't you?" I said, reaching for my tea because I didn't want to talk about this.

Hell, I didn't want to think about it.

"I would, and I own that. You know Dylan's it for me. I was man enough to say it."

"And if Dylan lived on the other side of the country from you, and she loved her job and her life there, and yours was here while you raised a child on your own… How would you own that?" I kept my voice low, watching the hallway to make sure they weren't coming back yet.

Wolf glanced at my uncle, and then he leaned forward and rubbed his hands together before his eyes met mine. "However the fuck I needed to. Life is short, man. Don't spend it making things difficult. Trust your gut. Do whatever it takes."

"Easier said than done. I have a daughter to think about."

My uncle set his glass down on the coffee table in front of us. "I've got five daughters, and I get it. You're a great father, Cage. But you're allowed to be happy, too. And your daughter will only benefit from that. You're not doing her any favors if you're sacrificing your own happiness for hers."

"Yet, you've remained single all these years since Aunt Beth passed away. Focused on your girls and not yourself." My aunt had lost her battle with cancer, and Uncle Jack had been a widow for more than a decade.

"Is that what you think? That I don't date because I'm sacrificing for my girls?" he asked as he shook his head. "I'd do anything for them, you know that. And for a few years, sure, I knew they needed my full attention, and I wanted to be there. They'd lost their mother and were grieving. Hell, we'll always be grieving for her. But that's not why I've remained single."

I looked up at him. "Why, then?"

"Because I already met the love of my life. I don't know if there's a second chance at that, you know? But I can tell you this much, Cage," he said, clearing his throat. "If I had a chance to spend one more minute with Beth in this lifetime, I would move fucking mountains to make it happen. Life is short, son. Don't waste it trying to do the right thing for everyone else. Because who even knows what that is?"

I nodded as I processed his words.

"Wow. I always thought you didn't date because you were afraid of Dilly bringing the wrath down on any woman who came into your life," Wolf said, as the corners of his lips turned up.

"Well, that, too." Uncle Jack laughed before looking back at me. "Don't overthink it. You've got a great kid, and she's more resilient than you think she is."

But that still didn't solve the problem.

Sure, Gracie was resilient.

But that didn't mean I could uproot her life and move her across the country. Hell, we didn't even know if that was what Presley wanted anyway.

This was temporary.

I knew the agreement when we started this thing.

I looked up to see Dylan walk into the room with Presley beside her, holding baby Hugh.

And for a brief second, I saw a glimpse of the future.

One I knew was impossible, but it didn't stop me from thinking about it.

twenty-three

· · ·

Presley

MY FATHER WAS DOING SO WELL that he'd sailed through physical therapy this morning, and I'd had breakfast with him and my mom before heading to the spa to check on the progress.

Lola and I walked through the space as she pointed out the walls that had been taken down, and I could really see her vision now.

"Wow. I can't believe how quickly things are coming along," I said.

"Right? And the good news is that they are staying on budget. We haven't had to dip into the contingency fund at all yet." My best friend smiled.

"This is so great, Lo. I'm so proud of you for making it all happen. Are we still on track to open in late spring?"

"Yep. I've even had a few interviews this week for massage therapists, and I met with two potential yoga teachers. Everyone in town is excited about it. Of course, Mrs. Runither asked if I would have a male masseuse available for her."

"Of course, she did. I went there with Cage and Gracie for dinner last night, and she was doing everything she could to flirt with him, and he was having none of it," I said, and her head fell back in laughter.

"You sure do spend a lot of time with them. You going to be okay when you leave? Have you guys talked about how that's going to look?"

"I mean, we live on opposite sides of the country." I shrugged, that heavy feeling landing on my chest. "We knew this before we started anything. I just didn't plan to get in this deep, you know?"

It was the truth. I hadn't expected to spend this much time with Cage.

With Gracie.

With his family.

Most importantly, I hadn't expected to feel all these things. All these feelings.

"Yeah, I was just happy you guys were on good terms again, but boy, did it go from zero to one hundred fast." She chuckled. "I should have known it. That's how you guys always were. If you were in the same room, you were going to find a way to be right next to one another."

I nodded as I ran my hand over the white quartz countertop they'd just installed at the front desk. Everything was going to be light and airy.

"And when we aren't in the same room, we both find a way to survive on our own. Eileen just sent my calendar over, and they have my days pretty packed with meetings and conference calls the day I arrive back at the office. So, we'll both be busy diving back into our lives."

"And you'll just go back to being on your own and spending long hours at the office?" she asked, as she crossed her arms over her chest and leaned against the wall.

"I guess so, Lo. It's worked for the last few years just fine. I love my job, you know that. And that magazine article has brought all sorts of attention to me and the firm."

"I understand how much you love your work, but the

attention will eventually die down, so don't let that make you feel pressure now. You're allowed to do what you want. And I worry that it will be more challenging to go back to that old way of life after these last few weeks. I haven't seen this side of you since we were teenagers."

"And what side is that?" I raised a brow, irritated that she wanted to point out how difficult it was going to be for me back home. I was returning to a city that I loved. And an office where my name was going to be listed on the outside of a building where I'd been working for years. This was what I'd wanted for so long. I didn't want to let this dark cloud ruin it.

"The side where your smile is genuine. Your laugh is real and not sarcastic. The one where you take Honey out for a ride in the mornings, and you let yourself be in the moment. The one where you're all glowy from all the sex you're having." She barked out a laugh and held up her hand to stop me. "The one where you fill me in every day on how proud you are of Gracie's riding and that you have her paintings taped all over your refrigerator. My God, can you imagine having paintings taped to your fancy refrigerator in the penthouse?"

"Your point?"

"This just feels like… you." Her gaze softened, and my heart squeezed at her words.

"This has nothing to do with the fact that you live here now, and you want me to come run the spa with you?" I chuckled, trying to make light of the situation. There was no sense in analyzing it. Sure, I was enjoying myself, the way one enjoys being on vacation.

But this wasn't my real life.

"Obviously, I'd love to work side by side with you every day. But it's not why I'm saying this. I'm not a completely selfish asshole. If I were, I'd be jealous that you're having all the sex while I'm sleeping alone in my bed every night." She chuckled. "I just want you to be happy, Pres. And you just seem really… happy lately."

"Maybe that's because I'm finally divorced. The scandal with Wes has died down. My contract for our partnership is ready to be signed when I return. I just signed a huge client that I will be lead on. Do any of those things sound like fair reasons to be happy?"

She forced a smile and nodded. "Yeah. Those are good reasons, too."

She was finally going to drop it and give me a break. We both knew that Cage and Gracie were the reasons that I'd been so happy lately. I just didn't want to say it out loud.

Because I knew that it wouldn't change anything.

So, I was just going to be thankful for the time that I had and carry it with me when I left.

———

"Well, we're just so grateful that you've accepted the position," I said to Dr. Jake, the new equestrian physician my father had hired. He'd interviewed several people for the position, but Jake Rowling lived one town over, and he was looking for a full-time position since relocating out west from Chicago a few weeks ago.

"The timing couldn't be better. I grew up in Garden Grove, so I'm happy to be back where my roots are. My wife and I like small-town living. But I didn't want to open a clinic there, so this is the perfect fit. Not a bad commute either, and you've got a gorgeous property, and horses are my strong suit." He smiled, flashing me his pearly whites. To most, he'd probably be considered good-looking. Unfortunately, I preferred the strong, broody, frowning guy who was just walking up with Gracie's hand in his.

And he was definitely frowning as his gaze moved from me to Dr. Jake.

"Presley!" Gracie shouted as she dropped her father's hand and started running toward me. I caught her in my arms and breathed in all the goodness. Seeing her every day filled me in a way I hadn't known possible.

"Hi, baby girl," I said as I ran my fingers through her pretty curls. She smelled like strawberries and sweetness today, and I freaking loved it. "Dr. Jake, this is Gracie and her father, Dr. Reynolds."

Jake extended his hand to Cage, who was still frowning and looked like he wanted to punch the guy in the face.

"Hey, nice to meet you both. Dr. Reynolds, you've been covering for me until I got here, huh?" Dr. Jake said, clearly not great at reading the room because he didn't seem to notice how agitated Cage was when he pulled his hand away abruptly.

"Yes. You must be the new guy." Cage folded his arms over his chest.

"I don't know. I've been called the good guy most of my life," Dr. Jake said, with a wink in my direction, and I chuckled along with him. A deep growl left Cage's throat, which only made the whole situation funnier.

"Good for you. Let's hope you can take better care of these animals than the last guy did."

"Not a doubt in my mind. I'm on it. And how old are you, Gracie?" He turned his attention to her, and Cage stepped closer because he couldn't help but be protective at all times.

"I'm five years old, but I'll be six years old really soon. Presley and me ride together almost every day."

"Yeah? Well, when she heads back to New York next week, I'd be happy to take over for her so you can keep coming out to the ranch and riding." Jake smiled, and I knew he meant well, but Cage narrowed his gaze at the man like he'd just committed a crime.

"That won't be necessary. I'll be continuing her lessons."

His voice was harsh, and Jake nodded before taking a step back.

"All right, then. You all have a good lesson. Presley, I'll come find you before I leave." He winked again, and I had to put my hand over my mouth to keep from laughing at the way Cage was glaring at the man who seemed completely unaware.

I set Gracie down, and she took off running toward Sally's stall.

"I don't like him," Cage said, keeping his voice low.

"Really? I couldn't tell."

"Why the fuck is he called Dr. Jake? I'm assuming that's his first name."

"He likes it. It's less formal."

"It's stupid," he said, running a hand over the scruff on his jaw.

"You're just finding any reason not to like him, aren't you?"

He glanced over at me. "That fucker's eyes were all over you. And then he tried kissing up to my daughter to win some points with you."

"I was standing in front of him. Where else would his eyes be?"

"Trust me. It's a dude thing. He wants you."

"You know you're ridiculous, right? He's married and has a baby on the way."

"So he says." He stopped in front of the stall.

"He showed me a picture of his beautiful wife, and he's already requested time off when she has the baby. Take it down a notch, Cowboy. You seem a little jealous." I smacked him on the ass playfully before walking past him to help Gracie get saddled up.

The next hour was spent with me working with Gracie and Sally. Cage went to talk with Dr. Jake about the horses. Hopefully, he'd ease up now that he knew he was married.

"She likes the sound of your voice," I said.

"How do you know?" Gracie asked.

"I can tell by the way her head moves the slightest bit every time you speak. She loves you."

"I love her. I hope Daddy lets me keep coming after you leave."

"I think he will. And your barn will be done soon, so I'll bet you'll get a horse of your own."

"I don't want any other horse. I love Sally, and she's my girl. Right, Presley?"

"Yep. When you know, you know."

"I know about you," she said, and she looked over at me with those big brown eyes and smiled.

"What do you know about me?" I held the reins and continued walking in a circle, leading Sally along.

"I know that you feel like you're mine."

My heart nearly exploded at her words.

"You do?"

"I do. I told Daddy I wish we could keep you forever."

A lump formed in my throat, and I nodded. I couldn't find words to reply, and I blinked several times to push away the tears that threatened to fall.

I finally pulled myself together.

"You feel like you're mine, too. And I'll keep you in here forever," I said, placing my hand over my heart.

"I love riding with you. And I love painting with you. And I love your pretty hair and your riding boots, and your laugh makes me happy."

A tear slipped down my cheek, and I quickly swiped it away as a weepy laugh left my mouth. "I love your laugh and your smile and your face and your pink boots and your pretty paintings. I love listening to you read and tell me about your day and what all the kids had for lunch. And I really love the way it feels when I hold your hand."

"Presley! I love holding your hand, too. What does it feel like to you?"

Forever.

"It feels sweet and special. And your hands are always toasty and warm." I chuckled.

"Because Daddy makes me wear mittens to school when none of the other kids are wearing them."

"That's because he loves you so much," I said, as we kept walking, and I fought the urge to pull her down and wrap her in my arms.

"You know what else I love about you?"

"What?" I asked, trying to hide the smile from my face.

"I love how happy Daddy is when you come to our house or when he sees you here. I know why he has us both in his heart now."

"Why is that?" I asked as I saw Cage out of my peripheral moving closer.

"Because we're his girls, and he loves us." And then she leaned down and whispered. "But don't tell him I told you. He's at work, and he doesn't like to talk about it."

I gave her a wink as I led Sally over to her father. I helped her off the horse, and we made our way toward the stall.

"Did things go a little better this time?" I asked him, my voice all tease.

"I guess. I still don't trust him."

I rolled my eyes and slipped my hand in his. "And why is that?"

"His teeth are too white, and he's too friendly."

"Sounds about right." I laughed.

After Sally was settled, we walked toward Cage's truck. He buckled Gracie into her booster seat, and I slipped into the passenger side as he climbed into the driver's seat and got himself buckled. He adjusted the rearview mirror to look at his daughter and then glanced over at me. His hand moved to my seat belt to make sure it had snapped all the way in before he pulled the truck down the driveway.

And there was no doubt about it.

His daughter had his heart.

But I think she was right.

I was fairly certain that I had a piece of it, too.

twenty-four

. . .

Cage

BRINKLEY

Are we all avoiding the topic because we're
afraid of Cage?

FINN

Definitely.

GEORGIA

I'm not afraid of Cage. But I know he doesn't
want to talk about it.

HUGH

He's definitely closed-lipped about it.

HE IS ON THIS FUCKING THREAD. What are
you talking about?

BRINKLEY

It's a group text. Of course, you're on it.

You're talking about me like I'm not here.

FINN

Hmmm… I wonder why we're afraid of you.
You're the only one who texts in all caps.

HUGH

Just worried about you, brother.

Why are you worried about me? I'm. Fucking.
Fine. And I wanted to write THAT in all caps,
but I didn't, for fear of you calling in the
National Guard.

GEORGIA

But you did the period after every word,
which was very effective.

FINN

Only you can appear pissed off in a text
message.

It's a gift. And I'm not pissed. THIS IS MY
NORMAL STATE.

BRINKLEY

I'm not afraid of you, so I'll say it. Presley is
leaving in two days. You spend a lot of time
together, so you must feel something
about it.

HUGH

We're here for you if you want to talk about it.

What is there to talk about? I knew she was
leaving. We had a plan, and we stuck to it.
That's it.

FINN

We've got openings for extras at Big Sky Ranch. I had no idea you were such a good actor. Do you want me to throw your name into the hat?

Why can't you just accept that I'm okay?

BRINKLEY

Why can't you just accept that you're not?

I SCRUBBED a hand down the back of my neck. Fucking Brinkley never knew when to stop pushing. None of them did.

HUGH

It's okay to not be okay. You know that, right? We all see how you are together, so we know it's going to suck when she leaves. That's all it is, brother. We're worried about you.

GEORGIA

I've cried twice today thinking about her leaving, and I don't see her as much as you do. So I know it has to hurt.

FINN

Weren't you the guy who told me to stop being a <cat emoji> with Reese? So, apparently, you can dish it out, but you can't take it? I'm here to call you out on your bullshit, just as you would for me. STOP BEING A PUSSY AND TELL HER HOW YOU FEEL.

I'm not being a pussy, you dickwanker. Nothing has changed between her and me. I admit it. But at the end of the day, it's not about admitting it. I think we both know it. But we have different lives, and mine is here with my daughter, and hers is in New York, conquering the world. I would never ask Presley to give up her dreams for me. So, can we stop analyzing it now? I've got bad luck when it comes to love. There's no sense wallowing. Shit happens. I got to have these last few weeks with her, and it's been fucking amazing. Never thought I'd get that much, so I'll take it. And my daughter fucking loves her and will probably be as devastated as I'll be when she leaves. There. Now we're all fucking cleansed. Can we stop talking about this now?

GEORGIA

Honest and vulnerable. I'm crying.

BRINKLEY

This is big. Huge. Impressive. You love her enough to put her needs first.

FINN

I've got to tell you… I did not see an emotional confession coming from you in my lifetime. Kudos, brother. I still think you should tell her. I know you think she knows, just like I thought Reese knew how I felt, but saying it can be pretty freeing.

It can also put a lot of pressure on her. I'm not looking to guilt her into a life she doesn't want. Trust me, she knows how I feel.

HUGH

I like seeing this from you, brother. Good shit.

I'm glad you're all so pleased. Love sucks. Thanks for the pep talk.

FINN

You still have Maxine. She's never leaving Cottonwood Cove, and I don't think she's ever planning to leave your house.

It's coming to an end. She's destroying my house. She can get out of her playpen now. She chewed up part of the throw rug in the family room. She dug up some plants. She needs to go back home.

BRINKLEY

Hey, can I just throw something out there regarding Presley?

I'd expect nothing less. I asked to stop talking about it, and you want to ask more questions. Shocker. Fire away.

BRINKLEY

What if you guys have two homes? You live half the time in New York and half the time here? Like Lincoln and I do?

You don't have children. Gracie can't be attending school on two coasts. She needs stability. And I don't even know that Presley wants this package deal. We don't talk about the future because we know this is temporary. She's looking forward to going back to her life, and it's one that we don't fit into. So, no sense in pushing something that won't work and setting myself up for rejection.

BRINKLEY

Let me noodle on this.

Please don't. Let me enjoy my last two days with her, and then you can all analyze the hell out of me after.

HUGH

We'll be at your house with a case of beer, and you can wallow as much as you want to, all right?

FINN

We got you, brother.

GEORGIA

You know alcohol is a depressant. He'll feel worse the next day.

HUGH

That's kind of the point. You get loaded. Feel worse. Wallow. And then move on.

Great. Looking forward to a miserable week. I have to go. One of Mr. Wigglestein's baby mamas is ready to give birth.

FINN

It's the circle of life. It makes me emotional.

For fuck's sake. <eyeroll emoji>

BRINKLEY

So deep, Finny.

HUGH

You are all over the place lately.

FINN

It must be the pregnancy hormones. You know I'm having a baby, right?

I barked out a laugh, which was probably why he said it. I turned off my phone and got back to work. My siblings were good at dragging shit up that I didn't want to think about.

No sense in getting worked up now. Time was ticking, and I would deal with the repercussions later.

———

We'd finished dinner, and Presley sat on the bathroom floor with me while Gracie splashed in the tub. Tomorrow night, Gracie was going to sleep at my parents' house so we could spend our final night alone together.

But tonight, Presley had requested that we just stay here, the three of us. She loved my daughter, and it meant the fucking world to me. Presley used the suds to gather all of Gracie's hair and make a big cone on top of her head, which had them both laughing hysterically.

"We get to spend all day tomorrow together, too. Right, Presley?" Gracie asked.

"Of course. We're going to take the horses out one last time and paint, and you said you wanted to play in the garden, too. That sounds like a dreamy day."

"And then you and Daddy are going to have a big people's night tomorrow before you leave, and I'll be with Grammie and Poppy." Gracie's eyes watered as she looked between us.

"You love going to Grammie and Poppy's," I reminded her.

"I know. I just don't want to say goodbye to Presley."

It was interesting to me how honest kids could be. They didn't think about how their words affected others; they just said what they felt. And it was like a shot to the fucking heart because I felt the same way.

When it all came down to it, I didn't want to say goodbye to her either.

"Goodbye doesn't mean forever. It just means I won't be here every day. But you can FaceTime me whenever you want. And I'll be back for the opening in a few months." Presley's eyes were watering now, too.

This was too much.

Too heavy.

"You'll be okay, I promise," I said abruptly, and they both looked at me like I had three heads. "Come on. Let's get you dried off. It's time for bed."

"Can Presley stay and tuck me in?"

I reached for the towel, turning my back to both of them and squeezing my eyes closed. How the fuck was I going to get her through these next few days when I was miserable myself?

Before I could answer, Presley spoke.

"Of course, I'll stay. I'd love to tuck you in and get some sweet snuggle time."

"Yay!" Gracie cheered, and I rolled my eyes because we were just getting in deeper and deeper the closer we got to her leaving.

My daughter insisted on having Presley dry her off and help her into her nightgown. Once her teeth were clean and her hair was brushed, they both climbed into Gracie's little bed, where Presley read her a few books, and then my daughter wanted to talk about the books because she was dragging shit out. I left to clean up the dishes from dinner, and when I came back, they were both sound asleep.

Presley was lying on her side with Gracie pressed to her chest and her head tucked beneath her chin.

I flipped the light off but stood in the doorway, staring at them. The light from the moon was shining through the opening between the curtain panels, providing just enough light to make out their silhouettes.

Bob Picklepants moseyed right past me, moving at a

snail's pace but finding the energy to jump up onto the bed and curl up at their feet.

As if he wanted to be as close to all that goodness as I did.

Maybe the lazy bastard was smarter than I'd given him credit for.

I made my way out to the kitchen and took Maxine out back, and when I stepped back inside, Presley was standing there smiling as I put the pig back into her playpen for the night. It was the only time she didn't try to escape.

"Hey," she whispered. "Sorry that I fell asleep for a little bit. Her bed is so cozy."

"You don't need to apologize. Bob's probably devastated that you left," I teased, as I pressed her back up against the counter. My hand spread across the side of her neck, and I kissed her hard.

Her hands were in my hair, and our kiss was feverish and out of control. Hell, I just needed to savor every last minute with this woman. I could feel the walls closing in around me, and I just wanted more.

I gripped her ass and lifted her up onto the counter before pulling my mouth from hers. Her hands were on each side of my face.

"I should head home. I'll be back early, though. I promised my parents I'd have breakfast with them and then do a quick walk with my dad. And then I'm all yours for the rest of the day and night." She waggled her brows.

We were cautious not to have sleepovers when Gracie was home, although, at this point, there were a ton of other things I'd let go too far, so I didn't know why we'd stuck with that rule.

"I want to make you feel good first," I said, and my hands slipped beneath her long, cream-colored skirt, and my finger slid up her lean thighs. I stopped at the edge of her panties and ran my thumb over her lace-covered pussy. She gasped as her hooded gaze found mine.

"I thought you'd want to wait until tomorrow night." Her teeth sank into her bottom lip.

"I need to make you feel good, Raven." I slipped my fingers beneath the lace to find her soaked, and I hissed, squeezing my eyes closed as I tried to tamper down my raging erection.

Her legs fell open, and she tugged my mouth back down to hers. I slipped one finger inside, and then a second, as her walls tightened around my digits. I thrust in and out as my lips meshed with hers. She rocked against me and groaned. I slipped my fingers out, moving both hands to each side of her face as I took in her wild, dark eyes filled with need.

I pushed her legs farther apart and took the dainty lace between my fingers before tearing it in half, giving me better access. I pushed her skirt all the way up and buried my face between her thighs. I thrust my fingers back into her as my mouth covered her clit. She leaned back on her elbows and bucked against me as her breaths filled the air around us. I replaced my fingers with my tongue, diving deep into her heat, and my thumb pressed into her clit, just where I knew she needed me.

"Oh my god, Cage," she panted, and it was the hottest sound I'd ever heard.

I moved faster, sliding in and out of her, as she tugged at my hair and ground up against my face.

Harder.

Needier.

More.

And then she exploded, her walls tightening around my tongue, as she went over the edge. I held her there, savoring every last bit of her sweetness.

Once her breathing slowed, I pulled back and helped her sit forward, tucking her wild waves behind her ear.

Her gaze searched mine. "Thank you. How about I return the favor?"

She jumped off the counter and led me to the pantry, pulling the door closed before she was on her knees. She unbuttoned my jeans and pulled the zipper down, shoving the denim along with my boxer briefs down my thighs, allowing my cock to spring free.

She looked up at me and licked her lips, and I tangled my fingers in her hair.

She teased the tip of my dick, swirling her tongue around in circles before wrapping her mouth around me.

She was warm and wet, and she knew exactly what I liked.

She took her time while I fucked her mouth and set the pace.

Her hands were on my ass, taking me deeper.

I was doing all I could to hold on and savor it, because I knew it would never be better than this.

"Fuck, Presley," I whisper-hissed and tugged at her head to give her warning that I was going to come.

But she stayed right there as white lights exploded behind my eyes, and I pumped into her mouth and groaned as I came so hard I couldn't see straight.

When she finally pulled back, she looked up at me and smiled.

Our gazes locked as I stroked her hair away from her gorgeous face.

Because this wasn't some stupid fling or friends with benefits.

I loved this woman fiercely.

And I knew she loved me, too.

twenty-five

. . .

Presley

MY FATHER and I finished our last loop with the sun shining down on us this morning.

"I think that's a long enough walk for one day," I said, as we made our way up the driveway after a two-mile walk. We'd been walking every morning this last week, and he appeared to be almost back to his old self.

"Yeah. I'm going to miss these walks," he said as he pulled off his jacket. "It's nice having the sun out again, isn't it?"

"Yeah, it's definitely warming up. I think it's still fairly cold in New York."

"Are you ready to go back and take the legal world by storm?" he asked as we stopped in front of the barn so he could check on the horses.

That had been the first thing he wanted to do once he was up and moving.

"Sure. I'm looking forward to getting back to my routine." I ran my hand along Honey's back.

"And you'll be back for the opening of Tranquility?" he asked, and I couldn't help but laugh.

"Yes. And Mom seems quite pleased that we went with her name," I said.

"She sure is. And she told me about the mural you're painting. She went into an awfully long, boring description about birds."

I shook my head. "Yeah. It's a long story. But I'm glad that she's excited about it."

"Well, you heard her at breakfast. She's agreed to spend more time here now. If I had things my way, we'd live here full time. This is where I feel the most at home."

I understood that better than he knew.

Better than I wanted to admit to myself.

I had obligations and responsibilities.

People relied on me at the firm.

"You sure do spend an awful lot of time with Cage and Gracie. Is that going to be hard when you leave?" He paused his brushing Honey to look up at me.

"Sure. But we knew it would come to an end. It's been nice getting to spend time with them, but it always had an expiration date. No one is going to get hurt this time." Last night had been emotional. Both my time with Gracie and my time with Cage. Something had shifted. Like we all knew the end was looming, so we were holding on tighter. Making every second count.

He nodded. "I'm sure you'll see them when you come back into town."

"I don't really know how it will work, Dad," I said, my voice cracking on the last word. I was trying desperately to be strong, but I was dying on the inside. I wasn't ready to say goodbye to them.

To us.

"You can't be so stoic that you don't tell someone how you feel. If you don't know how it will work, why don't you talk to him about it? You're leaving tomorrow. It seems like the right time to have the conversation."

I nodded and blinked several times to keep the tears away.

Once I was home, I would be busy, and I'd forget about how much fun I was having here.

At least, that was what I was desperately counting on.

———

"I love our new paintings, Presley," Gracie said as Cage and I settled on a blanket beneath the large tree in the front yard. She'd wanted to come sit out here so she could pick me a pretty arrangement from the wildflowers growing a few feet away in a little garden Brinkley and Gracie had planted together a few months ago. It had snowed, and of course, they had all died, but Cage told me that he'd gone and bought a few flower beds and filled them a few days ago after the snow had melted so she'd think they were back in bloom.

This man.

"I love them, too. But yours is my favorite." I squeezed her little hand.

God, I loved this girl.

It was an unexplainable kind of love.

I missed her when she was at school, or if I went a whole day without seeing her, I couldn't wait to see her the following day. It was almost an ache that I had when she wasn't around.

"Yours is my favorite, too," she said before her eyes grew wide. "Daddy!"

"I'm right here." He chuckled. "What's up?"

He was sprawled out on the blanket, looking all rugged and sexy. We were grateful for the sunshine that was out today, and I knew our time was coming to an end, so I wanted to savor every last bit of time with them. I'd taken so many pictures of Cage and Gracie and a bunch of the three of us on my phone.

I think a part of me knew how painful it was going to be once I didn't get to see them every day. And I didn't know how much contact Cage would want to have once I was gone. I was going to talk to him about it today. Let him know that I wasn't ready to say goodbye.

"Auntie Brinks got me a watering can. I left it in the house by the front door. Can I go grab it?"

"Yes. And I pulled the hose out so you can fill it up over by your garden."

"Be right back," she said, and she took off running. Cage and I both watched her as she hurried inside and then came running back outside, so excited she didn't even close the front door all the way.

"Slow down, Gracie girl. There's no rush. We don't need you falling and getting hurt," he said, and she looked back at him and smiled as she ran right past us toward her garden.

"You're so protective. I love it."

"I think sometimes I feel extra pressure, you know?" he said, and I sat forward to give him my full attention.

"What do you mean?"

"Well, I think when you have two parents, whether they are together or not, you still have someone to share some of that responsibility with. But for me, any time I think about doing anything, I have this voice in the back of my head reminding me that I'm all she has. I can't take risks or be selfish because if something happens to me, she doesn't have a parent. And it works both ways because I don't have someone reasoning with me about being too protective. My instinct is to keep her safe, and that's what I do."

My heart sank at his words.

How could I bring up trying to make this work, trying to find a way to see one another once a month or something like that, when he had a child to think of?

He couldn't make me his priority, and I would never ask him to, because one of the things I loved about him most now, was how he was as a father.

"You aren't alone, though. You have your family, and you

know, I, um," I stumbled over my words. "I would love to be part of your life, and Gracie's life."

He reached for my hand, and his gaze locked with mine.

"How would that work? I mean, I can't uproot her life, you know? I've got a practice here, and family, and a home."

But I'm not here.

I wanted to say it, but I couldn't.

"I know. I get it, Cage. I do. My life is there, and I don't know anything else. I've been working so long toward this goal that I can't see a different path." I shook my head and looked away. "I would never ask you to move. I just, I don't know. I'm not ready for this to be over."

He leaned forward and used the pad of his thumb to swipe the tear rolling down my cheek away. "I'm not either. But I don't have a solution. Not a realistic one, at least. I mean, I could come visit once or twice a year. You could come here that often. But what kind of relationship is that?"

I nodded. "Maybe once I establish myself as partner, I can make some demands in a couple of years. I can request to work remotely."

I was reaching. The partners would never agree to that. I worked sixty-hour weeks. That was the way I'd been able to advance my career. Working long hours, doing whatever it took. And I'd loved it because I had nothing else in my life.

Before now.

"How about we just see how it goes, huh? But I need you to know something," he said, leaning forward so his mouth was inches from mine. "I love you. I've always loved you, and I always will. Time may not ever be on our side, but I want you to know that. I need you to know that. No matter how long we go without talking or seeing one another, you own this." He took my hand and pressed it to his heart.

"I love you, too, and I always will," I said, my voice shaky.

"One day at a time, Raven."

And just as I was going to lean forward and kiss him, I heard a shriek in the distance.

"Daddy! Maxine got out!" Gracie's voice was laced with panic, and Cage was up and moving before I processed what was happening.

I pushed to my feet, and my world started to spin as I ran after them.

Cage was moving so fast as his deep voice traveled through the air. "Gracie! Stop!"

She was a good distance ahead of him, but I'd never seen someone run so fast in my life. He was a blur he was moving so fast. He shouted again and sprinted just as a loud screech had my legs freezing. The sound of brakes straining and tires skidding. A blue car spun in the road as I saw Cage dive through the air to reach his daughter. It was like something out of a movie.

This couldn't be real.

His large body slammed over the hood of the car, a loud bang as he dented the metal. Gracie's hair flew around them as they disappeared from my line of sight.

There were screams and cries, and I pumped my arms and ran as fast as I could. No sound left my lips as I saw the driver get out of the car. His lips were moving, but I couldn't hear anything. I moved around to the front of the car to get to the other side, as Cage lay on the ground with Gracie in his arms as she shrieked and cried.

"Call 911!" I shouted to the driver as I hurried over to them.

Tears made it difficult to see.

"Daddy!" Gracie just kept saying his name as he scrambled to sit forward, his hands on her cheeks and her shoulders as if he couldn't believe she was okay.

Blood and dirt and tears smeared together on her face.

"Oh my God. Are you okay?" My voice shook as I squatted down and tried to assess them. His forehead was bleeding badly, and his hands were scraped raw. I tugged off my sweater and wrapped it around Gracie as her little body shook.

The driver hurried over to us as sirens blared in the distance.

"Are you okay?" Cage asked his daughter over and over. "Gracie, are you okay?"

"Daddy, I'm sorry. I didn't want Maxine to get hurt." Her little sobs tore my heart to shreds.

Cage pushed to his feet, Gracie tucked protectively to his body, startling me and the driver when he got up.

"I don't think you should move," I said.

"Maxine!" Gracie shouted, and I saw the pig tucked in the bushes on the other side of the road.

"Maxine's fine," I said. "She's okay. Tell me what hurts."

My hands were running down her arms and legs, wiping the blood from her forehead only to realize it wasn't coming from her. It was coming from her father.

"Nothing is hurting, but my daddy is bleeding," she wailed. It was the most gut-wrenching sound, and I struggled to stay upright.

"Cage, you're bleeding badly," I said as I reached for his face and tried to find where it was coming from. I pressed my hand to his forehead, which was gushing blood now, and urged him to sit on the curb, but he refused.

He wouldn't let me take Gracie, and I was fairly certain that he was in shock.

The paramedics were there, and they told him they needed to take her, and he still refused.

"She stays with me," he said, his voice shaky now.

"Cage," the man said, making it clear that they knew one another. "We need to assess both of you. She will be right here. But you're bleeding badly, and we need to see where it's coming from. We're going to take you both to the hospital, okay? But you need to let her go."

Cage turned to look at me. "Do not leave her alone. Promise me you'll stay with her."

"Of course I will." My voice wobbled as the man pried Gracie from Cage's arms, and she shrieked and tried to hold onto him.

I took her hand in mine. "I'm right here, Gracie. I'm right here with you."

Several paramedics sprang into action. Gracie was placed on a gurney, and a female medic was asking her questions and flashing a light in her eyes as she squeezed my hand and continued to cry for her father, and then she pointed at Maxine, who was still standing in the bushes, shaking.

I looked over to see four paramedics working on Cage, as one was calling something into the radio, but it was all a blur. The driver of the car stood there staring and looking a little shocked as the police officer questioned him.

The officer came over to speak to me as they were loading Gracie into the ambulance, and I cut him off. "You'll have to talk to us at the hospital. I need you to go get that pig and just shove her inside the house and pull the door closed, please. She's friendly. Can you do that?"

He nodded. "Of course."

Gracie and Cage were loaded into two different ambulances, and my heart split in two as I saw the pain in his eyes when he looked over at me.

"You stay with her, Presley. Call my parents."

I nodded as the tears rolled down my cheeks, and I kept hold of Gracie's hand and moved inside the ambulance.

I dialed Alana, and when I tried to speak, the words were jumbled as the lump in my throat made it difficult to talk.

"You need to come to the hospital," was all I was able to get out.

"We're on our way," she said. Her voice was even, but I heard the fear.

I ended the call and turned my attention to Gracie, who

was looking up at me. Her dark eyes were a mix of sadness and fear.

"Hey, I'm right here. I'm not going anywhere, okay? Daddy's right behind us."

She nodded and sniffed as the medic wiped some of the blood from her forehead and searched her head for any injuries.

"You're going to be okay. It looks like you got away with very few scratches," she said, patting her on the shoulder.

"Is Daddy mad at me, Presley?" she asked, as more tears slipped down her cheeks.

"Of course not. He's just so happy you're okay."

"But I'm not supposed to go in the street. I was just trying to catch Maxine. I didn't see the car."

"I know you didn't. Everything is going to be okay. I promise."

And I just hoped like hell that it was true.

twenty-six

. . .

Cage

I'D MADE some big mistakes in my life.

And plenty of them.

But this... this would go down as the worst.

This would be my reminder of how easy it was to fuck up so badly that there was no return.

I closed my eyes as the paramedic pressed something to my forehead. I was pissed that I was in this ambulance while my daughter was in another one.

My baby girl.

I'd never get that image out of my head.

Her hair flying behind her while she ran after that mother-fucking pig. I'd kept an animal that wasn't even mine, and it nearly cost my daughter her life.

But it wasn't the pig I was pissed at.

It was myself.

I'd taken my eyes off her. I'd been so wrapped up in Presley that I wasn't paying attention.

I knew better.

Gracie was a kid.

I'd moved as fast as I could. I saw that car out of my peripheral.

I'd hear the screeching of those tires against the pavement for the rest of my life.

How fucking close that car came to her.

I'd snatched her up just as the bumper was about to make contact with her. I'd wrapped her in my arms and rolled onto my back across the hood, my head slamming into the windshield, and I'd prayed like hell that I wouldn't crush her.

I had one fucking job in this lifetime that mattered. I was given this little girl to care for.

The best gift I'd ever received.

And I'd been so fucking selfish. So caught up in my own bullshit.

It was destructive, and I'd received a warning that I was going to heed starting right fucking now.

When we pulled up to the hospital, they wheeled me out of the ambulance, and I tugged at a few cords hanging on me and surged forward.

"Where's my fucking daughter?" I asked, and I didn't hide that I was losing my patience quickly.

"Cage, she's inside with Presley and your dad. She's just fine. Stop giving them a hard time and let them do their job. You're covered in blood, and they need to make sure you're okay." My mother's voice pulled me from my rant.

"I'm fine. Is all this necessary?" I asked, and the paramedic nodded. "You've got a big gash on your head, and I'm guessing you're going to need stitches."

"Fuck," I growled as they wheeled me inside, and my mother told me to lie back on the bed.

I was a grown-ass man, but I knew when my mom was angry and worried, and she was definitely a mix of both.

They took me into the back room, and a doctor came and did the same tests the paramedics had just done before pulling back the bandage to look at my head. "Hey, I'm Dr. Locket. You took a good shot to the head. Luckily, you clearly have a hard head," he said, and the dude looked like he was maybe in his mid-twenties.

"No doubt about that. He's always had a hard head," my mother said as her gaze locked with mine, and without speaking a word, she basically threatened my life with a look.

Don't you dare move. Let them take care of you.

The next three hours were spent getting a CT scan and a ton of X-rays and stitches. Everything had panned out exactly as I'd said.

I was fine.

I had road rash on my back and arm and one broken rib. Everyone seemed shocked that I didn't break anything else. I didn't feel anything as far as physical pain. I was anxious to see Gracie and Presley, and that was all that mattered at the moment.

My brothers and sisters were all at the hospital now, and Brinkley and Georgia stopped in the room to tell me that Gracie was eating ice cream in the cafeteria with Presley. Finn, Reese, Hugh, Lila, Maddox, and Lincoln were with them.

I'd asked Presley not to leave my daughter's side, and she'd done exactly what I'd asked.

The relief I felt that Gracie hadn't been hurt was indescribable.

"Barely a scratch on her," her doctor had said.

"Can you text Presley and ask her to bring Gracie here? I need to see her." The nurse finished cleaning up my back and I thanked her.

"Of course. But I promise, she's fine." Georgia patted me on the shoulder and then typed into her phone.

"Cage, you need to listen to what the doctor said. You took a bad hit to the head," my father said.

"Yep. I heard him. Gracie and I will stay at your house tonight if that'll make you feel better." I wasn't doing it for myself. I was doing it for my daughter, and to give my parents some peace of mind. If I were to have a reaction, I wouldn't want Gracie to be home alone with me—but I felt physically fine.

I didn't miss the look that passed between my mother and my sisters, and Brinkley came to sit beside me on the bed.

"It's your last night with Presley. I'm sure she'd want to stay at the house with you and Gracie," she said. They knew I was supposed to take her out tonight. Gracie was supposed to sleep at my parents' house. But that all seemed like it was a million years ago now.

I was hurting my girls by dragging this out.

I'd been distracted earlier with Presley, and that was on me.

All on me.

And she was leaving tomorrow, so I wasn't going to have her stay up all night worrying about me having a concussion or Gracie being upset.

"No. We'll sleep at your house." I cleared my throat just as Presley walked in with Gracie's hand in hers. When my daughter's eyes locked with mine, she took off in a run, and I pulled her onto my lap, trying hard not to wince as I wrapped my arms around her, and she started sobbing.

"I'm sorry, Daddy."

"Don't apologize." My voice came off harsher than I meant it to, and I pulled her back and tipped her chin up to look at me. "You did nothing wrong. Daddy was the one who should have been watching."

"I didn't see the car." Her little voice wobbled, and I was so fucking pissed at myself that she'd had to experience this shit. She'd probably have nightmares about it now. I could have stopped this from happening.

I *should* have stopped this from happening.

"Gracie, you shouldn't have had to be looking out for a car. This is on Daddy, not you. Okay?"

She nodded as the tears fell down her face, and Presley hurried over with some tissue and helped clean her up.

"You all right?" Presley asked. Her dark eyes were puffy from crying, and I knew this day had taken a toll on her, as well. I saw the sadness on both of my girls' faces, and it was a reminder that I'd pretty much failed everyone today. My family stepped out of the room when the nurse came in with my release papers.

"I'm good to go," I said as Presley stared at the bandage on my forehead as if she didn't believe me.

"Those stitches will need to be checked in a few days. I know Dr. Locket went over all the concussion side effects with you, so you need to call the hospital if you have any concerns," the nurse said as she handed me a pen, and I signed at the bottom of the release papers.

"Got it." I pushed to my feet and set Gracie down. When we walked out of the room, she ran to my father, and he scooped her up. I could feel Presley's eyes on me as she walked beside me and reached for my hand. We paused outside the hospital and said our goodbyes to everyone, but I was quiet and ready to get out of there. Hugh handed me my truck keys but shot me a warning look not to drive and motioned to where my truck was parked a few feet from where we stood. I thanked them for coming and then asked my parents to take Gracie to their car and said that I'd meet them there shortly.

My parents hugged Presley, and I bent down to meet Gracie's eyes. "Say your goodbyes to Presley. She's leaving tomorrow."

I could tell Presley wanted to say something, but the look on my face must have been why she didn't. She leaned down and pulled my daughter into her arms.

"I love you, Gracie girl. I'll be FaceTiming you real soon, okay?"

Gracie broke down in tears, and I squeezed my eyes shut and wondered how I'd allowed this to happen. How I'd fucked up so badly and let things get this far.

"I love you, Presley. I'm going to miss you so much."

"I'll miss you more, sweet girl." Presley's voice shook. I glanced at my parents, and my mother swiped at the tear running down her cheek.

Jesus. Everyone was a fucking mess.

I helped Gracie to her feet, and my dad carried her to the car as I turned toward Presley, who pulled out a tissue from her purse and wiped away her tears.

"I can change my flight. I already texted Phillip to tell him I need a few more days," she said. "I didn't want to say anything in front of Gracie, but I can stay. I can be there for you two tonight and tomorrow. For as long as you need me."

"No. You need to get back. You can't put your life on hold for us." I shoved my hands into my pockets because I knew this conversation was going to suck. I'd known it was coming, and I'd put it off.

"But I can, Cage. I can be there for you guys right now."

"And what? This will just suck in three days when we say goodbye again? Why drag it out? We knew this was coming. I'm sorry for messing up our last night together and bailing on our date, but maybe it's for the best."

Her gaze narrowed, and I saw the hurt there. "You're upset and hurt, and I want to help you. I want to help Gracie. I don't care about our date. You dove over a moving car, and your head cracked the windshield. It was fucking scary. It's okay to tell me you're upset. I'm upset. I was so fucking scared when I saw that car moving toward her."

"I know you were." I reached for her cheek, tucking the hair behind her ear. "It was fucking scary. And it could have been avoided. *Should* have been avoided. But I was so wrapped up in us that I wasn't watching my daughter. That is on me. I knew better."

"What? This wasn't your fault. Maxine got out of the house. It was an accident." Her bottom lip quivered, and tears streamed down her face.

"But it shouldn't have happened. I failed both of you today. She could have been killed, and look what I put you through. I know it was an accident, but what are we doing, Pres? You're leaving. And extending a day or two or three doesn't change anything. It's going to hurt like hell either way. So why delay the inevitable."

"We can visit," she said, her voice shaking so badly that it took all I had not to pull her into my arms. But if I held her right now, I'd never let go. I'd take that extra day. Push for two or three more. And be in the same fucking place I am right now. Gracie had said goodbye. I needed to do the same.

Pull off the fucking bandage.

"I can't be flying across the country for an occasional visit. I can't leave my daughter every time I want to see you because it would be all the fucking time, Presley. That wouldn't be right. And we saw what happens when I start acting selfish. You and me… we've never been temporary. We both know that. So I'm going to give you the keys to my truck. Hugh parked it right over there." I pointed to the side of the hospital where it sat in temporary parking. "I'd drive you home if I thought I could do it safely. Just take the truck. Leave it parked at the barn, and I'll pick it up tomorrow or later in the week. Put the keys under the floor mat for me, all right?"

"This is goodbye, then?" She shrugged and looked away, using the back of her hand to wipe away the liquid that continued to leak from her eyes.

"Time has never been on our side, has it?" I asked, as my hand moved to the side of her neck. My thumb traced along her jaw.

"No. It doesn't quite seem fair." She looked away as I put the keys in her hand and took a step back. "Cage."

"Yep?"

"I love Gracie. You know that. I'm so sorry about what happened today."

"Not your fault, and I know that you love her. And she loves you, too. I probably fucked up letting her fall right along with me." I continued to step backward because walking away from Presley had always been the hardest thing I'd ever done. It was like going against everything I knew was right for me. Good for me.

Yet she wasn't mine.

Never really had been.

"It wasn't your fault, either." She clutched her hands to her chest. "I love you."

"That's never been our problem." I let out a long breath. "I love you, too. Always have. Always will. And I love you enough to let you fly the way you were meant to, Raven."

And with those words, I turned and got the fuck out of there.

I climbed into my parents' car and didn't look back. I asked my father to drop my mother and my daughter off, and then we'd go grab some clothes from the house. I was fucking exhausted, but there was something I had to take care of.

Gracie cried on the drive to their home, and I just held her little hand in mine. I didn't have words to take away her pain. I was exhausted and numb, and I needed this day to end. I kissed her on the cheek when they got out of the car, and then we made our way to my house.

I packed a bag for Gracie, grabbed a few things for me, and led both Bob and Maxine to the car.

"We're stopping at the Langleys' house. Maxine is going home."

My father glanced over at me. "Do you think that's a good idea right now? Gracie just went through something traumatic and then had to say goodbye to Presley. Maybe you should give it a few days."

"This fucking pig nearly cost Gracie her life. Hell, Maxine could have been hit by that car, too. It wasn't a good idea for me to take her in the first place. I can't be a good father with so many distractions." My voice broke on the last word, and my father nodded and backed down the driveway.

When we pulled up in front of their house, I led Maxine to the front door. When Martha opened it, she covered her mouth with both hands. Her eyes were swollen from crying.

"I heard what happened. I'm so sorry, Dr. Reynolds."

"It's time you take responsibility for your pet. She belongs to you, not me." My tone was harsh, and I couldn't fucking believe that a sharp pain hit my chest when I handed her the leash.

I hated this fucking pig.

She'd led Gracie to that road today.

It was probably just hitting me that my daughter was going to be crushed.

That I'd just said goodbye to the woman that I loved.

But this was for the better.

It was time to make things right.

Saying goodbye was never easy, and the fact that I'd been careless about putting my daughter in a position to have her heart broken was a reminder that it was time to wake the fuck up.

I wouldn't make that mistake again.

———

The next few days were brutal. The weather was gray and rainy, and my daughter was not herself. No matter what the fuck I did, she was... sad. I'd slept on her bedroom floor every night since the accident. She'd cried herself to sleep, and I couldn't bring myself to leave her. She cried for Presley every day and asked if we could call her. But I knew time would heal her heart, so I thought it best if we let a few weeks pass. Otherwise, this would just keep being an issue.

She was clearly disappointed in me for taking Maxine

back home, but she was so sad about Presley that she just wasn't speaking much at all right now.

I'd let her miss two days of school, and I'd canceled my appointments at work to stay home with her. After one night at my parents' house, we returned home.

Even Bob Picklepants was a sad sack. I hadn't known the bastard could appear so miserable because he was rarely awake long enough to display any real emotion. But he'd just stayed in bed the last few days, and he'd barely eaten.

I was losing control of my home.

My family.

And I couldn't eat. Couldn't sleep. I'd lie awake listening to the sound of Gracie breathing, and I felt completely empty inside.

Like I'd lost my capacity for joy.

I'd broken my daughter's heart by introducing her to a woman she'd grown attached to.

And I wasn't ready to deal with the fact that I was grieving the loss of Presley Duncan all over again.

And it hurt like hell.

twenty-seven

· · ·

Presley

IT HAD BEEN two weeks since I'd returned to the city. Wes had emptied the penthouse of his personal belongings and left everything else. But nothing about it felt like home anymore. I'd never realized how sterile and cold the apartment was.

I'd stared at the artwork last night and wondered why I'd had that hanging in my home. It was dark and kind of creepy. I'd taken all the paintings down and stacked them near the door. I was having them delivered to Wes because he loved them, and he should have them.

I'd taped Gracie's paintings to my living room wall until the frames I ordered arrived. They comforted me and made me feel close to them.

But my body ached. Physically ached.

I was hardly eating or sleeping. My communication with Cage was minimal. I'd sent a daily text asking how he and Gracie were feeling. His responses were short and to the point.

How's Gracie doing?

CAGE

She's hanging in there.

How about you?

CAGE

Same. You?

I'm okay.

CAGE

Okay.

It was the same thing each day, and it was killing me. My heart hurt so badly, and I couldn't talk to anyone about it.

I'd broken down in front of Lola when she'd taken me to the airport, and she'd been calling every day since I'd returned home. I'd put on a brave face because she would worry if she knew how much I was hurting.

How much being away from them was chipping away at me.

How I longed to see Gracie ride Sally. I closed my eyes, and I could see her sweet smile. Smell the strawberry shampoo that always wafted around her. I could hear her laugh.

Hear the way Cage said my name in that deep, gruff voice.

Feel his arms wrapped around me.

It was an ache that wasn't going away.

I cried in the shower as I washed my hair and glanced around the space. The shower could hold a dozen people, yet I was completely alone.

I was living in a sterile fucking museum that didn't even feel like me anymore.

Something had shifted in me when I'd watched Gracie run

toward the road. I still heard the sound of the tires screeching against the pavement every night when I closed my eyes. Maybe it was a maternal instinct, but the thought of what could have happened to her haunted me.

Knowing she was okay now was all that mattered.

All the things that I'd thought were so important just weeks ago seemed so unimportant now. My name being on the side of a building next to two men that I had very little respect for seemed shallow and stupid now.

I pulled myself together as I dried my hair and slipped into my navy suit. Today, we were meeting with A.R.C. Network. It was a big day. An important day. Our first in-person meeting. It was my time to shine in front of the partners and the new client. And I felt… nothing.

I applied my makeup and slipped into my nude heels.

I followed my old routine and grabbed coffee on Fifth Avenue. It was my favorite.

After the first sip, I was completely unimpressed.

Cove coffee was sweeter. I'd grown used to it.

I made my way up to the top floor and to the conference room to set up my PowerPoint.

"There she is," Phillip said, as he came around the table and glanced down at my computer screen. "Are you ready?"

"Yes. I'm ready." I forced a smile.

"Are you feeling okay?"

"I feel fine."

"You look a little pale," he said. "You've been working long hours since you returned. You've got nothing to prove, Presley. You're a partner at this firm. You can go home at a normal time. You've put in the work. We all know it."

What they didn't know was that burying myself in work was the only thing that distracted me from drowning in sadness at the moment.

"I'm just catching up. I'm fine. I promise."

He nodded and held up his hands. "You know I just

worry about you. You're more like a daughter to me than Brianna is at this point."

"She's still not responding?" I asked as I connected my laptop to the screen on the wall.

"Nah. She's got enough reason to hate me, and I can't fault her for that. I'm late to the game." That was the thing I admired most about Phillip. He owned his stuff. He was an admitted workaholic who'd chosen his profession over his family.

"But you can just keep trying. It might not be the perfect relationship, but you can find a way to be in her life. I think she probably just wants you to fight for her." I'd been surprised by the way my relationship with my mother had shifted when I was home. It wasn't perfect, but we were talking more than we ever had. She was sending me text messages about ravens, which was weird as hell, but I appreciated that she felt like we'd bonded over this.

Even if it was like throwing salt in a wound every time she sent me a fun fact about the nickname that the man I loved called me.

I'd asked her if Cage and Gracie had been by the house to ride, and she said she hadn't seen them. She'd asked Dr. Jake, and he'd said the same.

It killed me that she wasn't riding.

I knew how much she looked forward to it.

But it wasn't my place to tell Cage how to raise his daughter. She was his child, not mine, even if there were moments where she felt like mine.

Where I wished she were mine.

Wished that *they* were mine.

"I'll keep that in mind every time she ignores me, and I'll just keep trying." Phillip smirked.

"Good morning," Grant said as he walked into the conference room with Ben on his heels.

I gave another forced smile. Neither of them had asked

how my father was doing. Neither had asked if I was okay with the divorce.

They weren't my friends; they were my work associates.

I'd spent years trying to get their approval, and now, I just didn't care if I had it or not. Because I didn't approve of them.

They were both assholes. Ben would stab his best friend in the back if it made him a dollar, and Grant was not shy about the fact that he was sleeping with his secretary, Stacy, not caring that we socialized with his wife at work events.

I chuckled as I heard Cage's voice in my head. *"They're a bunch of selfish pricks."*

That was happening a lot since I'd been back. When I'd cry at night, I'd hear him.

"You're okay, Raven. You've got this. You were meant to fly."

I'd always had so many goals. So many dreams. But now that I was actually living the one I'd worked so hard for… it was a bit of a letdown.

Nothing was really different.

These two guys didn't respect me any more than they did a few months ago.

And I didn't feel the joy that I thought I would feel.

A part of me wondered if I was still in a loveless marriage with Wes, if all of this today would feel so much grander. Because this was all that mattered for the longest time.

And now, knowing that there was something better I could have in Cottonwood Cove made all of this feel like less than.

"Dan Walker and his team are here," Stacy said, and I didn't miss the way her heated gaze landed on Grant. She was half his age, and the man had no shame.

He disgusts me.

"You can send them back," I said, shooting a glare in Grant's direction just because he bothered me more than ever now. I didn't care for men who disrespected women, and Grant was a fucking womanizer.

He raised a brow at me before turning his attention to the door as Dan Walker and his team were escorted into the room. We shook hands and made some quick small talk about the weather. I'd had some pastries and coffee brought in, and I invited them to fix a plate before everyone took their seats.

I stood in front of them and went over a few things about what we would be doing for them now that they were official clients of the firm.

I'd be in charge of cleaning up their messes now, amongst other legal things that would arise.

"There's a disgruntled employee you should be prepared for," Dan said as he cleared his throat. "She's going to claim we had an affair and say whatever she needs to say to squeeze some money out of me."

I didn't miss the way Margo closed her eyes briefly and looked away. As if she were irritated by the situation but also irritated by her boss, judging by the look she gave him when he wasn't looking. It was my job to be aware of all of these things. Prepare for the storm that might be coming.

"Why was she fired?" I asked, because I needed to know what we were dealing with.

"She was Margo's admin. She wasn't doing her job." Dan set his pen down and stared at me, completely lacking any emotion.

Margo opened her mouth and then closed it.

"Did you want her fired, as well?" I asked the woman, who was clearly struggling with something.

She glanced at her boss and then back at me. "She was very good at her job, from my perspective. I wasn't the one who asked for her to be terminated."

There was an awkward silence.

"Sometimes we're too close to the situation to see that it's a problem. We can speak alone after the meeting," Dan said to me, as his gaze moved to each of my partners, and we all nodded.

"I'm guessing you just need to throw money at the situation to make it go away. But that's what we do best, right?" Margo said, reaching for her coffee and taking a sip like she hadn't just dropped a bomb on the room.

The next hour was tense as the passive-aggressive behavior made it clear that there wasn't a whole lot of love amongst this group.

We'd said our goodbyes, and Dan Walker stayed back for just a few moments. He didn't even take his seat after his team vacated the room, and he'd told them that he'd meet them at the car.

"You should be prepared for Tara to say that we had an inappropriate relationship. Just offer a settlement and make it go away."

Grant and Ben chuckled, as if he'd just said something charming or cute. Phillip glanced at me, waiting for me to handle things.

"How old is she?" It was a fair question. A young woman being intimidated by an older man was not going to go away.

"Twenty-seven or twenty-eight." He crossed his arms over his chest. Dan was in his mid-fifties, so she was half his age.

"Was there an inappropriate relationship?" I asked, my gaze locking with his.

"Does it matter?"

"It does to me." My voice came out harsher than I'd expected. "I like to know what I'm dealing with."

"I'm recently divorced, which makes me single. There's no scandal here."

Sure. Aside from you being president of the company she works for. Okay, genius. Way to justify your actions. She's half your age, and you're her superior.

"No harm, no foul. We've got you," Grant said, and I seethed that he'd just spoken for me.

"Great. That's why I hired you." Dan extended his arm to each of us, and I held his stare when he shook my hand.

He didn't intimidate me. He was just another guy with a big salary that thought he was above the law.

And my job was to protect him. It made me sick.

Ben offered to walk him out, and Phillip pulled to door closed, knowing what was coming.

"How dare you," I said to Grant. *"No harm, no foul?* Such brilliant legal advice you're offering."

"He's the goddamn client. A very important one, might I add. Do you really think she's ready to be the point on this?" He directed his question at Phillip, and I chuckled.

"Don't act like I'm not in the room. I'm aware that he's the client. But if he does something that we have to clean up, he needs to be aware that he fucked up, or he'll keep doing it. It's not rocket science. She's got him by the balls, and you know it. Maybe it just scares you because you understand it a little too well," I said, immediately regretting the words as soon as they left my mouth.

Fighting with the other partners was not going to make things easier for me. I knew how to play the game. He'd be gunning for me now more than ever because I'd actually just insinuated that I knew what everyone in this office knew.

"How dare you," he shot back. "What is this? You're a scorned woman now that your husband cheated on you and the whole world knows it? At least some men have the decency to be discreet."

My head fell back in maniacal laughter because I couldn't believe the audacity of this jackass.

"Ah, yes. It would have been so much better if he'd been discreet. Because then I'd have been trapped with a cheating piece of shit for years to come." I smirked as I stepped closer to him.

"All right. That's enough. This is not helping," Phillip said. "Grant, go to your office. I'll speak to you later. Let me talk to Presley alone, please."

"Well, we all know whose side you're going to take,

Phillip. But she needs to have a bit more couth than what she displayed today."

Grant stormed out of the office, and Phillip pulled the door closed before motioning for me to sit across from him. "What's going on with you?"

"Are you seriously siding with that snake? He's just mad that I called him out. And I did need to ask Dan if the rumors were true. I need to have all the information in order to represent the company best."

Phillip smiled. He was a kind man. A good man. He was honest and fair. Sure, he'd been married to his job, but as far as I knew, he'd never been a cheating slimeball like Grant. He'd remained friends with his ex-wives, so that was telling.

"You know that Grant is right, and I do tend to side with you. I've gone to bat for you." He held his hands up when I started to interrupt. "I've done it because I believe in you. You're good to your core, and I know this firm needs that. We don't have enough good here; we need to keep things balanced."

I rolled my eyes. "Well, thank you."

"I'm not looking for gratitude. I'm looking for honesty. What you asked Dan was fair. Could you have excused us from the room and asked him alone? Sure. But it wouldn't have mattered because you would have filled us in anyway. I wasn't bothered by that. You were direct with him, as you should be. However, calling Grant out was unprofessional, and you know it. It's not like you to lose your temper. I've noticed a difference since you returned, so how about you tell me what's really going on?"

"Obviously, I think Grant is a bit of a slimeball," I said.

"I'm a lawyer. You're avoiding the question."

"I've told you about my ex-boyfriend, Cage, who I dated for a long time before I met Wes."

"Yes, I remember you speaking of him often when you first came to work here."

"Well, I spent a lot of time with him and his daughter when I was back home." I blew out a breath. Only with Phillip could I say this. With him, I wouldn't feel judged. "I'm really missing them, which I hadn't expected. And I just don't know what I'm doing with my life anymore. I know it's not the right thing to say to my mentor who has just made me a partner, which I've been dreaming of for so long." I shook my head as a lump formed in my throat.

His gaze softened, and he smiled. "Wow. All those years married to Wes, and I never saw it."

"Saw what?"

"That look in your eyes. The one that tells me you've found something that matters more than work."

"It'll pass." I cleared my throat, embarrassed by how much I'd just shared, yet it felt good to say it to someone.

"Presley," he said, waiting for my eyes to meet his. "Maybe it shouldn't pass."

"What does that mean?"

"It means exactly that. Sometimes life throws you a curveball, and it's the one you need to go for. Listen, I think you're brilliant, or I wouldn't have pushed for you to become a partner. And this firm needs you, no doubt about it. But learn from my mistakes. I'm a sixty-five-year-old man who has been married three times and his only child won't speak to him. There are more important things in life than work. It just took me way too long to realize it."

A tear ran down my cheek and landed on the table. "They live there. I live here. Realizing it isn't the problem. I know that I belong with them. I just don't know how to make it happen."

"Semantics. Could you live there and be a partner? No. I'm not going to lie to you or sugarcoat things. But if it's the real deal, does it really matter? You're a wealthy young woman. This isn't about money. You're successful. Maybe you could have the best of both worlds. It just might look different than you imagined, but that doesn't mean it's a bad thing."

I nodded, although I had no idea how to make that my reality.

twenty-eight

. . .

Cage

I'D HAD a hell of a day at the office. I'd seen back-to-back clients, and I'd ended my day with a visit from Martha Langley. She'd informed me that Maxine was depressed and not eating, and she was at her wit's end. She'd decided to give her to a pig rescue a few towns over.

There were days that I felt more like a therapist than a veterinarian. And my daughter had not snapped back the way I'd hoped, and neither had I. I couldn't even make fun of Bob because Gracie and I were as pathetic as he was now. None of us felt like doing much lately.

I'd offered to take Gracie riding, but she'd turned me down. The only thing she liked to do lately was paint, and she'd paint this depressing sky with birds flying around, and I was starting to get concerned. I'd asked my mother to come over and see her this afternoon after school. Maybe I was reading into it, but I was worried about my girl.

When I pulled up to the pickup line and they opened the back door, Gracie squealed. "Maxine?"

Ah, did I leave out the fact that I took the little porker home and told Martha I'd be adopting her? She was part of the fucking family, whether I liked it or not.

And I'd actually missed her, even if she was a big pain in the ass.

The gaping hole in my heart was definitely due to the woman I loved living on the opposite side of the country. But if bringing Maxine back to the house could help repair some of the sadness for my daughter, I'd do it.

"Buckle up and I'll explain." I waved to her teacher and looked in the rearview mirror as Maxine made all sorts of heavy groans and loved on my little girl.

"Is she visiting, Daddy?"

"Nope. She's going to live with us permanently."

"Like Bob Picklepants?" Gracie gasped. It was the first genuine smile I'd seen from my little girl since the day of the accident and the day we both said goodbye to Presley.

I wondered if it was leftover trauma or if this was all because she missed her. Maybe she'd never get over it the way I never truly had all those years ago.

"Yep. Bob Picklepants Reynolds and Maxine Langley Reynolds are both official members of the family. But things are going to change. Uncle Hugh and Uncle Finn are going to help me build a proper pen for her this weekend. She's going to take over the mudroom when she's inside the house, and we'll have a sturdy gate built to keep her in there. The barn is finished, and she's going to have a place out there with the other animals, as well."

"I'm happy she's coming home to live with us, Daddy."

"Yeah? I'm glad you're happy. And Grammie is coming over to see you this afternoon."

"Okay." It was her eyes. Her fucking eyes were the dead giveaway. Even with that fat porker sitting beside her in the back seat, her eyes still told the story.

She was heartbroken.

It was easy for me to recognize it because I saw it in my own reflection every time I looked in the goddamn mirror.

"Tell me about your day," I said as I turned down our street.

"It was fine."

That was code for *I don't want to talk about it* in Gracie speak. I could respect that. Hell, I didn't feel like talking most of the time.

We pulled into the garage and made our way inside to find my mother setting some cookies out on a plate. She knew I was worried about Gracie, and I knew that she was, too. It had been three weeks since Presley left, and my daughter was still not herself.

"Hey, Gracie girl. I brought you some cookies," my mom said as she wrapped her granddaughter up in a hug.

"Hi, Grammie. Maxine is coming back home," she said as she set her backpack on the chair.

"I heard. That must make you happy, huh?"

Gracie nodded and declined the cookies. "I'm not hungry right now. Can I go paint, Daddy?"

"Yeah. Why don't you show Grammie what you're painting."

An endless slew of gray skies and black birds. It was alarming. Maybe my mom could get her to throw some sunshine into the picture or a fucking rainbow.

They disappeared upstairs, and I spent some time getting the mudroom cleaned out for Maxine. Hugh was going to pick up some wood this week, and we'd build a gate that would contain her in there for when she wasn't allowed to roam around the house. He and Finn said they'd help build a larger pen in the backyard for her, as well. So, we'd get that started this weekend.

I finished up and pulled a pizza out of the freezer and popped it into the oven. It was all I was up for tonight. I'd add some carrots and broccoli on the side, so I didn't feel like a complete fuckup where my daughter was concerned.

My mother and Gracie had been upstairs for hours, and they came down with a stack of paintings.

"Hey, can you come join us on the couch?" my mom asked.

Gracie sat beside her, and I took the chair across from them. "Did you have fun painting? I put your favorite pizza in the oven. I thought we'd keep it simple tonight."

She nodded as she handed me several paintings. They were all the same dark and gloomy painting she'd been making for weeks, with three black blobs in the sky like the clouds of death.

"Nice," I said, trying to fake it, because they were about as depressing as it got.

"Tell Daddy what the paintings are," my mother said, stroking the hair away from her face.

"It's our family."

Jesus. If this was a family photo, I'd clearly failed as a father.

I glanced out the window to see that it was raining again, so maybe the weather was just a reflection of that.

"I see. These black spots are us?"

"Those are birds, Daddy. Me and Presley are both ravens. We like to fly free on our horses. And you're a raven because you want to stay right by us."

Three birds.

Three fucking ravens.

I studied the photo. "Why is the sky always gloomy? You do remember that sometimes it's sunny outside, right?"

"The sky is gray because our family is in a storm right now. Because we aren't together."

My mother raised a brow at me, letting me know I'd misread the painting.

Really? Was I suddenly supposed to be some deep-thinking artistic guy?

I thought it was just a depressing photo with black blobs and an endless gray sky.

But this was a punch to the gut in a different way.

"But you know that Presley doesn't live here, right?"

She nodded. "I want us all to live together. Presley loves us; she told me so. And we love her."

"I know that. But that isn't always enough, Gracie girl." I stood and lifted her before settling her on my lap as I sat beside my mom. "I know that it hurts, because it hurts me, too. And I'm sure she's hurting just like we are."

"I don't like her being all alone. I know she's missing us a lot. I called her on your phone when you were in the shower a few days ago. And she told me so."

I startled. That was out of character for Gracie not to tell me something like that. Not to ask to make a call. Sure, she'd asked me to show her how to call my mother and my siblings before. And she'd called Presley once when I was sitting beside her on the couch a few weeks ago. But she was fucking five years old. Since when was she that resourceful to figure it out on her own?

"You shouldn't use Daddy's phone without asking."

She shrugged like that was a moot point and not worth answering.

What the fuck is happening?

My mom chuckled and looked between us. "Tell us why you called her and why you didn't tell Daddy that you did."

"Because I miss her. And my heart hurts. And Daddy doesn't want to talk about it. And Presley told me her heart hurts, too."

"It's not that I don't want to talk about it. I just don't know how to fix it," I admitted. It was the truth.

"You know what Mrs. Clifton says when you don't know what to do?"

If I had a nickel for every time Mrs. motherfucking Clifton was quoted with her kindergarten advice that had too many hidden messages to dissect, I'd be a very wealthy man.

"What does she say?" I asked, bracing myself for some

singsong bullshit about how the rainbow will lead you to your pot of gold.

"She says maybe you're thinking too hard."

Riveting advice, Mrs. Clifton.

What was she advising to do when you didn't know what to do? Just not think about it?

"So, we shouldn't think about how to fix it?" I was already exhausted from this riddle of madness.

"You shouldn't *over*think it." My daughter quirked a brow as her gaze locked with mine. She clearly had my mother's gift for therapy, and she was challenging me to go deeper.

But without overthinking.

Or, if I'd heard her correctly, not to think at all.

"All right. I won't overthink it." Whatever the fuck that meant.

"Daddy," she said, placing her hand on my cheek. "Mrs. Clifton says the answers are simple."

Well, Mrs. Clifton didn't have a clue what the fucking problem was, so she wasn't really in a position to say the answer was simple, was she?

"I know that lots of things in life are solved in a simple way. Maxine, for example, was an easy solution. The Langleys were going to give her to a farm, and I knew you wanted her to live with us. So, it was simple. Mrs. Clifton is a genius."

My mother chuckled which made Gracie smile, and I was grateful for that.

"He's trying, sweetheart," Mom said. "Tell us how you think we can fix you and Daddy and Presley being sad."

"It's simple. We want to be together, so we should be together."

My teeth clenched so hard that there was an ache in my jaw, and I made a mental note to give Mrs. Clifton a piece of my mind the next time I saw her. Not everything had a solution. Not every problem in life was fixable.

"It's not that simple, Gracie girl." My words came out harsher than I meant them to.

"But it is." Her gaze softened, and I stared into those pretty chocolate-brown eyes. I wanted to give this little girl the world. "If Presley can't move here right now, then we should move there. Because being here without her doesn't make us happy."

My eyes widened. "You've got your whole family here. Grammie and Pops and all your aunts and uncles."

"But they don't live with us in our house. Auntie Brinks lives in New York like Presley sometimes. And we still see her a lot here. Right, Grammie? We can visit lots."

My mother smiled, and her eyes were wet with emotion. "Absolutely, sweetheart. You're right. I moved away from my family to be with Pops when we decided to get married and start a family of our own."

I was still processing her words. "You have your school here."

"I bet they have schools in New York City. And you could be an animal doctor there."

I glanced at my mother, who was nodding at me. "Life is short, Cage. Happiness is more important than your zip code. Your daughter is a wise little girl."

"We've got a pig and a dog. And what about our house?" I said, wondering how the fuck they suddenly had it all figured out.

"Presley likes it here. We can have our house here, too. Maybe when her work's all done, we can come back and live by Grammie and Pops. But I miss Presley, and I think she needs us, Daddy."

"We're just going to walk away from our life here, just like that?" I asked, looking between my daughter and my mother.

"You're not walking away from your life, Cage. You're walking toward it. Bob would do fine as a city dog. He doesn't care to be outside much anyway. And you can find a country house outside of the city, or Dad and I will take Maxine for as long as you need us to. I just have one question for you," she said.

"What?"

"Are you happy here without her? Don't overthink all the reasons why it can't work. My question is, can you live without Presley?"

"No." It was a simple answer when it came down to it. I wasn't eating or sleeping much. I'd just been going through the motions and trying to show up for my daughter. But what was I teaching her about life? To settle because change is too hard? What kind of lesson was that?

I wanted Gracie to live large, to love big, to chase after every single damn dream she had in life.

"You want to move to New York to be with Presley?" I asked, my gaze locked with hers.

"Yes. I want us to be together like a real family. I don't feel right since she left."

"Neither do I."

"What are we going to do, Daddy?" she asked as her cheek settled against my chest.

"I'll tell you what we're going to do. We're going to go get our girl."

Gracie jumped to our feet. "We are?"

"I think we should. Are you coming with me?"

"I'm coming with you, Daddy. Let's go get the other piece of our hearts."

Damn, my little girl was wiser than her years.

And now that we'd come up with a plan, I was ready to jump on a fucking plane right now.

"Great. Let's fly out in the morning. We'll surprise her at work."

"I love surprises!" Gracie shouted.

I normally despised surprises.

But this one I could get on board with.

twenty-nine

. . .

Presley

THE FRAMES for Gracie's artwork arrived this morning, and I was choosing different mat colors to match each one. I'd have enough for a whole gallery wall now. This was the kind of art that I wanted in my home.

It had meaning to me.

Because she was my little girl, in a way. I'd felt that connection to her instantly, and I'd come to learn that there was nothing more important than that.

Family.

Love.

It was what life was all about.

I'd spent the last few days really thinking about it. About what mattered most. What mattered to me.

And after receiving the phone call from Gracie, I knew they missed me as much as I missed them.

I wrapped each frame in bubble wrap when my phone rang. I moved around a stack of boxes to find my cell and saw Phillip's name light up.

"Hey. I was just about to call you. I don't think I'm coming in today, but I got the client info you sent over, and I will be digging into it this afternoon," I said.

"Sounds great. How are you feeling? Are you starting to feel better?"

"Yep. I actually feel really good. Thanks for helping me figure things out."

"You got it. I'm glad I could help. I wanted to let you know that we just sent a courier over to your place with some files for you while you're working from home. So be on the lookout. They should be there soon if you want to let your doorman know."

"Thank you so much, Phillip. For everything."

"Of course. Let's talk soon."

I ended the call and dialed the front desk to let them know to send the courier right up when he arrived.

I was finding my new normal now, and it was the most at peace I'd felt in my life since before I went to law school. When I thought I had life all figured out. Now I knew that I didn't need to have it all figured out. I just had to trust my gut and stop doing what everyone else wanted me to do and figure out what I wanted.

It wasn't easy.

Pleasing people, chasing dreams that might not even be your own—they become a part of you. And when you sit down and really think about what you want out of your life, it's not always the path that you're on.

There was a knock on the door, and I shoved a few boxes against the wall before pulling it open.

My jaw fell open as Cage and Gracie stood there, with her little hand in his and him with his typical stoic smirk, giving nothing away.

"Presley!" Gracie shouted before lunging into my arms.

I wrapped her up and breathed her in, and the most overwhelming burst of emotions took over. Sobs left my throat, and tears dripped down my face. I didn't try to stop them this time; I wanted to live in them.

To remember why I felt this way.

"I missed you," I said as we both sobbed.

"Uh, can I come inside?" Cage's deep voice startled me, and I chuckled through the sobs.

"Of course." I kissed Gracie's cheek, and she squirmed out of my arms and walked over to her father. She took his hand, blinking up at me with tears still running down her face.

"Hey," he said.

"Hey yourself. What are you two doing here?"

Gracie looked up at her father, and he winked at her. "We came to get our girl."

"Oh, yeah? What are you going to do once you have her?"

"I'm going to fight like hell to keep her this time," he said.

"What if she never really left, and she's been yours all along?" I asked, my voice shaking.

He dropped Gracie's hand and moved so fast it took my breath away. He had me in his arms, and he kissed me hard. "I've been yours all along, too. I don't want to make the same mistakes we made before. I want to do it differently this time."

"Me, too," I whispered, as I stared up into those sapphire blues.

He kissed me hard again and then led me to the couch before pulling me onto his lap. Gracie came over, and I settled her on my lap, and we all three laughed at how ridiculous we were.

But I couldn't get close enough.

Cage and Gracie were like breathing air to me. My world didn't work without them now.

"We're here to tell you that we don't want to live without you. Gracie helped me see things clearly with all her paintings," he said, and his gaze softened.

"Tell me."

"You and I have weathered a lot of storms, Presley. And we always let those come between us. But this, now… you and me, my daughter—we've gotten through the storm, and now it's time to rebuild. However that looks, whatever it takes, we don't care, as long as we're together after the storm."

"Because we're all ravens. Right, Daddy?"

"Well, they do mate for life, according to my mother," I said, my voice trembling.

"They sure as shit do. Maddox got us out on his plane first thing this morning, and we went straight to your office."

"Daddy yelled at a man because your name wasn't on the building," Gracie said, placing her hands over her mouth to keep from laughing.

"I'm guessing Phillip sent you here and told me you were the courier?" I shook my head in disbelief.

"Yeah. We had a bit of a rough start when some ass—I mean, some guy copped an attitude when I asked why your name wasn't on the building. We had a few words before Phillip came out and broke things up. He said you were working from home today, and you'd explain your name not being on the building because it wasn't his doing; it was yours."

I nodded as Gracie's head settled beneath my chin, and her strawberry shampoo flooded my senses. "There's only one place that I want my name."

"Where's that?"

I ran my finger over his heart. "Right here next to Gracie's... exactly where it belongs."

"I don't understand why you can't have both."

"Because I don't *want* both. I want this," I said, stroking Gracie's cheek and looking at the man I loved. The man I'd loved my whole adult life.

Before, during, and after the storm.

"I want to wake up and have breakfast with you two, and I want to take Gracie to school. I want to ride horses together and sit out by the water and daydream as a family. I want to paint and go for walks where there aren't horns honking every second. I want to watch you get frustrated when Mrs. Runither says inappropriate things to you, and I want to help Lola at the spa. I want Gracie to know my parents, and I want to do Sunday dinners with all the Reynolds. I guess… I want a life. A real one. One that matters. And when I'm with you two, I know it's where I belong."

"But you love your job. And we came here because we don't want you to give that up. Gracie and I looked up schools on the flight, and she's excited to wear a uniform. I can work anywhere. I've got plenty of experience, and I can handle city dogs. I won't be dealing with the madness of a small-town clinic, and I'm good with that. If we're together, I'm good with all of it."

"Thank you for being willing," I said, blinking away the tears as Gracie pulled back to look at me when she heard the shake in my voice.

"Presley, don't be sad. We want to live here with you. And be a family. And Daddy's going to stop overthinking."

I laughed and shook my head. "That's what I want, too. But I can do that in Cottonwood Cove. I don't want this life anymore. It doesn't fill me the way I thought it did."

"What about your job?" Cage asked, his brows pinched together with concern. "I'm never going to be okay with clipping your wings. You know that."

"I'd never let you clip my wings," I said, leaning forward to give him a chaste kiss. "I'm a consultant at the firm now. I can do that remotely. In fact, I've already started. I have movers coming tomorrow to take everything home. I guess you two just beat me to the surprise."

"You're moving to Cottonwood Cove?" Gracie squealed, then jumped up and danced around the room.

"I am."

"You're sure?" Cage asked, his voice still filled with uncertainty.

"I've had a lot of time to think about it, and being away

from you two has been really hard. Harder than I expected." I nodded and swallowed the big lump in my throat. "But it's given me time to think. I don't love what I do. I don't love the office I work in. I love Phillip, and he's going to let me choose the clients I want to be involved with. It will be a very part-time position to keep my feet in the water. But I'm going to work at the spa with Lola part time, too, and I figure you two can fill the rest of my time, huh?"

"We can ride every day," Gracie said. "The barn is done, and we can have horses at our house now."

"That would make things convenient, as long as you two want a new roommate." I smiled.

"Gracie." Cage's voice was deep and steady as his eyes stayed locked on mine. "Go find the bathroom and wash your hands."

"My hands aren't dirty," she said, staring down at them with confusion.

"In the wise words of Mrs. Clifton, *don't overthink it*. Wash your hands, and you can go look around the apartment."

"Okay." She kissed my cheek before kissing her father's cheek and running down the hallway in the direction I pointed her in.

"Hey, I need you to know we're ready to move here. For you. To support you and to be with you."

"I love that you're willing to do that for me. And I'd take you up on it if I had any desire to stay here. But I don't. We can keep the place or sell it. I don't want to live here anymore. I want to live in my favorite small town, with my favorite grumpy man and his amazing little girl."

He pulled me down and kissed me like his life depended on it. In the way only Cage Reynolds could kiss me.

When he pulled back, he smiled. "All right. I can work with this plan. But you need to know that Maxine is back, and she might get a little jealous."

"I thought you took her back to the Langleys?" I asked, my fingers running along his day-old scruff.

"They were giving her up, so I said we'd take her."

"I can handle Maxine. I guess you're just a big softy now, huh?"

He shifted the slightest bit, making sure I felt the erection that was suddenly poking me in the ass. "Nothing soft here. But that kid of mine insisted on coming with me to get our girl back, so I'm guessing that means I've got to keep things under control for a little bit longer, which isn't easy, considering it's been three weeks since I've been buried deep inside that sweet puss—" He was cut off when Gracie came running into the room.

"That bathtub is like a swimming pool. Can I take a bath in there tonight?" Gracie asked.

"Of course, you can," I said. "And I have all the bubbles, too."

"Sounds great. Is it time for bed already?" Cage waggled his brows at me.

"Daddy, we haven't had dinner yet. It's still sunny outside."

"Damn," he whispered against my ear. "Bedtime can't come soon enough. She's going to torture me, isn't she?"

I laughed. "I promise I'll make it worth the wait."

"I'd wait a lifetime for you." His hand found the side of my neck, and my gaze locked with his. "In some ways, I feel like I have."

"We've still got a lot of life left to live, Cowboy."

"Then let's get to living now. I'm done waiting."

"So am I," I said, as my forehead rested against his.

"Are you two going to get married?" Gracie asked, pressing her face against ours.

I laughed. Cage groaned. This was our new normal.

"He hasn't asked yet. It's not like I haven't waited years for this proposal," I teased.

"Were you waiting for me while you were married to someone else?" He tickled me, and Gracie jumped on his back.

"Presley was married to someone else, and Daddy was married to me, and now we're all getting married!" she squealed.

"I'd marry you right here, right now," Cage said as his heated gaze locked with mine.

"Is that your way of asking?" I asked as I ran my hand over his cheek.

"I'll ask any damn way you want me to."

"I don't care how you do it. Just make it official."

"Yeah?" he asked.

Gracie clapped her hands as her hair hung around her dad's face. "Make it official, Daddy." Cage shifted his daughter to the side and set her feet on the floor beside him as he pushed to his feet to stand.

He moved across the room and glanced around at the moving boxes before coming back with a black Sharpie.

I raised a brow, and Gracie watched with wide eyes as her father dropped down on one knee. "Presley Duncan, you were the first girl I ever loved, and you're the only woman I've ever loved. I've belonged to you since that first day I saw you in the stables, and then I watched you fly through the air on your horse, and I swear you've owned me from that day on. I will move to a big city or live in a small town and be the happiest man in the world if I have you by my side, raising my little girl with me."

The tears blurred my vision, but I nodded. "Yes. I want forever with you and Gracie."

When he moved back, he had this wicked grin on his face as he pulled out the marker and took my hand in his. He drew a black line around my ring finger and then handed me the marker. I drew the same line around his finger before turning my attention to the little girl standing beside him with the biggest smile on her face.

"How about you? Can I keep you forever, Gracie Reynolds?"

Her teeth sank into her bottom lip, and she nodded. "You want to marry me, too, Presley?"

"More than anything."

"Me, too," she said, and I took her hand and drew the same ring around her finger before she lunged forward and hugged me tight.

Cage got this soft look in his eyes that I didn't see often, and his tongue swiped out along his bottom lip. The move was so sexy that I fought the urge to groan.

He handed the marker to Gracie. "How about you go put this in the kitchen and let me kiss my future bride without you watching."

Gracie giggled and ran off to the kitchen as Cage pulled me forward, and his hand covered the back of my head as my lips crashed into his.

And I was completely overcome with emotion.

Because I'd never felt happiness the way I did right here, right now.

I'd found my forever, and I was never letting go.

thirty

. . .

Cage

IT WAS my favorite day of the year, next to the day that I'd made Presley Reynolds my wife. We hadn't wanted to wait, and we didn't want anything formal or fancy.

We just wanted forever, and we wanted it right away.

We'd both felt like we'd waited long enough for one another. So, a week after we'd returned to Cottonwood Cove, we'd gotten married on her family's property, overlooking the water. It was the place I'd first laid eyes on her.

Her mom was horrified by the lack of formality, but it was exactly what we'd both wanted. My family, her family, and a couple of friends, and we'd made it official. She'd worn a long white skirt and a pretty white top that fell off her shoulder, with her favorite cowboy boots. I'd worn a gray dress shirt that she and Gracie had picked out for me with my best dark jeans and boots. And Gracie wore a matching outfit to Presley's because she wanted to look just like the bride, which was cute as hell.

Presley had had a tiny ring designed for Gracie, as a promise to be her mom from that moment on. Gracie had asked Presley in return if she could start calling her mama.

I wasn't a guy who allowed himself to get weepy, but that

day, man—seeing my girls love on one another like they had brought me to tears.

Of course, Finn and Hugh never stopped razzing me about it, even if I tried to say a bee had stung me in the eye.

And I didn't even care.

It would go down as one of the best days of my life.

But today was June 23. The day I'd met Presley and the day my daughter was born. We'd thought about waiting to get married on the same day, but Presley felt strongly that we should keep today about Gracie. She didn't want anything to take away from that.

So, we celebrated our secret anniversary this morning with my head buried between her beautiful fucking thighs as she cried out my name.

It was a perfect way to start my day.

And now… it was my little girl's sixth birthday. It was my wife's first time getting to celebrate it, so she'd gone batshit crazy and invited the whole damn town to our house. Everyone from Gracie's class was there, along with Mrs. Clifton, who I hugged extra tight in thanks for the whole *don't overthink everything* talk, which she didn't even know had been a game changer for me.

Gracie had wanted a rodeo theme, and Presley had transformed our yard into a full rodeo. There were arches with pink and white balloons and some sort of cow print everywhere you looked, a backdrop for photos, cowboy hats for everyone, and cups that read *Gracie's Rodeo Party* on them.

It was a little over the top, but I wouldn't change a thing.

The cake looked more like a wedding cake, with a sparkly cowboy hat sitting on the top tier, and my daughter held on to her mama's hand as everyone sang to her.

These were the moments that knocked the air out of my lungs.

Not the over-the-top decorations or the fact that my siblings had joined together to buy my daughter a horse, even though Sally had been moved over to our barn and had been officially given to Gracie by her new grandparents.

What little girl needed a second horse?

No, it wasn't that. Nor was it that Presley and Gracie had ordered some sort of plaid rodeo top for Bob Picklepants, who spent the entire party lying out in the field with all that chaos moving around him, or the weird pink tutu that our giant pig, Maxine, was sporting at the party.

It was seeing Gracie's hand tucked inside my wife's hand.

It was seeing the way Presley's honey-brown eyes watched my daughter do the simplest things, like playing in the garden or painting.

It was catching them during bath time, talking about horses and ravens.

It was Sunday night dinners with everyone I loved most in the world laughing and talking and having a good time.

My father came up to stand beside me as I watched Presley and Gracie pass out slices of cake to everyone.

"You all right? You look a little… unlike yourself," Dad said.

"This is the new Cage. He's kinder and gentler," Hugh said, as he came up behind me and slapped me on the back.

"Nah. I think he's menstruating again. He gets all quiet and emotional every time his wife and daughter are in the room," Finn said, and he barked out a laugh and stood beside me.

"Oh, did you get my message that I needed to borrow some of your tampons, you pussy whipped motherfucker?" I hissed.

More laughter.

"You boys have a sick way of being happy," my father said as he shook his head and made his way toward my mom, who was waving him over to come dance with his granddaughter.

"You do look happy, brother." Finn bumped me with his shoulder.

"Yeah. I'm pretty fucking happy. You sappy bastards don't look too bad yourselves."

"You've been a little quiet today." Finn turned his attention to Hugh. "I see the way you and Lila keep looking at one another with this suspicious smile on your faces."

"We aren't going to announce it until Sunday dinner, but I'll tell you two if you can manage to keep a fucking secret for a few days."

"He's clearly talking to you because we know I can keep a secret," I said. "My nickname growing up wasn't 'loose lips Reynolds'." I smirked at Finn, who found the made-up nickname hilarious.

"What's going on?" he asked Hugh.

"Lila's pregnant. We've been trying for a while, and she took a test this morning."

I wrapped an arm around him and shook him a little bit. "Atta boy. Congratulations, brother."

Finn did the same thing, and we both promised not to say a word until they announced it.

I tipped the can of beer to my lips, and my chest squeezed.

This must be what it feels like to be chronically happy.

Speaking of chronically happy… Georgia came bounding up to us with a scowling Brinkley behind her.

"Who shit in your cornflakes?" I asked Brinkley.

"Oh, I don't know. I guess *injustice* shit in my cornflakes," she said, crossing her arms over her chest. "That little punk kid over there just tripped me during the potato sack game. I was going for gold, and he stuck his foot out and took me out."

I glanced over to where she was pointing and laughed so loud they all startled. "That's Preston. The little shit is always up to no good, but I didn't think he was smart enough to take you down, Brinks."

"You do realize we're talking about a six-year-old, right?" Georgia asked, shaking her head in disbelief.

"I don't know. I'm pretty good at reading people, and that kid is giving mob boss vibes," Finn said.

"I agree. I'm fairly certain he's the kid who stole my goody bag off the table when I was eating." Hugh shrugged.

"Speaking of rule breakers…" Brinkley narrowed her gaze at Finn. "You're the only one who hasn't gotten your final fitting for your tux. My wedding is in two weeks, you slacker."

For once, she wasn't giving me shit. Presley had dragged me down to the tailor's to get my fitting done last week.

"Hey. I'm with child. My mind is all over the place."

Hugh's head fell back in laughter. "Your wife is carrying a baby. You can't keep using that excuse."

"Really? Well, guys, Hugh and Lila are pregnant. But it's a big secret." Finn had a wicked grin on his face.

"You asshole. I was going to tell you guys at dinner on Sunday. No one knows. We just found out this morning."

Georgia and Brinkley both lunged at the big ole teddy bear and hugged him.

"Well, now I feel guilty," Georgia said.

"Why?" Brinkley asked.

"I've got a bun in the oven, too. We wanted to wait until after your wedding to announce it. So, keep this between us for now."

"Oh, man, Cage looks like he's going to start crying again. All these babies are making the big grump weepy." Finn dodged my hand when I tried to twist his ear off his fucking head.

"It's the sun shining in my eyes," I said, and they all burst into laughter.

I looked up to see Presley walking toward me, and her gaze locked with mine.

I was the happiest man in the world, there was no denying it.

And I didn't care who knew it.

———

Gracie had gone to Piper's house for a sleepover, and Presley and I had taken the boat out on the water to watch the sun go down. I couldn't take my eyes off her wearing this sexy white bikini.

I pulled over at my favorite spot in the cove and tugged my wife to her feet. I picked her up and held her like a baby before I jumped off the side of the boat. She squealed as we flew through the air and plunged into the cool water.

My hands found her waist, and I pulled her up with me as our heads broke through the surface of the water.

"Hey, Mrs. Reynolds," I said, as she pushed her wet, long hair away from her face.

"Hey yourself, Mr. Reynolds. You're going to pay for that."

"You know how much I like it when you're wet," I teased, and she nipped at my bottom lip.

"Such a filthy mouth, Cowboy."

"And you fucking love it."

"I do."

"Thanks for marrying me, baby."

"Thanks for loving me."

"Always have. Always will." I moved us a few feet from where the boat was docked until my feet hit the bottom of the ocean floor, and my hands moved to her ass and lifted. Her legs wrapped around my waist.

"Same." She leaned down to kiss me.

"So, I wanted to talk to you about something."

"Okay. Let's hear it."

"How do you feel about having more children?" I asked.

I'd been thinking about it since the day we'd said our vows. Gracie was asking us daily when we were going to give her a brother or a sister.

"I like the idea. But there's something I wanted to talk to you about first," she said, her hand moving to the side of my face as she swiped away the water droplets and smiled at me.

"I'm listening."

"Well, Gracie is calling me mama now, and…" She looked away for a few seconds before coming back to me, her eyes wet with emotion. "It means so much to me because I love her like she's mine."

"She is yours, baby."

"I want to make it official." She blinked several times as the tears mixed with the water droplets on her face.

"You want to adopt her?"

"I do. I want her to know that I took the steps to make sure we were a family in every way. And it's important to me that we start that process before we bring another child into the world. I don't want her to feel like anything is different for her, you know?"

God damn. The way I loved this woman. It shouldn't even be possible to love someone this much.

This hard.

This real.

"All right. Let's get the process started."

"Just like that?" she asked, the corners of her lips turning up.

"Just like that."

"Great. I've already looked into it, and with her biological mother having signed away her rights, there shouldn't be any problem."

"I love that you love her the way that you do."

"I loved her the first moment I laid eyes on her, if I'm being honest. I felt this connection to her, maybe because she was yours. She had that little ballet outfit on, and her dark eyes and her rosy cheeks were so sweet. And then when she started taking riding lessons from me, it just grew stronger. There's just something about that little girl."

"I couldn't agree more. She's a raven like her mother."

"She is, isn't she? So maybe we get you a little cowboy or cowgirl next. How does that sound?"

"I'll take as many as you're willing to have."

"I like the sound of that. How about I go off the pill this month, but we start practicing right now?"

My hands moved to push my swim trunks down, and I slid the fabric between her legs to the side and teased her with my tip. "Is this what you want, baby?"

"I want you. All of you. Always."

I plunged into her with one thrust, and she gasped. "I'm all yours, Presley Reynolds."

She rode me up and down, slowly at first, and then faster as we found our rhythm. I tugged her head down to mine, seeking her sweet mouth.

I kissed her as she glided up and down my cock like the raven that she was.

Faster.

Harder.

Free.

My hand moved between us, as I could feel how close she was. I pressed against her clit as she exploded around me, and I thrust into her one more time before I followed her right over the edge.

Just like I always would.

This woman owned every inch of me, and I'd spend the rest of my life making sure she knew it.

Once our breathing settled, she placed a hand on each side of my face, and the corners of her lips turned up. "I think we're going to have lots of fun making babies, Cage Reynolds."

"Count on it."

"I'm glad we weathered the storm," she said. "We came out the other side even stronger, didn't we?"

"The best part is after the storm. After you realize that you made it. You're still standing. Your heart's still beating, and you found your way to one another. That's exactly what we did."

"We made it, didn't we?"

"I'd go through it all over again if it led me to you."

"And now we have forever together," she said, as her forehead rested against mine.

"I'm counting on it."

We stood there wrapped up in one another as the sun disappeared behind the clouds.

There was no doubt in my mind that I was the luckiest man alive.

My raven had found her way home.

And I was going to keep her this time.

Forever.

epilogue

. . .

Presley

BRINKLEY AND LINCOLN had gotten married at the Cottonwood Cove Country Club, and the ceremony had been absolutely stunning. A few of Lincoln's teammates were there, and most of Cottonwood Cove had shown up for the big event.

I'd been honored to stand up for Brinkley, along with Georgia, who was her maid of honor, Lila, Reese, her sister-in-law, Tia, and all five of her cousins, Everly, Vivian, Dylan, Charlotte, and Ashlan. The wedding party was enormous.

Lincoln had asked his brother, Roman, to be his best man, along with Cage, Hugh, Finn, Maddox, his agent, Drew, and five of his teammates.

It was quite the celebration.

Gracie was the flower girl, and she'd looked absolutely adorable walking down the aisle, dropping pink flower petals everywhere.

She'd been busy dancing with all her uncles at the reception, and Cage had just cut in to slow dance with our little girl.

I'd settled at a table with Lola, who had become good

friends with all the Reynolds now. Dylan, Vivian, and Everly were all groaning over how good the cake was.

"This is your best cake yet," Dylan said before forking another bite.

"You say that about every cake I make." Vivian laughed.

"Hey, have you guys noticed that Dad has been talking to Lincoln's mom, Abi, for an awfully long time?" I followed Everly's line of sight to see Jack and Abi talking, and her head fell back in a full laugh.

Dylan stopped eating. "Really? What's her story?"

"Easy, killer. They're just talking."

"Hey." Brinkley sauntered over and waggled her brows. "Have you all noticed your father and my mother-in-law, Abi, have been awfully chatty through the entire reception?"

"Does Dad have game?" Dylan gaped. "Abi is beautiful. And she's a good woman, right?"

Brinkley laughed. "Yes. And your dad is a good-looking guy. They actually look really cute together. Why didn't I think of this?"

Ashlan and Charlotte sat down and leaned in as Ashlan whisper-shouted. "Are we talking about Dad and his hot lady?"

"That's my mother-in-law," Brinkley said over her laughter, just as Tia walked up and wrapped an arm around the bride.

"Are you having fun?" Brinkley asked.

"Yes. Best wedding ever. But if one more lady asks me if my brother is single, I'm going to hurl," Tia said over her laughter.

"In his defense, he does look like a *GQ* model, and he's stealing all the attention in the room, which is saying a lot with the men in attendance at this wedding. He's too young for me, but damn, that is one fine-looking man," Lola sang out, and everyone agreed, aside from Tia, who was rolling her eyes and making it clear she was annoyed.

"Well, good luck to whoever finally wins him over. He's such a grump sometimes," she said.

Brinkley laughed. "He just needs the right girl to knock him on his ass. Just like his brother."

We all held up our champagne flutes and toasted to Brinkley and Lincoln.

"So, Brinks, do you think you guys will have kids right away?" Vivian asked.

"At the rate everyone around us is getting knocked up, this will come as a big surprise, but we want to wait a little bit. With Lincoln still playing professional football and me working full time, we travel so much, and we want to just enjoy married life. And we'll see how we feel after the next few seasons."

"Yeah, it's hard when your husband is on the road a lot or you're still trying to work. Now that Hawk coaches part time, he has a flexible schedule. But I'm telling you, Jackson and Emerson are a full-time job," Everly said.

"Tell me about it. I'm lucky to have Hadley and Paisley at an age where they can help me with Monroe. And she's an easy baby, which has made it possible for me to stay on deadline because my publisher is a real tyrant," Ashlan said over a fit of laughter as she looked at Georgia.

"Hey, your words are magic. The people can't get enough. I'm currently beta-reading her latest, and it is so good. The steam… don't even get me started," Georgia said. "Bossman thanks you for that."

Everyone laughed, and Dylan turned her attention to me. "Do you think you and Grumpy McNugget over there will have more kids?"

"Yes. I think so," I said, feeling my cheeks heat as they all smiled, and Georgia laid her head on my shoulder.

"I've never seen my brother happier," she said.

"Yeah, it's impossible to miss how happy he is now. But

he'll always pretend to be a big grump, won't he?" Dylan laughed, and we all agreed.

But I knew the man beneath that salty exterior. The way he loved big and would do anything for Gracie and me.

"Look at you," Everly said, reaching for my hand and squeezing. "You're glowing. And the way you and Gracie are together, it's just magical. You were the missing piece in their lives."

"Amen to that," Brinkley said, and she shook her head as if she'd known it all along. "I caught Cage smiling as he watched you before you lined up to walk down the aisle together. He's so happy, and I'm just so glad you guys found your way back to one another."

"Not surprising. Second-chance romance is so hot right now," Georgia said, and the corners of her lips turned up.

"I love that everything is a trope with you." Ashlan chuckled.

"Ohhhh… what's my trope?" Charlotte asked.

"You and Ledger are a best friend's brother mixed with a dash of second chance. The one who almost got away." She smirked.

"Luckily, no one got away, because you two were meant to be together, and Harper and Hudson are proof of that," Dylan said about her niece and nephew. Charlotte and Ledger had twins that were absolutely adorable. "What are me and the big, bad Wolf called in the romance world?"

"Well, that's an easy one," Georgia said as she and Ashlan both laughed before speaking at the same time. "Enemies-to-lovers!"

"I like it." Dylan waggled her brows. "I sure hated that man in the beginning, but now… I'm all about being lovers. I've been horny as hell since giving birth. I thought it was supposed to make me lose my sex drive, but that has not been the case."

More hysterical laughter sounded at the table.

"You did give birth to the easiest baby on the planet. Baby Hugh is a lot like his uncle. He's so mellow and chill," Vivian said.

"True. He's a dreamy baby. I'm sure the next one will be a real pistol, like his father. And I'll never sleep again." She rolled her eyes, feigning annoyance.

"Are you guys already trying again?" Georgia asked.

"Hells to the no. I need to give my vagina time to heal."

My head fell back as loud laughter rang out around the table.

"What? I popped a human out of there. She needs time, just like I need time. And Wolf is getting that ridiculous guard dog, so we'll be adjusting to all of that. Plus, I'm going back to work soon, and I can't wait," Dylan said before looking over at Georgia. "What's Vivi and Niko's trope? Hot, bad-boy firefighter meets straight-laced bakery owner with a hidden sexy side?"

"Oh my gosh. What is wrong with you?" Vivian said as a wide grin spread across her face.

"They are the classic friends-to-lovers. Good girl, bad boy. The makings of an epic love story." Georgia winked. "And clearly, you two can't get enough of one another at the rate you keep popping out babies."

Niko and Vivi had three kids now. Little Bee was the sweetest big sister to her two brothers, Clancy and Calum.

"That sexy husband of mine said he wanted to fill that house of ours with babies, and we've been busy doing that." Vivian smiled, and her cheeks pinked.

Gracie came running over to our table with her cousins, Jackson and Bee, right behind her. They ran over to their moms, and Gracie reached for my hand. I pulled her onto my lap and wrapped my arms around her.

Cage came up behind me and bent down to kiss my cheek as his arm came around both me and our daughter.

Everly held up her phone and snapped a picture of us.

"Such a beautiful family," she said, and she held up the phone to show me the photo.

We looked cozy and happy and content.

Which was exactly how I felt.

"Hey, how about a cousin picture with all of us and our babies?" Dylan asked as she started wrangling everyone up, and Romeo offered to take the photo.

Some of the babies were sleeping, but it only made it all the sweeter. We piled in, with all the hubbies holding some of the kids. Gracie was in her father's arms but refused to let go of my hand. I glanced up to find her watching me with the sweetest smile on her face.

We were surrounded by family and all the love one could ever wish for.

Cage's free hand found my ass, and he squeezed hard enough to make me yelp, which caused laughter to erupt around the group.

We finished taking photos, and Cage took my hand, Gracie still comfortably hooked on his hip with her head tucked beneath his neck.

"Come on. Let me take my girls home." He winked.

I nodded, but the truth was, as long as these two were beside me, I was already home.

The End

Do you want to read about Presley's big surprise for Cage and Gracie... Grab this special BONUS SCENE HERE:
https://dl.bookfunnel.com/sjkuqbaf1y

Thank you for reading the final book in the Cottonwood Cove series! Are you curious to see if Romeo Knight finds love? Pre-Order book 1 in Magnolia Falls series, Loving Romeo!

This is a Small Town, Enemies-to-Lovers, Sports Romance! Grab it HERE:

https://geni.us/lovingromeo

Do you want a sneak peek of Loving Romeo? Get ready to watch this bad boy boxer fall hard for the girl he's determined to hate. Keep reading for the first two chapters from Loving Romeo…

acknowledgments

Greg, my forever cowboy! I feel so lucky to call you mine. I love doing life with you! Love you SO MUCH! Thank you for supporting me and encouraging me to chase my dreams.

Chase & Hannah… I don't know how I got so lucky to be your mom! I feel like the luckiest mama in the world! I love you to the moon and back!

Willow, I am endlessly grateful for YOU! Thank you for always supporting me, listening, making me laugh, keeping me going and being the most amazing friend. Love you so much!

Catherine, thank you for your friendship and for all of your support! Cheers to making many more memories together for years to come. Love chain forever! Love you!

Kandi, I don't know how I existed without you before, and I'm just so grateful to be on this journey with you! I'd be lost without you! So thankful for your friendship! Thank you for pushing me, inspiring me to work through the tough days and for cheering me on every step of the way. I am forever grateful for you! Love you my sweet friend!

Elizabeth O'Roark, Endlessly grateful for your friendship, and you are stuck with me forever now! Thank you for making me laugh, talking things through and being such an amazing friend! Love you!

Jessica Prince, I am so thankful for you! Thank you for the encouraging messages and for your friendship! Love you!

Pathi, I can't put into words how thankful I am for YOU! Thank you for being such an amazing friend!! Thank you for believing in me and encouraging me to chase my dreams!! I love and appreciate you more than I can say!! Love you FOREVER!

Nat, I could not be happier to be on this journey with you! I am so excited for all the memories we will get to share and I feel so lucky to be working together again! Thank you for supporting me and most importantly, thank you for your friendship! So grateful for you! Love you!

Nina, I don't know how I ever made a decision without you. Thank you for always being there for me. From the little things to the big things. Thank you for encouraging me in every way! I am forever grateful for your friendship and to be on this journey with you! Cheers to many more years together! Love you!!

Valentine Grinstead, I absolutely adore you! You are such a bright light and I am so thankful for YOU! And I will forever love our date night in Paris!! Love you!

Kim Cermak, You complete me. LOL! I'd truly be lost without you! Thank you for all that you do for me every single day!! I absolutely adore you!!

Christine Miller, I am so grateful for you! Thank you for making my life so much easier and for all that you do for me!! I am SO THANKFUL for you!

Sarah Norris, thank you for the gorgeous graphics, for all of your support and for always being willing to help! I am incredibly grateful for YOU!

Meagan, Oh how I adore you! Thank you for being an amazing beta reader and an amazing friend! Your support means the world to me!! Thank you so much!! Love you!

Kelley Beckham, thank you for setting up all the "lives" with people who have now become forever friends! Thank you so much for all that you do to help me get my books out there! I am truly so grateful!

Amy Dindia, You are the absolute sweetest and I'm so

thankful for you. Thank you for creating absolutely perfect reels and TikToks for me. I am endlessly grateful for you!

Logan Chisolm, So thankful for your friendship and your support! Thank you for reading my words and for all that you do for me! I absolutely adore you! Xo

Doo, Abi, Meagan, Annette, Jennifer, Pathi, Natalie, Caroline and Diana, thank you for being the BEST beta readers EVER! Your feedback means the world to me. I am so thankful for you!!

Emily, Thank you for creating these gorgeous special edition covers! I love working with you so much!

Sue Grimshaw (Edits by Sue), I would be completely lost without you and I am so grateful to be on this journey with you. Thank you for being the voice that I rely on so much! Thank you for moving things around and doing what ever is needed to make the timeline work. I am FOREVER grateful for YOU!

Ellie (My Brothers Editor), So thankful for your friendship! I am so grateful for our chats and for all the laughs! Thank you for always making time for me no matter how challenging the timeline is! Love you forever!

Julie Deaton, thank you for helping me to put the best books out there possible. I am so grateful for you!

Jamie Ryter, I am so thankful for your feedback! Your comments are endlessly entertaining and they give me life when I need it most!! BEST COMMENTS EVER!! I am so thankful for you!!

Christine Estevez, thank you for your eagle eyes and being the last set of eyes on my book! I am so thankful for you! Your friendship truly means the world to me! Love you!

Crystal Eacker, I am so thankful for you! Thank you for doing whatever is needed! For making forms, beta audio reading, taking photos and making graphics!! You are such an amazing support and I'm forever grateful!

Jennifer, thank you for being an endless support system.

For running the Facebook group, posting, reviewing and doing whatever is needed for each release. Your friendship means the world to me! Love you!

Paige, I am so grateful for your friendship! I love our chats about decorating, pumpkin decor, books, kids, life, and everything in between! You are such a bright light in my life! Mother loves you! LOL!

Rachel Parker, I am endlessly grateful for your friendship! I love our chats. I love our LIVES! I love my Charlotte updates! And… I love you!

Sarah Sentz, thank you for always being so supportive and for making time to chat with me on every release! Thank you for helping spread the word about my books. I am forever grateful for you!!

Ashley Anastasio, I adore you and I am so happy that I finally got to hug you in person! I am forever grateful for your support and friendship! I appreciate all the love for my books!! It truly means the world to me!!

Erin & Tori, Thank you for all of your support and for reading my words! I am endlessly thankful for YOU!

Kayla Compton, I am so grateful for your support! I love that you and I share a love for our favorite lake!! Thank you for spreading the word about my books and all that you do to support me!

Mom, thank you for loving Cage & Presley and for cheering me on every step of the way! I am so thankful that we share this love of books with one another! Ride or die!! Love you!

Dad, you really are the reason that I keep chasing my dreams!! Thank you for teaching me to never give up. Love you!

Sandy, thank you for reading and supporting me throughout this journey! Love you!

Sammi, I am so thankful for your support and your friendship!! Love you!

Marni, I love you forever and I am endlessly thankful for your friendship!! Xo

Monica, if Bravo hadn't brought us together, I'm certain the book world would have! LOL! So thankful for your friendship!

To the JKL WILLOWS... I am forever grateful to you for your support and encouragement, my sweet friends!! Love you!

To all the bloggers, bookstagrammers and ARC readers who have posted, shared, and supported me—I can't begin to tell you how much it means to me. I love seeing the graphics that you make and the gorgeous posts that you share. I am forever grateful for your support!

To all the readers who take the time to pick up my books and take a chance on my words...THANK YOU for helping to make my dreams come true!!

keep up on new releases

Linktree Laurapavlovauthor
Newsletter Laurapavlov.com

other books by laura pavlov

Magnolia Falls Series
Loving Romeo
Wild River
Forbidden King
Beating Heart
Finding Hayes

Cottonwood Cove Series
Into the Tide
Under the Stars
On the Shore
Before the Sunset
After the Storm

Honey Mountain Series
Always Mine
Ever Mine
Make You Mine
Simply Mine
Only Mine

The Willow Springs Series
Frayed
Tangled
Charmed
Sealed
Claimed

Montgomery Brothers Series
Legacy
Peacekeeper
Rebel

A Love You More Rock Star Romance
More Jade
More of You
More of Us

The Shine Design Series
Beautifully Damaged
Beautifully Flawed

The G.D. Taylors Series with Willow Aster
Wanted Wed or Alive
The Bold and the Bullheaded
Another Motherfaker
Don't Cry Spilled MILF
Friends with Benefactors

follow me

Website laurapavlov.com
Goodreads @laurapavlov
Instagram @laurapavlovauthor
Facebook @laurapavlovauthor
Pav-Love's Readers @pav-love's readers
Amazon @laurapavlov
BookBub @laurapavlov
TikTok @laurapavlovauthor

www.ingramcontent.com/pod-product-compliance
Lightning Source LLC
Chambersburg PA
CBHW061416160726
47995CB00003B/629